THE DOUBLE RIDER

OTHER FIVE STAR WESTERNS
BY MAX BRAND:

THE DOUBLE RIDER

A WESTERN STORY

MAX BRAND®

FIVE STAR

A part of Gale, Cengage Learning

GALE
CENGAGE Learning®

Detroit • New York • San Francisco • New Haven, Conn • Waterville, Maine • London

LIBRARY OF CONGRESS CATALOGING-IN-PUBLICATION DATA

Brand, Max, 1892–1944.
    The Double Rider : a Western Story / by Max Brand. — First Edition.
        pages cm
    " 'The Double Rider' first appeared under the title 'Rippon Rides Double' as a six-part serial in Street & Smith's Western Story Magazine (10/18/30-11/22/30)"—T.p. verso.
    ISBN-13: 978-1-4328-2707-6 (hardcover)
    ISBN-10: 1-4328-2707-3 (hardcover)
    I. Title.
PS3511.A87D675 2013
813'.52—dc23   2013019109

Published in conjunction with Golden West Literary Agency.
Find us on Facebook– https://www.facebook.com/FiveStarCengage
Visit our website– http://www.gale.cengage.com/fivestar/
Contact Five Star™ Publishing at FiveStar@cengage.com

Printed in Mexico
2 3 4 5 6 7 17 16 15 14 13

ADDITIONAL COPYRIGHT INFORMATION

CHAPTER ONE

Of blue waters, breaking to green and white, Rippon dreamed. He dreamed of the flash of paddles, and the trembling brightness of a cascade behind him. As he envisioned that river, he felt that it might flow into his own burning throat and be accommodated there. Then he wakened and found himself in his camp on the desert. The ache and sting remained behind his tongue as he sat up. His head whirled a little, and with it the blue and white Tyndal Mountains in the distance seemed to whirl, also.

Instinctively he reached for his canteen, found it, shook it, and a mere rattling of the buckle answered him. The thing was empty. This was a dry camp, and the last drop of water he had poured down the throat of his bronco the night before, for it had been a hard march and a still harder one was before him. He had depended on water at Nigger Wells, and had found them dry; the very mud in the center of the hole was baked hard, and the slime was a green powder, deeply cracked across. So he had plugged steadily along through the evening until Baldy, the mustang, began to shake his head in a certain way.

Rippon knew what that head shake meant. He knew all the ways of Baldy, and the gestures of the horse meant for the rider as much as human speech—sometimes more. They were partners. They were old campaigners together. Roman-nosed, pot-bellied, ewe-necked, short-legged, Baldy was a cartoon in flesh. He had the short temper of an old rheumatic and the

7

cunning of a serpent. But Rippon loved him, and he loved Rippon. The man loved the horse because that dumpy mustang had a heart as big as his body and the soul of a fighter, because it had muscles of supple steel, the eye of an eagle, the foot of a mountain goat, and patience surpassing that of Job. The horse loved the man because in Rippon, Baldy found his first master. He enjoyed bucking every morning to warm himself up, and Rippon was as pleased by the exercise as the mustang. He delighted in shying at every bright-faced rock, every idle whirlpool of dust that rose in the wind, but Rippon was never troubled by those halts, those side-leaps. He sat in his saddle as though tied with ropes.

The mustang found himself matched and overmatched, but he kept on fighting, and both of them greatly enjoyed the fight.

Now Rippon rubbed his eyes and looked toward the mountains. They looked close, cool, and blue. He could almost see the trees prickling on the slopes like hair on an unshaven cheek. They looked very close indeed, and their cool blueness made him think of water. But he was not deceived. Tough as Baldy was, those foothills were a good fifty miles, and fifty miles, in Baldy's condition, would be a tremendous day's march. However, Rippon was not daunted.

A thousand miles away and forty days ago he had heard of the pleasant country beyond the Tyndal Mountains, the pleasant country through which the Tyndal River was running full to the bank all the year, and his heart, long drying in the desert, and his soul, burned by the desert sun, had yearned for the greenness of that distant land. He had made up his mind. He had sold—given away—his mining claim, the very next day, and with Baldy, and little else, he had begun his march.

His pack consisted of his slicker, three extra pairs of socks, a small sewing kit, a second flannel shirt, a change of underwear, cartridges for the rifle, the rifle itself, and some salt. He took with him neither coffee, sugar, flour, bacon, cooking utensils, nor any of the odds and ends that swell a pack and kill a horse. Rippon traveled with a theory. Animals lived everywhere, even on the hottest, widest desert. Wherever animals lived, his rifle would bring them down. With fire to cook, and salt to flavor the kill, he was content. He had lived on meat for all these days, and he did not allow himself to be troubled or deterred by certain cravings of appetite. He endured pain and monotony of effort as Baldy endured the same things—with a set eye and a sort of fierce enjoyment of his own discomfort.

Now he stood up and stretched himself. He was as ugly as his horse, but in a different way. Baldy was a dumpy grotesque. Rippon was a long and lean one. He looked loose-coupled, weak in the joints, too wide for his depth. His arms were narrow except at the points of the shoulders; his legs were narrow, too. He seemed to have no stomach, the ribs stood out so boldly above and around it. His neck was thin in front, but looked big from the back view. He had a big, arched nose, sunken cheeks, a crag of a jaw, and at the base of it there was generally a little projection of muscle under the skin, for his teeth were usually firmly locked together. His eyes were narrowed and wrinkled at the corners from squinting across the sun-brightened face of the desert. He was the sort of man about whom anyone would have said: "An ugly customer." He was brown almost to blackness. The print of his thirty-odd years was plainly in his features, and the loneliness of a solitary life and ways surrounded him with a certain atmosphere, such as that which surrounds a distant mountain, loftier than its fellows.

He was, in short, a man of the desert. He had been in other places, too. But the desert was his home. He could leave it with sudden repulsions, as he was leaving it now, but always the desert called him back again with a voice that he could not resist. He was desert-made, also. That leanness and looseness of his he had in common with the desert lobo, the wolf that seemed all hard bone and loosely rolling hide, but that had the strength of steel springs, coiled and ready for use, tireless, swift, and sure. His strength simply lay near the bone. There was no fat, no waste; he was the most economical surface that could be offered to the burning of the sun.

So he appeared as he stood up and rubbed the last sleep from his eyes. It was high time for him to be up. The night had ended. The dawn was there before him, flaming over the tops of the mountains. Far better for him and the mustang if he had wakened two hours earlier and begun the march in the cool of the day. So there was no time to be lost.

He took his breakfast in two seconds. That is to say, he pulled the belt two notches closer about his gaunt stomach. Then he turned about to look for the horse. But Baldy was not there! He could not believe the thing, at first. The ground was as flat as the palm of his hand. He could let his eye jump to a distant horizon in any direction. But unquestionably it was true. Baldy was not there. He had vanished as water might have vanished, as his own dream had vanished.

As soon as he was sure of this, he began to cut for sign. Miracles do not happen, even on the face of the desert, which some men believe is closest to God. Therefore, he cut for sign, moving in circles, at a dog-trot, for there was no time to be wasted. He found the sign that he wanted, presently.

Fifty yards away, a small trail came dimpling across the sand, the tiny impressions and the short steps that a burro would take. No, this must be a mule. This trail came up to the hoof prints of Baldy, where the mustang had been nosing away the sand to get closer to the roots of the scanty bunch grass. From that point, two trails went away, side-by-side. Had the man thought that Baldy was a stray? No, not with those hobbles on. Not with the sweaty saddle marks upon his back and the gray outline of the bridle straps still upon his head. The hobbles had been cut. Baldy was stepping out at once at a good pace.

No, he had been stolen!

Rippon looked at the distant mountains. At a stride they seemed to have receded to double their former distance. He had given the last of his water supply to Baldy. The horse was the point on which he had lavished his supply, because he had expected that the horse would have to do the work. Now a pain of foretaste shot from the back of his dry throat through all his veins, burning him. A day of fierce torture was before him; death might come before the end of it.

He went back to the place where he had camped. He lifted the rifle and dropped it again. He weighed the saddle and threw it down. He knew instantly that his own chances of winning through to water were by no means good. Burdened by even the smallest encumbrance he would surely fail.

He left everything behind him, therefore, except an extra pair of socks and a piece of soap. The soap was not for washing, not on this day. First he sat down, pulled off his boots, and, turning the socks he was wearing inside out, he rubbed the soap upon the wool. Thank heaven those socks were good wool. Cotton would file the skin off his feet and make them raw in no time. The soap would help, also, to avoid blisters. He pulled on the socks again, drew on the boots, and stood up. He raised his hat from his head, smoothed back his rather long hair, and resettled the hat. Then he started for the western mountains.

He went without haste, stepping short, patient of the backsliding of his feet in the loose surface sand of the desert. A short, quick step was the thing, leaning well forward, and in his soul he summoned up the enduring temper of a beast of burden.

He was a cold man, was Rippon. Emotions did not leap up and take him by the throat. But as he walked across the desert he knew with a perfect surety that death lay at the end of his march. Perhaps it would be his own death—the mad, raving death of the thirst-famished. But if he lived through to the mountains, it would be the death of the other man.

He thought about it without violence, without grinding of teeth. He felt, really, more of a mild curiosity about the thing that was to be. He had only his knife left to him. Perhaps the other man would die with that knife thrust through his heart. Perhaps it would be a matter of naked hands. Rippon looked down at his big, brown hands and smiled a little.

Who was the man? Well, never a white man. For too many generations the white men of the West had known the sacred code. To steal a man's horse in the desert was tenfold a vaster crime than to shoot him through the brain. No white man could have done the thing.

So he went steadily forward, patiently. It began to be hard to swallow. Later on, he could bite his arm and suck the salty blood. But it was too early for such an emergency measure. That would come a good deal later.

He followed the sign of the trail. It was easily read, and it pointed straight toward the central pass, at which he himself had been driving. Well, somewhere in that pass he might find his quarry.

He did not pray for vengeance. He did not look up to heaven and vow revenge. He merely looked down again to his big, sun-browned hands.

Chapter Two

By 9:00 a.m. the sun already burned him like a torch. It scalded his shoulders. It ate like an acid through his coat. It sank into his flesh. He could feel the moisture leaving his body. Acrid dryness remained.

By noon, he began to have dizzy fits. When these came, he stopped short and made sure that he was still aimed in the right direction. He waited for his head to clear and then he went on. In his throat and his tongue there was a torture. He first tried to turn his mind away from it. That was of no avail, for the torment that he tried to disdain swelled greater and greater. It mastered his mind; it mastered his imagination. Terror began to take hold of him. He thought of the many stories he had heard of men driven mad by thirst, wandering, shouting thick, indistinguishable words. So he turned his thoughts in the opposite direction. He centered his mind upon his own sufferings. He tried to picture the dryness of his throat. He calculated, coldly, the swelling of his tongue. Every effort at swallowing, and the indescribable suffering that accompanied it, he regarded with a sort of scientific detachment, as a thing only remotely connected with his own flesh and body. And, following this course, he found that the torment became more endurable. He almost forgot the thing in the contemplation of it.

He came suddenly, in a small, shallow draw, upon an abandoned mule. The saddle had been taken from its back long enough to allow the sweat to dry in ridges where the outer rim of the blanket had come. The animal was far gone. Its head was down under the ceaseless bludgeoning of the sun's force. Its lower lip was pendulous, far-hanging. Its eyes were almost closed. The dark lashes were so long that they reminded him with a strange force of the lashes of a pretty girl against her cheek—one touch of prettiness in a thing so ugly. One hip sagged. Its legs were braced, far apart. It was ready to die; it had given up the battle exactly where its master had abandoned it.

Rippon went on.

Through the sands, from this point, only one set of tracks proceeded. He could tell that it was the mustang's trail. Baldy had had thrush, once, in the left forehoof. Ever since, the hoof had been fitted with a shoe that had a bar across it to keep the hoof artificially spread. There could be no doubt that the thief had abandoned the mule, having exacted from it the last ounce of strength. Then he had taken the mustang and gone on. Upon the ground there were the prints of his feet where he had dismounted and changed saddles. He wore the boots of a cowpuncher, the high heel pointing in toward the ball of the foot, but, by the spread of the toes, he could guess that this was a heavy man. He measured his own print in the sand. A heavy man, and with a big foot, as large as his own, in fact.

He went on half a mile, following those tracks of the mustang. Then he paused. For a moment, he stared straight before him toward the mountains. In spite of his effort, he had made slow progress, and the blue valleys and their promise seemed even more distant than when he had started toward them at dawn.

He told himself that he would not look back. But he could not help it. He had to turn, and there behind him, he saw distinctly the silhouette of the dying mule.

"I won't be a fool," Rippon said aloud. "Besides, the mule's done for. Nothing can save him."

Nevertheless, he was a fool. He had to turn and go back to the animal. It seemed to him that the weight of the sun's heat redoubled as he went back. The wind failed utterly. Perspiration streamed down his face. The sheer dryness and torrid heat of the air turned the drops to salt. He began to feel that he was stifling. But he went clear back to the mule.

It was a young mule, gray-coated, tall, with a mule's slender shoulders, and hanging belly, and sloping rump. It was a good young mule, useful under the saddle or tugging at traces in a freight train. He tried to urge it forward. But it kept its eyes half closed and would not heed him. He cut out a long strip from the leg of his trousers. With that he made a lead rope, fastened it around the neck of the animal, and then pulled gently, because a strong force would break the strip of cloth.

The mule groaned. The human quality in the voice tore the heart of Rippon. Into his dry eyes rushed tears. He winked them away. And yet one or two rolled down his cheeks.

"I'm far gone," Rippon whispered to himself. "I've turned into a baby. I'm a regular woman. I'm no good."

At this, the mule lurched forward, and then began to walk behind him. He backed up before it. He began to talk to it, cursing gently, and the long ears of the mule answered him, sagging forward, and then back, giving it a whimsical, half-mocking look.

Rippon faced about and walked on toward the mountains, and the mule followed. Presently he stumbled upon a wind-riffle in the sand and fell flat on his face. The sand stung him like fire. The heat of the sand burned through his flannel shirt and roasted his stomach. His hat had fallen off. The weight of the sun struck the back of his head like a club, and he did not want to rise.

Then, against his heels, the forehoofs of the mule tapped lightly. He got to his knees. He waded on his knees through the sand and struggled to his feet.

"I'm finished," Rippon said. He turned and looked at the mule. Its long ears were cocked forward at him, as though it were smiling. "No, I'm not finished," Rippon debated. "I'm going to fight it through. I'm going to kill him."

He went on toward the mountains.

Suddenly he discovered that the torment sprang not from his throat and swollen tongue alone. It came from his feet, also. He could walk on them no longer. He sat down in the shadow of the mule, pulled off his boots, and looked at his feet. They were raw; they were bleeding. The boots of a cowpuncher never were made to stand such a strain as he was giving his feet. Flesh would not endure such a thing.

He looked at his feet. Then he looked upward, hopefully, at the mule. Perhaps that would be his salvation, but he saw, at once, that the knees of the beast were trembling. He had little power; the mule had less.

He set to work, patiently, there in the shadow of the mule. He cut off the uppers of the boots. With these, he made sandals. He made a thong to fit between his big and little toe, for each foot, and wound the thong up the calf of his leg. It was a clumsy sandal, but it would hold, only slipping on his foot a little. The sewing he did with his knife, boring holes through the leather and passing the strips through. He had a reserve supply of the soft leather of the tops of the boots, and this he took with him when he got up and proceeded, marching with the mule behind him.

Once or twice the mule pulled back, but, when Rippon looked over his shoulder, the poor beast trudged on. Its lips opened and closed, flopping together with an audible sound. Sometimes that clapping together of the lips kept time with his strides.

"The mule won't give up," Rippon told himself. "He's fighting for me . . . he's marching for me, because I want him to.

Not for himself." He looked up at the sky. The flame of it smote his brain and made him reel. "Oh, heaven," said Rippon, "let me get through. Let me find him."

He was walking through fire, and in the midst of the flames he could see only one picture, and this was of the thief—a big man, heavy, secure in his strength, stealing the horse by night and looking back under the stars, with a sneer, toward the figure of the sleeper. The fire had blue flames. Presently Rippon's eyes cleared and he saw that he was looking at the mountains. The flames were no longer blue. They were brown, streaked with green. Then a door opened in his mind and he saw that the flames were really the rolling mountain sides.

For he was closer now. When he looked at the mountains, he thought that they were only a step away, for he could see the rocks, the trees. When he looked at the desert under his feet it seemed an endless ocean to traverse. Therefore, he looked seldom at the trail of Baldy, and more often at the mountains. It kept his heart up.

His tongue began to swell still more. He did not bite his arm; he slashed it with the knife and sucked the blood. Afterward, it was easier to breathe, and he could walk better, too. Force out of his own body had given him power to proceed. The thought amused him and occupied his mind almost as much as his agony, for a time.

Then he told himself that he had only three miles to go. He closed his mind against itself. He walked an hour. Then he looked at the mountains and told himself that he had still three miles to go. This broke his heart, so completely that he dropped upon both knees and both hands, in the shade that the mule cast.

He saw the trembling legs of the mule and raised his head again to the terrible sky.

"Heaven won't let me fail," Rippon whispered.

He got to his feet. The word heaven stuck in his mind, oddly. He had used the word chiefly for cursing, before, but now it rang in his brain. Yet he knew that he had made an appeal, and that, somehow, he had been answered. He told himself that it was a thing to think of on another day, if this day were not the last, really.

He marched on. His jaw was set so hard that he was half choked, and his nostrils flared. Then, suddenly, he found himself walking uphill.

"There are no hills on the desert," Rippon said aloud.

He shook his head and made himself see. And behold, there were trees about him! No water, but trees, which must send their roots down to the sacred blessing of moisture. He looked back at the staggering mule and laughed, and the mule pricked its ears at the stifled, panting sound that it heard, unlike a human voice.

"I've won," said Rippon.

He rounded the top of the hill, and followed the trail of the mustang to the hollow—and stepped to the knees in water. He stood still, shocked, bewildered. But it was water, no mirage. He could feel the heaven of it on his raw, scalded feet. It was flowing water, and he was saved.

He looked back at the mule. A horse would founder itself with water, after such a march, but not a mule. So he let the beast drink. It waded in, belly-deep, and drank. Even in that starved moment, it did not plunge in its head up to the eyes, as a horse would have done, but barely touched the surface with its lips, and closed its eyes, and groaned softly.

Rippon groaned also, and drank in sips.

CHAPTER THREE

When Rippon had finished drinking and bathing, his full senses had returned to him, and he saw that he had walked into the evening. The sky was red. The water of the creek before him was as red as flame, also, taking the reflection.

Then he sat up, dripping, gradually raising his head until he could tell himself that he was no longer a walking nightmare, but a man. He had tobacco and thin, brown, wheat-straw papers. Out of these he made a cigarette and smoked. The smoke stung his puffed and cracked tongue but it comforted his very soul. It was food, equal to the drink that he had tasted.

At last, when his thoughts were again sober and cleared, he looked up toward the hanging buttresses, the crags, the darkness, the gathering mist of the pass. The mule would never help him to climb it. It stood by, after drinking, with fallen ears, hanging head, hanging lips. And its legs still trembled. It would have to spend whole days in this grassy hollow, beginning to eat, sleeping much, lounging under the trees during the heat of the sun. Then it would be well and fit again.

"I've saved the life . . . of a mule," Rippon said to himself, and he laughed a little, until the sound of his own voice, echoing, rather alarmed him and brought him suddenly to his feet with a beating heart.

The mule could remain there to rest, but the pass and the climb were for him and his tortured feet.

The vision of the thief never had left him, and now he began to climb upward, following the trail of Baldy where it appeared, now and again, on the ground. Rocks were most of the way, bruising his feet. He followed the trail until he was well committed to the pass, then the darkness closed slowly, softly over him.

By this time, he was quite high. A wind blew out of the east, straight up the pass. It was compressed and focused by the enclosing walls, and now that he had gained a sufficient height, the wind was iced by invisible snows—the real snows were higher above him.

All was blackness. The stars were no real help. Sometimes they left the water dark, where the stream ran down the middle of the pass, and he stepped into the snow water, benumbing his legs and feet. Sometimes the starlight reflected dimly on the face of a polished rock, as though that were water, and he side-stepped the place, only to look back and see that he had been avoiding good ground.

His feet were no longer an important torment, for now that his brain was clear and the delirium of the day's march was well behind him, he could put pain in its proper place. The cold of the wind froze all feeling out of his body. It left his mind clear as the stars above him, to reason and to resolve.

And he marched on. He was tireless. The long years of constant labor helped him. The perfectly fit body was a resource. But most of all there was the force of his indomitable mind to drive him, subduing body and the fatigues of the body to nothing.

A number of times he stumbled, and in the falls he cut his hands, his knees. Once he remained down long enough to hear the soft, musical conversation of the waters beside him, then he got up and went on again.

The trees loomed scatteringly, at first, then in close files, loftily, and the sweet, keen fragrance of the pines refreshed him.

The trees dwindled in height. They grew sparser. He reached timberline, where all the trees ceased at once, where the realm of the rocks began, and where the wind leaped off the snows of the peaks and drove through him until the furnace of the desert seemed a happy, sleepy dream, in comparison with this new pain.

But he marched on. He could stop anywhere and build a fire for himself, he knew. But he would not stop. He despised the weariness that numbed his body and beat in his brain. His hands, he told himself, were still strong. They had not been used. He kept flexing his fingers to make sure of their strength and to keep the blood flowing in them against the time when they would have to clutch a knife haft, or a throat.

He reached the crest of the pass. He knew it because the steady slant of the ground began to be downward. There was no stream beside him, at first. Then a new murmur of water began, faintly, and it ran in the direction in which he was going, so he knew that he had topped the divide.

At this, he stopped for a moment and looked up at the bright stars of the sky, placid, indifferent to him.

"They'll see something tonight," Rippon said to himself.

A moment later, as he strode along, a ray of light reached him like the point of a sword, a startling and bewildering thing in that frozen night. He could not help turning toward it.

"Perhaps it's the campfire of him," said Rippon.

He did not believe that such a thing could be, but he went on toward the fire. He stumbled against a rock. He recovered himself, and went on, again. The fire grew. A smell of roasting meat came to him—bacon. Then he smelled coffee. The goodness of those odors was past belief. His mouth filled with saliva, and he grinned as he stalked on through the darkness. Pain was forgotten. The troubles of the day grew small. He was about to eat; he was about to have food between his teeth, and against his palate, and passing down his throat into the vast emptiness of his maw.

But now he grew more careful, for he was so close that he could see the shadow of the fire tender bending here and there, wavering as the flames jumped. It was a good, big heartening fire. He stretched out his hands toward it, and he stretched out his desire toward it. At that moment, he heard a horse stamp, and, dropping to one knee so that he could see the better, looking up across the field of the fire, he made out the form of a horse grazing, a deep-bellied, Roman-nosed, ewe-necked horse—Baldy!

At this, he stayed down for a long moment, for he knew that he was at the end of this trail, and that he was about to kill a man. He never had taken a human life. There had been fights, from time to time, but always with the fists. Once he had had to use the barrel of his Colt to tap the head of a quarrelsome, drunken fellow, but, otherwise, his hands had been enough. Men, no matter how high their spirits or how wild with drink, usually sobered enough to avoid that grim face of his, those wide shoulders, significantly furnished at the tips with rounded knobs of muscle. But now he was about to take a human life, he told himself.

He had no conscience about it. No jury of Westerners would give him anything but praise, when his story was heard. His horse had been stolen from him when he was in the midst of the water famine on the desert, and for that sin there was only one proper punishment.

He went nearer to the fire, stepping softly, feeling his way with his wounded feet, making no noise, his eyes ever upon the form of the man by the fire.

The traveler had spread his blankets. His saddle was to serve as a pillow. The rifle and a holstered revolver lay beside the saddle. A coffee pot steamed on the edge of the fire, and the man was drinking from a tin cup that might hold half a pint or more. To Rippon, this was traveling deluxe. He came right up to the edge of the firelight, until he was facing the stranger, and as close to the latter as the thief was to his guns. There Rippon paused to survey his victim.

When the cup was lowered, he was disappointed. It was not the face of a strong man. Rather, it was a face that could have been strong but had lost its natural character. There was a highly arched nose, a well-made jaw, eyes protected under big, bony brows. It was a face like his own; the hair was sandy, like his. The eyes were blue-gray, like his. But there the resemblance ceased, for the face was pale as the belly of a dead fish. The years of this stranger must be about his own, but time had told more heavily upon him, and the features were partially masked or obscured by a flabbiness of loose flesh. Hanging folds, deep lines, appeared beside his mouth. His throat was gross. His body was deep, not with strength but with excess weight, and, as he sat, he sagged forward, his shoulders hanging.

His ride on a horse had fatigued him more than the terrible march of Rippon on foot had exhausted the latter. As he watched him, Rippon felt like a lean and active mountain lion with a fat house dog before it—heavier, but a foolishly easy prey. He had planned upon a robber, a man of action, and he had found a helpless bulk of flesh. How could he take this man in his hands and break him?

He gritted his teeth to rouse the ferocity that he had felt the moment before, but the hot rush of anger would not come, or else but slowly.

He feared that if he waited longer all his original impulse would leave him, so he stepped straight into the field of the firelight, as one throws himself into water where he must sink or swim. The stranger looked up at his face. It was amazing to see his calmness. Then he looked down at the feet of Rippon.

"You've had considerable of a walk," he said. "Sit down and rest your feet, stranger."

CHAPTER FOUR

But Rippon did not sit down. He dropped his big hands on his hips and spread his wounded feet more widely, so that he would be braced and ready to jump in, or out, or to either side. He merely stared at the thief, and the horse thief stared back at him.

Presently the head of the latter jerked up and his eyes narrowed with curiosity. "Hello," he said. "Who are you?"

"My name's Rippon."

"My name's Palding," said the stranger. "What's the matter? What's biting you?"

Still, Rippon would not answer. But he drew a little closer. He passed the boundary inside of which a man feels the physical presence of another, like a hand on the shoulder, sometimes like a blow in the face.

The horse thief seemed to feel the latter shock, for he winced back suddenly. Then, staring up at Rippon, his pale face grew still whiter, and his eyes widened.

"You're him, are you?" he asked.

"Yes," said Rippon, through his teeth, "I'm him."

Palding nodded. "You wanna be mean," he stated, "but you can't. You ain't feeling so mean, just now, as you are hungry. Am I right?"

Rippon, waiting, trying vainly to gather his rage about him like a cloak of thunder, looked steadily at the other, and, under sagging, weary eyelids, the man stared back at him, smiling a little, as one armed with a superior knowledge.

"I stole your horse. There he is," said Palding. "There's a good saddle on his back, and a pack as good as the one you left behind you. If you had guns, there are mine. If you had a hard march, I'll pay you in cash for it. I'll make it the best day's work you ever did. How does that sound to you? Now sit down and feed your face."

He said this in a dull voice that had rather a rasp to it, a trailing rasp of fatigue. It seemed as though life or death were small matters to him, he having already lived too much. The rage of Rippon dissipated like a mist when the morning breeze strikes it and shatters it. He sat down. A cup was handed to him and poured full of steaming coffee. As he drank it, fresh rashers of bacon were laid neatly in the frying pan, and in another moment he was eating with a great rush of appetite.

At first Rippon was uneasy. It did not seem to him that Palding or any other man could be so preternaturally calm in the face of a danger like this. He had a feeling that some confederate of the horse thief must be prowling on the edge of the night, ready to slip up and bury a knife in the back of their victim. He had to shrug this idea away, as the chill it generated slid down his spinal column.

So he loosened his belt, ate more, finished a third cup of coffee, and now he sat with the cold of the mountain night gripping at him from behind, and the warmth of the fire saving him in front. He began to smoke, and all this while he had not spoken a word. Now he said: "Palding, you've hypnotized me. I came here to throttle you, and, instead of that, I've eaten your chuck."

That smile of Palding that was part mockery and part understanding continued. "I'm only pulp," he said. "You couldn't put your hands on a thing like me. I'm only the mold and mildew of a man. That's why I stole your horse. I knew when the mule was going to fail that I couldn't make it on foot."

He said it without shame, as one who knows facts too well to read them as a personal blessing or a curse. His smile had a larger meaning to Rippon; it mocked the world and it mocked him who smiled. He despised existence because he despised himself.

"It seems to be a joke, but somehow I'm not laughing," said Rippon. He thrust out his feet toward the fire and looked down at them.

"It's not a joke," said Palding. "You've marched all day to kill a horse thief . . . and at the end of your march you've found a job, instead."

Rippon smoked and said nothing.

"A five-day job for five hundred dollars," said Palding. "Does that sound to you?"

"Where?"

"In the upper Tyndal Valley."

Rippon started. It was the goal of his journey, from the first. He had a strange, cold sense that fate had joined him to this flabby wreck of a man.

"What's the job? Marking cards, or working the brake on a roulette wheel?" he asked. Then he stiffened. "I want none of your business, Palding," he said fiercely.

But Palding was answering the first question, and he said: "Your job is playing decoy for gunmen to shoot at. You won't turn down an easy job like that . . . after the work you've done today."

"I just step out and get shot through the head, eh?" On the hard face of Rippon appeared a smile at last.

The other was nodding. "Want to know about it?" he asked. Without waiting for an answer he went on: "Twenty years ago I'm there in the Tyndal Valley . . . a hard, mean kid, tough as sole leather, and fond of a gun. I have words with young Sam Barrett, one day, and shoot him under the heart. He drops dead, and I start east. Too many Barretts in Tyndal Valley, and every Barrett is a fighting man. I make dust, and I never come back. I have too much sense. My father and mother die. I rent out the ranch and get danged little for the land, year in and year out. It's not good land . . . the land is too poor to sell, in fact. So there I am with one foot in Tyndal Valley and the other foot in Chicago, New Orleans, New York . . . wherever the going is easiest and the ponies are running to my ranch.

"At the end of twenty years I get a letter from old Charles Barrett. He says . . . 'My boy, come home and settle down. We've forgotten what you did twenty years ago. Anyway, it was a fair fight.' I read that letter and scratch my head. It wasn't a fair fight. Sam Barrett had a gun, but it wasn't loaded. I knew it. The Barretts guessed that I knew it. It was murder, and they want me for that murder. But they have something more in their minds. They want me in Tyndal Valley for something more than to kill me.

"I take a look at myself in the mirror. I'm finished, and I know it. I've lost my nerve. I can't handle cards any more, and I can't read the minds of the ponies any longer. I'm a hulk. Pretty soon I'll either starve or start cracking safes, which is the straightest road up the river. So I say to myself that I'll take the long chance and go to Tyndal Valley to see what's up the sleeve of Charlie Barrett and what I can make out of the old ranch. That's what I start to do, and then I meet you on the way. You'll take the long chance for me."

Rippon squinted at the arched nose, the long jaw, the wide shoulders of the other. The thought flared like a spurt of fire across his brain. "They've never seen you for twenty years," he said. "I'm to go down there and wear your name until the shooting's over. Is that it?"

"Maybe there'll be no shooting at all."

"You don't think that," stated Rippon.

"No, I don't. Otherwise, I wouldn't offer you a hundred dollars a day."

Suddenly the wind was still, but, looking north among the stars, Rippon could see the Great Bear flat on its back amidst masses of tumbling clouds.

"And another five hundred to pay for your day's work today."

"I'd be a fool," said Rippon.

"We're all fools, most of the time," said Palding. "Turn into those blankets and sleep. I'll keep the fire up."

"You'll take the horse and start on," Rippon surmised.

The smile never varied on the sagging face of Palding. "D'you think that I'd ride away and leave my luck stranded behind me?" he asked.

And Rippon, snapping his fingers with a sudden reckless decision, went to the blankets, rolled himself in them, and was instantly asleep.

It was a dreamless slumber, from which he wakened shivering, to see the rosy hair of the dawn blowing over the mountain tops. He sat up and gave a sweeping glance to the naked peaks, the white heads, the crooked ravines of the upper slopes, filled to the lips with packed snow. Then he turned toward the fire.

It still blazed high. Palding must have fed it industriously all night long, and, as Rippon looked at the bend of the back, the weary drooping of the head, he forgot the crimes known and admitted by the scoundrel and remembered only this strange vigil that had given him a comfortable sleep. As he had given to his horse the last of the water, so had he been tended by Palding. Pity grew up in the heart of Rippon, and some remained even when he faced the big man, a moment later, and saw the half-suppressed and mocking smile.

CHAPTER FIVE

Rain scoured the highlands as Rippon came over them—rain rattled, and beat, and dashed against the slicker that he was wearing. And a cold wind started his feet aching, though they were wrapped in two pairs of socks and comfortable enough in the big boots that Palding had given to him. However, he dropped below the storm presently as he came down into the upper valley of the Tyndal River. Still, as he looked back, he could see the thunderheads standing around the peaks, quivering with lightning, now and then, but the valley was clear of clouds and the slant afternoon sun soon warmed his body and his heart.

The river widened from time to time as creeks ran down to join the main course. He saw a cascade flashing in the distance, and there were broken flashes on every green hillside down which the rills of rain water were running. It was like his dream in the desert, but more green, more crystal-clear, more beautiful. He had forgotten all about the rich fragrance of wet earth and growing grass; now it rose enchantingly into his face. And he saw cattle browsing, not the lean, hollow-ribbed creatures of the desert, but sleek-sided round tubs of fat beef and comfort. He saw sheep grazing, in closely formed wedges, upon the upper slopes. It was not the richest valley in the world. The rocks that showed their faces, here and there, were a token of the shallowness of the soil in most places, but to Rippon it was a dream of pastoral happiness.

He was so rejoiced that he half forgot the dangerous mission upon which he was riding, until the slant of the sun's rays warned him that the day was already wearing old, and, passing the crossroads and the bridge, he knew that he was close to the house of Charles Barrett. Yes, that was it on the hill to his right, clustered around by trees.

The journey had required no more than four hours; he was so late in arriving because he had spent the entire morning studying, with Tom Palding as his tutor. A map had been given to him to pore over and make out the features of it thoroughly. There had been talk about some of the Barretts. Not too much, but only the faces and the names that a man might be apt to remember after twenty years. There was Charles Barrett, first of all, who looked like a fox; young Jeremy Barrett, who looked like a lion with a yellow mane; and old Mrs. Mary Barrett, who had the color of a corpse and the penetrating wit of a fiend.

The rôle of Rippon was to be thoroughly non-committal. He was to listen much and to answer little, but he was to find out what mysterious change of heart had moved Charles Barrett to write that letter, and to make sure, if he could, that a Palding could safely live in the valley. Five days. One to get to the house, and four to live in the valley. And $500 for those five days.

"You'll earn it, I'm thinking," said the rascal, Palding, with his odd frankness. "Those five hundred dollars I've given you may belong to a dead man before the next sunrise."

Rippon could not help wondering at his own willingness to ride on the mission. It was indeed as if hypnotism had been used on him, but he guessed shrewdly that the chief hypnotic influence had been the danger itself. He was drawn forward by the power of the hidden mystery, as Bluebeard's wife toward the forbidden chamber.

He turned off the main road, unbarred and pushed open the gate, and, in spite of Baldy's prancing, he shoved the bar home again behind him. Then he rode up the lane to the Barrett house. The trees loomed big before him, glistening in the sun's yellow light. He passed through them and saw the house itself, two stories high, but the stories low and the structure having that rambling and patchwork appearance that surely tells of many periods of building. There was a kitchen garden at one side, fenced around with wire net, but holes had been broken through the netting, and there were a number of chickens inside the enclosure, foolishly strutting, or scratching, or picking at leaves with a judicial air. In front of the house was a long hitching rack, with holes pawed out in front of it, and the hitching bar itself gnawed almost through, in places.

The look of this place was home-like to Rippon. He dismounted, tethered Baldy, and rapped at the first door he saw. It was opened by a girl with her sleeves rolled up to the elbow and a gingham apron girdled around her. She had a dish rag in one hand. There was a sharp taint of pepper in the air, and she was sniffing a little, and her eyes watering from the strength of the spice.

"Hello," said Rippon. "Are you Linda Barrett?"

"No," said the girl. "I'm only Maisry. I'm only hired help."

She had a voice like a child's, thin and sweet. She was a pretty youngster, though her good looks were not improved by the way her hair was dragged back to a knot at the back of her head, or by the largeness of the smudge of soot across her nose. The front of the gingham apron was thoroughly wet with dishwater.

"I'm Tom Palding, Maisry," said Rippon. "I'm pleased to know you. Can you tell me where I'll find Charles Barrett?"

"My Jiminy," said the girl softly, and looked at him for a moment. "Are you a Palding?" Then she pointed. "Mister Barrett, he's over at the straw stack. He's cutting out a bunch of straw, I guess."

Rippon went over to the corral fence, slid between the bars, and walked out to the straw stack. There he saw Charles Barrett. He knew by Palding's description as surely as from a photograph. It was a thin, pointed face. The man was small. But he had a good, round chest and thick arms. He must be fifty, according to Palding, but he looked not a day older than forty.

"Hello," said Rippon.

"Hello to yourself," said the other. He let go of the backbreaking hay knife with only one hand, and frowned slightly as he looked down toward Rippon.

"You dunno who I am, I guess," said Rippon.

"I dunno that I do," said the rancher. He rubbed the heel of his hand across his dripping forehead and looked again, impatiently. "Well, who are you?" he asked. "Who sent you here, young man?"

Rippon rested an elbow on the top of a fence post. "I'm an old neighbor of yours, Barrett. Maybe you can guess the rest."

At this, Barrett straightened entirely and peered sharply down. His eyes sparkled, and made him appear more like a fox than ever. "You're not Tom Palding, are you?" he asked. "By the powers, you are!" He came hurriedly down the ladder, and, jumping the fence that secured the stack from the corralled animals, he confronted Rippon. He looked even smaller than he had on the bench of the stack where he was working. He looked still more powerful, also. "So you're Tom Palding, are you?" he said. "You were quite a boy. But I never reckoned you'd make this kind of a man. Shall we shake, Tom?"

"We might as well," said Rippon.

He took the stubby hand. It gripped him with a sudden might, amazing in so small a man, but Rippon merely smiled a little and then turned his own fingers of iron. The rancher gave up at once.

"I wanted to see if you're what you look," he said. "You are.

33

You're real. I'm gonna be glad to see you, before I know it. Come on into the house."

Rippon went with him to the house and knew that he was being surveyed every step of the way.

"I heard you were mostly breaking faro banks," said Barrett. "You look like you'd been mostly breaking broncos."

"I've broke some pitching broncos," said Rippon, "but the faro banks have always broke me. That's nothing new, I guess."

They reached the house. He felt that he had passed the first inspection fairly well, and once he could get this little fox of a man to lower the bars of judgment, all would be well, perhaps. For the five days, at the least.

They went in through the kitchen door.

"Maisry, we'll have another man for dinner," said the rancher. "Fetch in a pot of coffee, now."

They sat in the dining room opposite one another at the end of a long table that was composed of heavy planks laid across strong sawbucks. The floor was spur-scarred and heel-worn. The walls were utterly bare, except for two picture calendars, one of which showed the head of a race horse, and the other a girl in colors, with a sheaf of wheat straws between her white teeth. The naked boards had warped, here and there, leaving big cracks, and even a murmur would probably sound from one end of the ramshackle house to the other. They could plainly hear Maisry moving about in the kitchen, the floor creaking under her tread, the bail of the coffee pot falling with a clank against its side. Charles Barrett was still examining his guest with a stony eye of doubt when the girl brought in the cups and the pot.

"What'll you drink besides coffee or without coffee?" asked Barrett. "I've got some Old Crow, brandy. . . ."

"I drink whiskey," began Rippon, naturally, but then he saw, from the corner of his eye, that the girl was shaking her head violently toward him, and he added, as smoothly as he could. "But I don't drink a thing in your house, Barrett. Not till I know you better and why you want me here."

CHAPTER SIX

They stared at one another across the planks of the table, while the small brown hands of Maisry filled the coffee cups, and then put the pot at hand. She left the room before Barrett spoke.

"You've grown into a hard man, Tom," he said.

"Yes," said Rippon. "I'm pretty hard."

"You don't smile so much, like you did when you were a kid."

"No, I don't smile so much," Rippon responded.

Why had the girl warned him against the whiskey? Or was it against taking a drink of any kind in this house? The latter meaning, no doubt.

"You don't seem like Tom Palding," said the rancher. "But you've got the looks he'd have on growing up."

"I want to know why you've asked me out here," Rippon said again.

"I told you why I asked you. You tell me why you came?"

"Curiosity. I wanted to see the old place. What made you write?"

"Because twenty years is long enough for a dead man to be remembered," said Barrett.

"Not for you," Rippon replied. "You're not the kind to forget."

He saw the lips of the other compress a little. Then Barrett nodded. "You're not a fool, Tom," he said. "You never were. Not even as a kid. You knew when a man carried an empty gun, for one thing." As he said it, the center of his cheek was pinched with white, and his jaws locked hard on the last word.

Rippon sipped his coffee and watched his man over the rim of the tin cup. It appeared plain that he would earn his $500 before the end of the fifth day.

"You mean Sam Barrett's gun," he said calmly. His nerves tingled, but he kept his voice quiet. He had been ready to face the danger; he had forgotten about the shame. "I never knew a thing about that gun."

It was true, for that knowledge had been the murderer's— Tom Palding's.

Barrett dismissed the subject with a stiff gesture. His fingers never were straightened, entirely; they were hooked a bit from holding reins or pitchforks and hay knives.

"We'll drop Sam Barrett," he said. "You want to know why I asked you to come out here. I'll tell you. It wasn't for fun."

"No, I guess it wasn't." Rippon nodded.

"It was not for murder, either," said Barrett. "There come the boys in." He added this aside. The two dining room windows were flashing with red light now. From the distance, horses whinnied, hoofs pounded, and Rippon had a sudden failing of the heart as he realized that many men were now at the beck and call of this indomitable little tight-lipped man.

"I'm glad it wasn't for murder," said Rippon. "I hoped it wouldn't be for that."

"I wrote you another letter five years back," said Barrett.

Rippon nodded. Nothing had been said to him about this.

"You write back," said the rancher, "that no matter how much I want to buy your ranch, you won't sell it. You'll see me damned first. You don't want Barrett money. You'd rather have Barrett blood. Well, I wanted to get you to change your mind. That's why I asked you out here."

The girl came in from the kitchen, bearing a load of table dinnerware. "It's time for me to set the table," she said.

"You keep out of here," answered Barrett. "Dinner can wait a while."

As she retreated, the kitchen doors opened again and three burly youngsters came in close together.

"You don't remember these?" asked Barrett. "Harry, Joe, and Charlie, Junior . . . my boys. Harry, Joe, and Charlie, here's somebody you ain't seen for a good many years. You were kind of young to remember him, then. This is Tom Palding."

They stopped as though each had been struck heavily in the face. They looked fixedly at Rippon as if he were a snake. Then they glanced at one another.

"How are you, boys?" asked Rippon.

But he did not rise. He merely studied them, face by face. There was nothing of the father about them. They were built on an ampler scale. Their faces were more open, and none of the fox appeared. Three hardier, braver-appearing men he never had seen. They maintained their silence in spite of their father's introduction and the greeting from Rippon.

Charles Barrett did not reprove them. "Where's your cousin, Jeremy?" he asked.

That was the leonine member of the tribe, Rippon remembered.

"He's sleeking down his bay mare," said Harry Barrett, and still he stared at Rippon with a steady malignance.

"Well, you tell him to be handy. You all be handy. It's pretty nigh to eating time."

They went out of the room without a word. Each, as he went through the doorway, turned a baleful eye over his shoulder upon Rippon, and then the door was closed, softly, as if by one whose mind was filled with thought.

"What do you think of those boys?" asked Barrett.

"Three good, useful lads," said Rippon. "Well raised, too.

Nice, smooth manners. Regular thoroughbreds, anybody could see."

A smile twitched the corners of Barrett's mouth and went out again. "Let's get back to the matter of selling that ranch of yours," he said.

"All right."

"There's four hundred and fifty-five acres of it."

"Yes."

"Mostly rocks."

"A good many rocks."

"Fifteen dollars an acre is a gift, for land like that. You couldn't raise a quarter of a ton of hay an acre on it . . . but you're always sure of twenty ton of rocks. What do you say to fifteen dollars an acre?"

"I'm not selling the land," said Rippon.

Barrett smiled. "I'll make my top price right off the reel. Twenty dollars an acre. That's nine thousand and something. I'll call it ten thousand flat. I'm not a skinflint."

"It's not a bad price," said Rippon.

"Bad price?" Barrett cried out suddenly. He flushed with emotion. "You try to get the same price out of anybody else. Yes, or within three or four thousand dollars of that price! But I want the land. It fits into mine. It rounds me off. That's why I want it. It takes a danged elbow out of my ribs and gives me breathing room."

"I'm thinking," said Rippon.

"You've seen enough to save you a lot of time in thinking," said Barrett. And he chopped down the edge of his fist suddenly upon the table. The heavy planks quivered through all their length and breadth.

"I've seen you and your three boys," Rippon said. "Yes, I've seen quite a lot of persuasion around here, if that's what you mean."

"That's what I mean," said Barrett.

Here the kitchen door was pushed open again and in the doorway stood Jeremy Barrett. Rippon knew him at a glance, so well had Palding described him, and so easy was it for the description to fit him. Lion *was* the name for him.

"Hello, Jeremy," said Rippon.

"It's Tom Palding," said Charles Barrett quietly.

The yellow eyes of Jeremy burned at Rippon with a sudden flame, and then, without a word, he closed the door and shut himself from the room.

"Have you seen enough persuasion?" asked Charles Barrett softly.

Suddenly Rippon was smiling, not at his host, but at himself, his folly, and his fate, for what could be more absurd than the position in which he found himself, or more uniquely terrible? Because he had taken the name of Palding, he was in a trap. Because he lacked the authority to sign Tom Palding's name, he would have to stay there until the springing of the trap broke his back.

"Charles," said Rippon, "will you tell me short and simple?"

"Yes," answered Charles Barrett. "I'll tell you like ABC. You make that sale to me, or else you explain yourself to Jeremy and the rest. You explain to them that you really didn't know that Sam Barrett's gun was empty. You can explain that, I suppose?" He leaned back in his chair and sighed like a man who has finished a hard day's work.

"It only took a simple thing to catch me," said Rippon, nodding his head a little.

"Yes," said Barrett. "I still can't believe it. It doesn't seem possible that you've been such a fool. Well, we'll get on to the business, then you'll have to take my check on. . . ."

Rippon shook his head, and at this Barrett suddenly sprang to his feet, and, leaning over the table, he said through his teeth:

"You're not going to try to bargain with me, Tom, are you? You don't think that I care much whether it's land or murder, do you? By glory, as I see you sitting there with your cursed, sneaking smile, Tom, I've half a mind not to let you live, no matter what you do. I'll ask you once more. Do you make the sale to me? It's the last time I'll ask you, mind."

But Rippon merely smiled.

"Harry! Jeremy!" shouted Barrett suddenly.

And Rippon heard the quick answering of footfalls coming toward either door of the room.

CHAPTER SEVEN

On the right hip of Rippon was Palding's gun. It was a new Colt, accurate as a rifle, hard-shooting, and perfectly balanced for the grip of Rippon. He had tried that gun in the morning, and knew how many inches of hard pine wood a bullet from that Colt had whipped cleanly through.

For this weapon he now reached, but he changed his mind instantly. Through the two doors, the four young men were striding into the room—the three sons of Charles Barrett through one, and the leonine Jeremy Barrett from the kitchen, with a wisp of steam clinging about his shoulders like a thin cloud about a mountain height.

So Rippon did not draw a gun. Instead, he got up from his chair, and, with a long backward stride, he put his shoulders against the wall. He was ready to fight before he died, but there was no use making the gesture that would bring on the end suddenly.

"You see 'em, Tom," said Charles. "Now I give you the last chance that you'll ever have in the world."

"You sent me a safe-conduct . . . or that's what it amounts to," said Rippon. "Here it is." He took out the letter that Palding had given to him and laid it on the edge of the table.

Charles Barrett snatched up the letter hastily, and ripped it across. "What's the use of honor when you're treating with a murderer?" he asked. "Can you tell me that?" He cast the pieces of the letter to one side. "Will you answer me?" he commanded angrily.

Jeremy Barrett stooped and picked up the fallen pieces of the letter. He pieced them together along the edge of the tear.

"I'll not sell," said Rippon.

"You're about two-thirds crazy, it looks to me," said one of the Barrett boys.

"He's gonna get what mad dogs all have to get," said Harry.

"Where is he?" demanded a hard, cold voice near the right-hand door.

"It's Cousin Mary," said Charles Barrett. "Keep that door closed. Don't let her in."

Big Harry Barrett strode to the door and put his shoulders against it just as the knob was turned.

"Who's holding this door?" asked the dry, lifeless voice.

Harry, perturbed, looked over his shoulder at his father, and the latter made a mute gesture ordering him to persist in barring the way.

"It's me. It's Harry," he said.

"It's Harry, is it?" said the woman. "Harry, d'you know that this is your cousin, Mary Barrett?"

"I know that, ma'am," said Harry Barrett, looking over his shoulder again for help.

"Open that door this minute! D'you hear me?"

"Cousin Mary . . . ma'am," said the poor boy, stuttering a little.

"Don't cousin me. Open the door! They tell me that the murderer of my boy is in that room. Open the door and let me in!"

"I can't . . . ," said Harry.

But, as though a crushingly superior weight were applied from the outside, the door now forced slowly open, and Harry Barrett stood aside to let his cousin enter.

Mary Barrett, according to Palding, had a face like a corpse. No other description could have suited her at all. Like a white, dead thing she stood there in the doorway, staring at Rippon. Her hair, her eyebrows, her skin seemed all of one tone, and the fixed eyes seemed to have a film over them. She wore a tightly fitted black jacket that pinched her severely across the stomach and puffed foolishly high at the shoulders. In one of her bony old hands, deformed with work, she carried a lace handkerchief, thin as a bit of mist. She had on a gray woolen skirt and shoes fit for a farm boy, made of extremely heavy leather, but scrupulously polished with black.

Now that she stood in the room, she turned her head deliberately from one person to the other. The high, tight collar pulled painfully at her neck as she moved it.

"Is that him?" she said. She lifted her arm and pointed it directly at Rippon.

"That's him," said Charles Barrett. "That's the man that murdered your boy Sam."

"And are you gonna murder him to pay it back?" she asked.

The ugly word made even Charles Barrett stir a little.

"He'll get no more than comes to him," Harry Barrett said in defense.

"Heaven bless you, child," said the woman. "Did you think that I was trying to save him? Murder is as murder does. That's a saying, or ought to be one. Murder is as murder does, and my boy Sam has been lying waiting for twenty years for this day to come. Twenty years he's been lying there in the churchyard with his face turned up. . . ."

"Look here, Cousin Mary," said Charles Barrett. "Don't you get yourself too excited and. . . ."

"Oh, I ain't excited, Charlie," she said. "Not a bit. I know what Sam has been waiting for, though. I tell you what, Charlie. My boy's soul could never leave the ground for hell or heaven, until Tom Palding died . . . until a Barrett killed Tom Palding, as Tom killed my boy Sam." She started across the room toward Rippon.

Charles Barrett held out an arm to bar her progress. "You stay back, Mary," he said. "You're close enough now."

"I gotta lay my hand on him," said Mary Barrett. "I've laid my eyes on him, and now I've gotta lay my hand on him before he dies."

Her power so overawed all the others in the room that even Charles Barrett could not stand against her for a moment. He gave back and she walked straight up to Rippon. The latter shrank from her bony hand that was stretched toward him.

"Keep away from me, will you?" he said.

Suddenly she grinned at him. The sight of his disgust and his fear caused her the most violent joy. Her eyes flared at Rippon, and now she laid the tips of her fingers against his breast. Was it only a stroke of his imagination, or did a real chill flow out from her touch and pass into his very heart?

With her fingers resting against him in this fashion, she looked up to his face and said slowly: "If I could put twenty years into a curse, I'd curse you, Tommy. But I can't do that. I can only look you in the eye and hope that you'll see something in me that'll be worth remembering." Then she suddenly screamed: "Look me in the eye, look me in the eye! You looked at my boy Sam! You looked down a gun barrel into his eye. Look at me now!"

Rippon, terrified even where there was no reason for physical fear, dragged his eyes to hers and met the look of her steadily, though it cost him a most untold effort of the will.

The glare of triumph dimmed a little in her eyes, eventually. A shadow of doubt and of wonder took its place. She stepped back from Rippon and shook her finger at him. "Have you gone and made yourself honest, Tommy?" she said. "You ain't such a sneak and a liar, quite, as you used to be. Have you gone and made yourself honest?"

"Mary," interrupted Charles Barrett, "it's time for you to get out of this. You get along with you, Mary. We've got a little business to attend to."

"Oh, Charlie," she said, "it's like seeing another man."

A vague hope flickered up for a moment before the eyes of Rippon. If the old woman really doubted his identity, might he not quickly convince her that he was not Tom Palding, after all? But no—her next words removed that faintest hope.

"It's like seeing another man," she repeated, "except that the same face is there, and the same sneaking heart is somewhere inside of him. But he's more of a man. Thank goodness for that. It would need something more than the killing of a dog to make up for my Sammy. Hush, Charlie. Don't be pulling at my arm. You won't get me away any the sooner for all that."

"Cousin Mary," said Barrett solemnly, "it ain't the sort of a time when we want to have a woman around. It ain't the sort of a time. It ain't right. So will you get away from us, now?"

"I'll get away," she said. "I'm only gonna ask one thing of you, Charlie."

"Ask me, and I'll do it if I can."

"Did you get him here fair, or crooked?"

"What difference does that make?" asked Charles Barrett.

"Oh, Charlie, the difference of leaving my boy to sleep sound or to wake up out of the ground and curse us all. That's the kind of a difference that it makes."

"Jeremy," said Charles Barrett, "will you take her out of the room?"

Jeremy still remained fixed in place, with the letter in his hand, as though it were a copious document and needed many minutes for its perusal. Now he shook his head at Charles. "I won't budge to take her away," he said. "Cousin Mary, they invited Tom Palding down here to see us. They invited him safe and sound. It's all written down in Charlie's handwriting, right here. 'He'll be safe,' says the letter. The letter says it, in so many words."

He sighed, as the greatness of the difficulty overcame him. In his rage, his eye had been like a yellow glass, electric currents of light streaking out through it. Now the eyes grew dim, misty, like the eyes of a troubled child. He looked about him for help, his glance falling upon face after face.

"No, you're all Barretts," said Jeremy.

"You've started a good thing, Mary," said Charles Barrett angrily. "You've got Jeremy turning his hand against us, haven't you?"

"Him? Even Jeremy ain't a fool enough to want to let Tom Palding go!" cried the woman.

"I dunno," said Jeremy. "I feel sort of sick about it, just now. I feel sort of poorly about it. I've gotta make up my mind. Where's Maisry? She always helps me pretty good to make up my mind. Maisry!"

"Jeremy . . . you're mad!" shouted Charles Barrett. "Maisry ain't in the family. You can't ask her opinion. You can't tell her anything."

"You don't have to tell her," said Jeremy. "There ain't any need for that. She knows already. She knows all about us, already."

"Jeremy," pleaded Charles Barrett, "you're not going to be foolish? You're not going to ruin everything?"

"You're always calling me foolish," Jeremy said. "But I've gotta make up my mind. Maisry, come here!"

The kitchen door opened a crack. The frightened face of Maisry appeared.

"Maisry, you come and be the judge," said Jeremy Barrett.

CHAPTER EIGHT

"Get out, Maisry!" Charles Barrett yelled. "Get back into that kitchen where you belong!"

She shrank away. She would have closed the door and disappeared, but Jeremy reached back his long arm and caught her by the wrist.

"Let me go, Jeremy," she whimpered. "I don't want to come in, and they don't want me. Let me go."

"Let her go!" commanded old Mary Barrett. "I've never seen you so half-witted, Jeremy. Let her go, this instant. Letting kitchen help into the Barrett affairs . . . why, I never heard of such a thing."

Instead, he drew her strongly into the room. She clung with her free hand to the jamb of the door for an instant, but the steady, insistent pressure of Jeremy dragged her on until she was standing at his side. Not to caress her, but as though to retain her beside him more gently and securely, he put his arm around the girl. Rippon watched the vast muscles rippling under the sleeve of the shirt. The man was a Hercules. He used his strength with the most extreme care, but little Maisry was as though walled in with solid iron. She could not move. She could only look vainly around her for help and then up at the face of Jeremy, biting her lip, while a tear or two came trickling down her face.

"I'm not going to let her go," said Jeremy Barrett, "and one of these days I'm going to. . . ." He paused in the midst of the sentence, and put the torn letter under the eyes of the girl from the kitchen.

"Maisry, don't you read a word of it!" commanded Mary Barrett.

"I don't want to read it."

"Close your eyes! Don't read a word, my girl, or it'll be the worse for you!" shouted Charles Barrett. He was in a terrible rage. It spotted his face with white and with purple.

"I don't want to see it," Maisry said.

At this, a rumble came out of the throat of Jeremy. It was a murmur of thunder such as comes before the storm, and plainly the storm was rising in his heart. It showed in his eyes, the yellow lightning flickering there.

"She'll do as I tell her to do," said Jeremy. "Who'll say no? Who says no to me, I want to know? Do you say it, Charlie?"

Charles Barrett seemed to lose half of his anger at a stroke. At least he controlled his voice instantly.

"You don't know what you're doing, Jeremy," he said. "That's what I mean to say. Putting our affairs into the hands of kitchen help. . . ."

"Aye, you're a proud man," said Jeremy. "But if our affairs are right, it won't matter whose hands they get into. And if they're wrong, they've gotta be made right. Who says that Maisry ain't to see this letter?"

"I say it!" cried Mary Barrett.

"You're talking out of a grave," replied Jeremy, looking toward her with an expression of the greatest loathing and disgust. "You've been mostly in a grave for twenty years. You're with Sam. You're buried with him. You've only stayed alive to plague us, I'm thinking."

"Jeremy!" cried one of the boys. "You can't talk like that to Cousin Mary!"

"Let him talk," Mary Barrett said with a dreadful smile.

"There ain't men enough in the Barrett family, now, to make sure that their women get decent treatment. There used to be a different kind and a better breed. But they've died out. Now, there's only the hulking brutes like Jeremy, that wipe their feet on a woman's heart . . . and the rest of the Barretts, they stand by and won't help."

"Will you all be quiet? Will you have sense?" said Charles Barrett. "You're wrangling together. And here's Tom Murderer Palding right in the same room with us. Have you forgot that?"

But these voices, and these words, came dimly and with a dream-like uncertainty to Rippon, for he was scanning eagerly the face of Maisry, flushed by the kitchen heat, and watching the hand in which she held the letter of Charles Barrett. He looked so keenly that he noted one of the fingernails was broken and that as the face was flushed by the heat of the stove, so the hand was pink from much immersion in dishwater. The grease, the stain of the kitchen work was upon her, and the smudge was still over her nose. She seemed touched by the labor and by the soil of it more deeply than any other man or woman he ever had known.

She seemed, in the midst of the concentration of her reading, to be aware of his scrutiny and the place of it, for, still reading, she raised a hand and rubbed at the mark of soot. She spread the blur but hardly diminished it. Then she lowered the paper and looked up at Jeremy with pain wrinkling her forehead.

"Tell me, Maisry," said Jeremy.

"They're only pretending," she answered in a faint voice, meant only for Jeremy but reaching Rippon because his ears were trained so deftly on her. "They're only pretending. They won't hurt Tom Palding. In the letter they say they won't."

He looked down at her. The same expression, almost exactly, was in his face as was in hers, a baffled and troubled pain, wrinkling his forehead. "No," he said, his deep voice sunk low into gentleness that never could be really gentle, "they won't hurt him. They were only pretending. Now you can go back to the kitchen."

As though she were a child too feeble to get to the door or to find the way, he ushered her to the kitchen, keeping his great arm loosely around her, opened the door for her, and saw her through, and then closed the door behind her.

Every eye in the room except Rippon's was now fixed upon Jeremy. For Rippon already knew what was in Jeremy's mind and he was more interested in the expressions of the others. The three boys were like three big wolfhounds, eager on the leash, ready to leap in for the battle; Charles Barrett fairly trembled with excitement and controlled fury; old Mary Barrett was whiter than ever, and her eyes were merest gleams of light. All of them were staring at Jeremy. One might have thought that they dared not attack Rippon or carry out their project against him without the special permission of this single man, Jeremy.

And perhaps it was true.

The man was not over-alert in the wits. He was slow-minded, dull in the brain. But, nevertheless, there was such force in him that to Rippon he seemed capable of balancing all the other people in the room—this one against those five. For one thing, there was no dread in him. For the other, in his eye and in his bearing, and in the rippling power of his arms, one could see that, when he struck, he was a thunderbolt for speed and inescapable weight. So the five of them stood there leaning against a leash, and that which held them was the single hand of Jeremy.

"Well, Charlie, you were only pretending, Maisry says," Jeremy said.

"Tell me one thing," said Charles Barrett. "Are you going to throw yourself into this? Are you going to go against everybody, Jeremy?"

Jeremy puckered his brow once more, and the bewildered look of the child again passed over his face, and dulled his eyes. He went to Rippon and put a hand on his shoulder. With an easy movement, he turned Rippon toward the light of the windows a little more.

What power in that hand, thought Rippon. *As well to close with a grizzly bear as to stand hand to hand with such a fellow as this. There is such strength in him that it passes ordinary human experience. Or could one find the same thing in the circus, or sometimes on the wrestling mat?*

Eagerly Jeremy was looking into the eyes of Rippon, and the latter, with a great effort, looked back.

"You never did a murder?" Jeremy asked suddenly.

"No," Rippon answered.

"He lies!" shouted Charles Barrett excitedly.

"He lies! Don't let him try to persuade you, Jeremy!" cried one of the boys.

"Ain't lying easier than murder?" asked Mary Barrett.

"You never did a murder," said Jeremy. "You thought that Sam's gun was loaded, that day. You thought it was a fair fight?"

"I didn't murder Sam Barrett," said Rippon.

The simple weight of truth was in his words and in his voice. He himself could feel the ring of the right metal, here.

Jeremy turned short around, patting Rippon on his back and half shielding him. "Maisry is right," said Jeremy. "You were only pretending. You wanted to scare him. Is that right?"

The answer came from Mary Barrett, and it stunned Rippon. "Of course, we're only pretending. You've just stepped in and spoiled a game, Jeremy."

Charles Barrett and the three boys looked at her in bewilderment. But she kept on nodding, with a cold and continual smile.

"That's it, of course," she persisted.

Jeremy rubbed his knuckles across his forehead. "I thought

you were serious," he said. "I really did. I suppose that I'll always be spoiling somebody's game. I suppose that I'll always be a danged fool." Then he took a great breath. "But I'm mighty glad, Charlie. You dunno how glad I am. I thought for a minute that you really wanted to do him in. All four of you." He turned back to Rippon. "You see, it's all right. The Barretts are hard, but they're not what you thought, eh?"

"I'll be going along, then," said Rippon.

"You've had nothing to eat," said Jeremy. "You can't go along without eating something."

"I want to get to my place," said Rippon.

He went toward the door, and Jeremy went with him. It seemed an incredible thing to Rippon that he was actually walking past the four tense faces of those men who wanted his life. But there he was, and now at the kitchen door, and then standing over Maisry, looking down at her. The door had closed behind him. From the other room, where the five were, he could feel the stony silence. Their rage was so complete and perfect a thing that it made a sort of music, pursuing him, but all the rage of all five of them could not stand against the force of that one man, Jeremy.

"You're free of them?" the girl asked, looking up at Rippon, startled.

"Yes," he said. "I thank you and Jeremy Barrett for it, too."

"Come along, come along," said Jeremy. "You don't have to thank anybody. It was only a game. They had to try to get back at you, a little. They're all honest. All the Barretts are, I hope. Come on along, Tom, and I'll ride a piece of the way with you."

They went out and mounted their horses, Rippon on Baldy, Jeremy on a low-made bay gelding with quarters fit to pull before a plow.

"Look at that," said Jeremy suddenly. "Maisry's crying about something. Look back there where Maisry's crying."

CHAPTER NINE

Only in time to see Maisry turning away from the door into the shadow of the interior did Rippon look back, but the droop of her head and shoulders told him that Jeremy was right.

The big man halted his horse and looked back; he seemed about to return.

"She's like that," said Jeremy. "You never can tell when she'll start crying. I eat sadness when I eat her cookery. There's no joy in her. She never is glad, hardly."

"She looks pretty gloomy," Rippon agreed.

"You wouldn't know. She isn't gloomy, though. You hate gloomy people because they seem to hate you. But she doesn't hate you. She's afraid. That's what makes her sad. She's afraid that the sky will fall on her head."

He started his horse again, as he said this, and, as though the words were still in his mind, he looked up to the sky. It was the red heart of the sunset time. The west, the south, the north were all banded with colors, dancing with flame, and to the east it seemed that the storm clouds over the Tyndal Mountains were a sea of fire gathered in vast combers and solid billows, ready to tumble down the upper slopes and sweep Tyndal Valley to the bare bones of its rocks.

That stupefying thought jumped full blown into the brain of Rippon and made his heart leap. He had to grip his hand hard before he could force the vision to dissipate. His nerves were hard-strained. Even when he used his will, the thought would not quite pass, and he saw himself buried in the gloom of the valley with a red ruin impending over his head. For the first day had not yet ended; he had only lived through it to the verge of the night when the real dangers might just begin. And more than four days remained before him.

"She's afraid that the sky will fall on her head," Jeremy Barrett was repeating. "Some people are that way . . . they think a terrible thing is always just about to happen."

"Who is she?" asked Rippon.

"She? Oh, she just happened along. She's always been cooking for Charlie. About a year, now, nearly. Well, yes, a year when August Fourteenth comes along. She'll have been here a year, by that time."

Rippon looked down at the road, which was going past them at the slow pulse of a walk. He could read in several things between the words of Jeremy. The big man knew the date of Maisry's coming as a mother knows the day her first child was born.

"She just happened along from where?" asked Rippon.

"I don't know. Somewhere east . . . or was it north? She talked a little to Mary Barrett. Mary said that we ought to keep our mouths shut and thank our stars for a good cook that would work so cheap. So everybody has stopped asking questions." He smiled a little. "What difference does it make, where she came from?" he asked.

"Only to her," said Rippon. He thought of the smudge of soot on the bridge of her nose and the pink stain around the corners of her eyes. "Yeah. She cries a good deal," said Rippon. "I'd guess that."

"Some girls seem to be pretty much like that," said Jeremy. "They cry because they're happy, and they cry because they're sad. They cry because they're not home, and they cry when they are. But the tears don't mean any more than rain in summer. Maisry, she's like that."

He looked to Rippon for confirmation, and Rippon nodded, a little absent of mind. They passed through the gate at the end of the lane; Jeremy closed it after them.

"I'm going on all the way with you," he said.

"Thanks," said Rippon. "I'll be mighty glad to have you."

"I ought to hate you, the way all the rest do," said Jeremy. "But I don't. When I heard your name, today, I thought that I could. But I couldn't. It's a funny thing." He shook his head at this mystery.

"Jeremy," said Rippon, "whatever I was in the old days, I'm not that now. I want you to believe that, for a day or two. I'm not the same man."

"No?" said Jeremy. "Well, maybe you're not. I've seen the weak pup get to be the best of the litter. So maybe you've changed. You used to be mean. But there are not so many corners inside your eyes now, as there used to be. I want to see you home. It's a hard thing for a man to go home alone. And the place is pretty badly broken down."

"Is it?"

"Yes. The red windmill fell down last year. Phil Barry fixed it up a little and hoisted it again, but it's shaky. I suppose Phil wrote to you about it, when he was renting the ground?"

"No, he didn't write to me."

"Phil never could make any money on the place. The ground is full of rocks."

"Well, Charlie Barrett wants it," said Rippon.

"Does he? You don't say."

"Yes. He wants it. He'll pay ten thousand flat. Didn't you hear him say that?"

"I don't know that I did. Ten thousand? It's not worth that."

"No," said Rippon. "It's not worth that. But he wants it to round off his place."

"Does he? The Tarleton place would suit him a lot better, and that's good pasture. Joe Tarleton cut a ton and a half of volunteer hay on the marsh meadows last year. It came up fine. It was full of wild oats. Joe ought to plow those marsh meadows."

"They were always rich," Rippon said, at a venture.

"Not when you were here. They were under water, then. Don't you remember that?"

"Of course I remember."

"That's where we used to skate. You couldn't forget that, in the winter?" persisted Jeremy.

"No, of course I don't forget."

"Why, it sounded like you had forgotten . . . like you thought that the meadows had been free of water when you were here."

"No. Not that." He wanted to change the subject. So he said: "Why doesn't he buy the Tarleton place instead of wanting mine?"

"Tarleton wants too much. He wants fifty an acre. It's only worth forty. Why won't you sell your place, Tom?"

The answer on the tip of Rippon's tongue was that he would sell in a moment—if he were Tom Palding. But he checked that retort. He merely said: "The old place means something to me."

"Does it? Well, you have changed."

"Everybody changes in twenty years."

"No, not everybody. Maisry, she won't change in twenty years. She'll always be the same."

"Do you think so?"

"Yes."

"She might learn to be sort of more jolly," said Rippon.

"No, she won't change a bit," Jeremy said almost angrily. "I don't want her to change. One reason that I like her is that she's sad. It hurts me, but it makes me happy. I'm going to marry her, someday, I think, but I don't suppose that I ever could make her entirely happy."

Rippon, listening, found it hard to believe his ears. The man was not a half-wit. He was simply naïve, like a child. He spoke out every thought that came to him.

"You can't understand Maisry," said Jeremy. "Look at the way she cried when we rode off. Why should she cry? Because of you. Because of me? Because we were riding off and the valley would be dark pretty soon? Because she was glad you were free from the house? You never can tell what makes Maisry sad. Anything makes her sad. Everything makes her sad. That's why I'm going to marry her."

They reached a bridge. It sounded solemnly beneath the beating hoofs of the horses, the echoes rolling up the shallow draw beneath.

They went on in utter silence for another mile, the horses jogging, the saddle leather creaking like metal under their knees. Then they came to the house.

"Well, there it is," said Jeremy.

He drew rein, and Rippon started a little. He had forgotten all about the way to the house. The mapping that he had done in his mind had been rubbed out, for the time being.

There was a dark mound of trees of several kinds. Above it, in the rising wind, the wheel and fan of the windmill were jerking back and forth, making a loud creaking. Rippon hated the thought of sleeping in the house, this night, with the noise of the rusted mill creaking above his head.

"Well, so long, Jeremy," he said.

"Hold on," said Jeremy. "It's kind of dark. I'd like to leave you in the light. I'll go in with you."

"Thanks," said Rippon. "I'd like to have you, too."

They rode up to the corral gate. "No, the bar's on this side," said Jeremy. "Have you forgot that?"

"It's twenty years," said Rippon.

"It's twenty years, but I wouldn't think you'd forget that. Mostly, people don't forget things like that."

"Well, I've forgotten."

Jeremy Barrett already had the corral gate open. They left the horses at the hitching rack near the little weighted gate that opened on the boardwalk toward the house. They walked in under the low-reaching branches of a fig tree; the gate came back with the drop of the weight and banged heavily. A creaking sound ran a short distance down the fence, on either side.

Then they went into the house. Hardly any light remained in the sky, but there was enough to show them that the pane was out of one back window. They climbed in through that. Rippon went first, and found the air inside was close, warm, unfragrant. No matter how long the shack had gone uninhabited, there was a sense of ghostly humanity wrapped in the thick of the shadows inside. He scratched a match.

They were in the dining room, and it was a wreck. A leak had formed in the roof, and the water, descending, had fallen on the table. The dripping water and summer heat had taken the surfacing off the table and turned it white; the boards were warped beyond belief. This room had been papered. Half the paper was gone from the walls and lay scattered on the floor, looking as though rats and mice had gnawed it.

They went into the adjoining kitchen. It was a greater wreckage still.

"You stay in here," said Jeremy. "I'll go bring in your pack."

CHAPTER TEN

Against this proffer, Rippon did not protest, and saw Jeremy Barrett open the back door and go out into the night. For his own part, with another match he examined the kitchen wall and found there a lantern in which, strange to say, there was oil. He heard it swishing about as he took the lantern from the hook. So he pried up the chimney and lit it. No doubt, it had been left there by the last renter of the ranch.

With this light—a dim one, on account of the smoked condition of the chimney—he went on with the exploration of the house. He found that the kitchen was not altogether unfurnished with pots and pans, though several of these had been eaten quite through with rust. Beyond the dining room, the hallway hummed and whistled with the force of the wind, which still rose, and outside he could hear the hurrying grind and screech of the windmill, as it turned on its pivot back and forth. This noise gave him a sense that there was a definite time limit, and that he must finish with his exploration before long.

He went into a bedroom. It was just in front of the dining room and it was in a state of disrepair almost as bad as that of the dining room. Yes, worse, for the flooring had broken through, due to the fall of part of the ceiling. Through the gap above, he could look into the emptiness and the gaunt ribs of the attic, where the old rafter sagged under the weight of the roofing.

The opposite bedroom, across the hall, was perfectly sound,

to his surprise. The roofing was whole, and the bed was covered with a neat white spread, turned and tucked snugly under the mattress. On two of the walls hung framed, glass-covered enlargements of photographs—one of an elderly man with a forked beard, and one of a woman with a frightened face and a high-busted gown.

He went into the parlor. It was a room worthy of the old name. There was a bookcase with a few books in it. There was a flowered carpet on the floor, the strips of it sharply defined where the nap had been worn away. He saw a horsehair sofa, a big leather-covered armchair, a memorial wreath—under glass— hanging from the wall. On the central table lay a copy of *The Pilgrim's Progress,* the cloth cover stamped with a cheap tooling of flowers. There was a family picture album, also, and, opening this, he had hardly glanced through two or three pages before he saw a picture of Tom Palding.

There was no doubt of it. It was Tom as he must have appeared years before, dressed up for Sunday and church. He had on narrow trousers, a jacket with sleeves a good deal too short, gloves that barely reached the wrist, and he held his hat in his hand. His hair was brushed slick and straight back from the face, and his head was turned just enough so that the big arching nose stood out prominently, half in profile.

It was Tom Palding. All the passage of the twenty years could not mask or conceal that homely face. It had given a covering of gross flesh, but that was all. It had deepened the lines at the corners of the mouth. Time had accentuated the weakness without developing at the same time the incipient strength of the lad. Yet it was the indubitable Tom Palding with whom he had sat there among the mountains, balanced between a desire to kill and to help the rascal.

He took the photograph out of its page in the album. He lighted a match to one corner of it, and watched the curling of the cardboard as the flame climbed, turning the board flaming yellow, then red, then to twisting wafers of black carbon. These wafers turned yet thinner and smaller into little gray flakes of ash that broke away and drifted on the air. But he could not leave that photograph to bear a silent witness against him and accuse him of being not Tom Palding at all, but an interloper. There was, in fact, so much difference in his face and that of the picture—especially about the eyes—that he wondered any of the people of Tyndal Valley could have taken him seriously for the missing man.

However, the others in Tyndal Valley had not seen Tom for twenty years, and who would come to Tyndal Valley to claim that identity as a thing of any price? He was taken for granted, simply because he presented himself, because he was almost of a height with the other, and, above all, because their features were of the same general cast.

He dropped the last thin rim of the picture that remained in his scorching fingertips. He kicked the caked ashes to a dust, where they lay upon the carpet before him. Then, rubbing his hands, he picked up the lantern and prepared to return to the rear of the house.

He was not happy. That was certain. He was not a whit happy, and he wished with all his might—for the second time that day—that he had not allowed himself to be tempted by the wiles of plausible Tom Palding.

But there he was, committed to a strange task, and, much as he disliked it, he felt that he could not give it up. His sense of honor was not a thing that troubled him very often. Only in great issues it was sure to crop up as an unwelcome guest, and this was one of the occasions. For the task that had been assigned to him, and that he had accepted, must be done. A promise given was, to Rippon, a sacred obligation.

In the kitchen he opened the stove and saw that the firebox

seemed in good condition. He was finishing that examination when Jeremy came in with the pack. He said that he had turned Baldy into the pasture adjoining the corral. The pasture fence was sound and would hold the mustang, probably, unless it were a jumper.

Then they went out together. Jeremy Barrett held the lantern while Rippon, with the hand axe that he had found in the pack of Tom Palding, cut for firewood some brush that grew not ten paces from the back door. It was a tall, strong growth, and its size was a comment upon the many years the house had gone untenanted.

Rippon took the firewood back into the house and built in the stove a roaring fire, for which he opened the dampers above and the face of the firebox below. A rank steam and smoke issued from the stove. Summer mold and winter damp had invaded it and now had to be burned out, sending an acrid, stifling odor through the room. They opened the back door and the window; the wind came in and helped to scour the fumes away until, at last, the business was done, and the fire was burning cheerfully and sweetly with a good, gay, crackling sound.

Jeremy, meanwhile, was scouring out a frying pan, rubbing it with sand to get off the rust. When it was washed and clean, they sliced bacon into it, and stirred up flapjacks with flour from Tom Palding's sack. What was becoming of Tom Palding now, Rippon wondered? How was he managing there on the mountain heights without a gun, without ammunition, without a horse, without food? He had matches and a knife, and very little else, but the problem of self-maintenance had not seemed to concern the mind of Palding in the least when the two parted. Well, if his hands were empty, his wits were full.

And here sat Rippon, at last, eating doughy flapjacks and bacon and drinking strong black coffee at the kitchen table in the Palding house, while opposite him sat the enemy against whom he had been most strongly warned, the lion about whom Palding had not been able to say enough—Jeremy Barrett himself!

They finished. They sat smoking after dinner, puffing at pipes and looking at one another through the twists of blue-brown smoke.

"Tell me, Jeremy," Rippon said. "What made you do it?"

"What?" said Jeremy. "There in the house? Well, I hate to see numbers win. I hate to see one dog go down under a pack. But mostly it was because Maisry looked at you kindly. Maisry liked you, Tom. That's why I had to help you. I saw in her eyes, when she looked, that she liked you pretty well."

"She's a good girl and a mighty strange one," said Rippon. "But I don't mean what happened there in the house. I mean what's happened here. Why did you stay here with me till I'd had dinner?"

Jeremy puffed for a moment and looked at the ceiling as though he were repeating the question. "Well," he said, "I wanted to see you settled in. That was all."

"More than that," insisted Rippon.

Jeremy stirred suddenly, and the chair groaned in protest against his moving weight. "Well, there's a lot of them," said Jeremy. "And I was no friend of yours, Tom. It was only Maisry that budged me, today. But I thought, afterward, that I ought to stand with you against the rest of 'em. They're a crowd. You're by yourself. I thought I'd put myself where they couldn't persuade me away from helping you. So I came along here with you, and now I've been under your roof and eaten food with you . . . and not even Charlie Barrett can get his slick tongue around that." He banged his fist suddenly on his knee. "I wish that you'd never come back into the valley, Tom," he admitted. "You're going to make a terrible mix-up. There's going to be hell to pay, because you've come back here among us." Then he got up from the table and stood at the door, for a minute, scowling at the floor and thumbing the brim of his sombrero. "I'm going back home now," he said. "Mind you, now, Tom, that you look pretty sharp, all the time. I wouldn't sit with no doors or windows open and a light in the room. There are Barretts and Barretts in Tyndal Valley, and there's some of them would be proud of the job to shoot you through the back, while you sat in here smoking."

"Thanks," said Rippon. "I know that I've got to watch myself."

"So long, then," said Jeremy Barrett.

"So long," said Rippon. "I'm thanking you, Jeremy. I'm thanking you more than I can put down in easy words."

To this expression of gratitude, big Jeremy Barrett returned no reply, but, after lingering for a moment in the door of the kitchen, about to step out onto the back porch, he turned suddenly about and came again into the room. There he planted his hands on the end of the table and leaned massively above his host.

"Tell me, Tom."

"Aye."

"What makes you stay here? Why won't you sell the land? What's the good of the old place to you, except to get yourself a chance to be killed?"

"Why, you've got the right answer already," said Rippon. "It's the old Palding place. There isn't any other. You see how it is, Jeremy?"

"Twenty years away from it, but you still love the ground?"

"For twenty years I feared the Barretts more than I liked the land. But I'm back."

This suggestion, Jeremy took into his mind and considered, nodding his head up and down, bewildered, but grappling firmly with the problem. At length he shook his head, as though admitting that the thing was far too much for him.

"Well," he said at last, "Maisry likes you pretty well, and that will do for me. I don't feel my blood rise up against you none. Good bye again, Tom."

He held out his hand, hesitantly, and Rippon took it with a powerful grip, for he knew that this giving of the hand was to Jeremy Barrett a great and significant gesture, even more important than taking food in the house of another. The old tokens and the old taboos had a meaning for Jeremy. He was as close to the soil and as close to a frontier as any Indian.

Then he went hastily out into the darkness. The boardwalk to the corral gate groaned and clattered under his stride, the gate slammed, and the noise of the hoofs moved away down the lane. Rippon was left alone.

He did not realize, until that moment, how the power of Jeremy had surrounded and supported him, all this while, like the power of ranged troops. Now, the moment the big man was gone, every danger was liable to leap in at him—they might be lurking in any place near the house, for that matter, waiting only for their own famous champion to disappear.

In the first place, there had to be some slight security. In the second place, there had to be sleep. In the past two days he had overtaxed even his own lean, wolfish, supple strength of brain and body. So he set about himself a lair for the night.

Into the bedroom that was in repair he took all his belongings except his guns and a single blanket. With his slicker and the rest of Palding's pack, he made the semblance of the outline of a human form under the spread that covered the bed. After he had done that, he went back into the dilapidated bedroom.

He took a long, stout thread from the sewing kit, and fastened this to the handle of the shutter, for the shutters opened inward. This done, he wrapped himself in the blanket and lay down with his rifle beside him and his revolver lying across his stomach. In his hand he grasped firmly the end of the thread, giving it a twist or two around his forefinger.

His plan was simple. That window looked upon the south, and a strong moon was shining. If he jerked open the shutter, the shaft of the moon's light might well reach to the door of his room and even illumine the narrow hall beyond it.

So he closed his eyes, put his trust in the subconscious mind that must mount watch over him, and instantly fell into a sound slumber.

He was cold; the boards were hard; dampness crept up from the floor and invaded his bones; then rats came out and began to prowl, sniffing at his face, in the darkness, nibbling at the edges of the blanket, ravenous and curious. But still he did not waken. He slept almost like the dead, without a dream except, toward the end, a flickering vision of Maisry, with the smudge of soot upon her nose.

That vision snapped out like an electric light and Rippon sat up, wide awake, cool, all his senses about him. There had been no noise louder than the scampering of the rats, to be sure, but the new sound had a different import. It was the faint, faint groan of wooden boards when a weight is softly pressed upon them. That sound was coming up the hall. It began at the kitchen, and it proceeded slowly, slowly. There were pauses. Sometimes it seemed farther away. Sometimes it seemed nearer. It was so small a sound that he was half inclined to call it a fiction of his mind and go to sleep again, but he remembered that he was in Tyndal Valley, and that thought kept him strictly on edge.

He freshened his grip on the end of the string. The forefinger was numb from the twist of the thread about it, stopping the circulation, so he unwound it, and held it in another way. His revolver he raised from his lap. He bunched his knees and laid the gun across them, pointing toward the place where, in the darkness, the doorway ought to be. To make sure of its place, he put a hand against the wall beside him. It had a damp, clammy feel, but by its direction he was able to place the door securely in his mental map of the room.

He was very cold. The dampness from the floor had invaded his bones, and he shook spasmodically. He only hoped that he would be able to keep his hand steady for the crucial moment. Then something seemed to breathe in the room.

He held himself hard. He could feel his eyes bulging, as they strained through the darkness toward the door, but he could make out nothing. There was only that extra sense that told him of a living presence near at hand. Perhaps it was not a man at all. Wolves had been known to den up in abandoned ranches.

A moment later something flickered before his eyes like distant lightning. He knew what it was. It was the ray from a dark lantern, unshuttered a mere crevice so as to allow a probing ray to fly before the stalker.

With this, all fear left Rippon. He was at ease. For the sense of the mysterious was gone the instant that he was sure he had to deal with human danger merely. Still he waited. Once or twice he looked down, to remove the strain from his eyes. Then he probed at the darkness again, and, finally, it seemed to him that when he saw the ray of light again it was turned from him, stabbing into the opposite room.

He was there—with helpers no doubt. He who had come for murder was there in the hallway, sliding the delicate finger of light toward the bed in which lay the crude dummy that was supposed to represent Tom Palding asleep in foolish security.

Where was the moon, now? Rippon looked over his shoulder toward the shutters. He could see a faint glimmer through a few of the chinks. He hoped that it was lying directly south from the aperture. In that case, the light would flow straight in over him, leaving his position in darkness, and strike across the hall.

In any case, now he must try. He put on the thread a pressure. He felt the shutter give a trifle. He had been a fool not to make the thread double, triple, so that it would stand the force of a powerful jerk. Now he had to draw upon it gently, as upon some intangible thing. And only slowly the shutter gave, widened. A shaft of moonlight shot over his shoulder, and now the shutter swung to its full width, and straight through the doorway and into the hall flooded the moon. It did that, but also he felt its silver mantle falling over his own head and shoulders.

Even now he could not see very distinctly. He could only make out two pairs of boots with spurred heels, the extremities of two pairs of legs standing there in the hall, and above them, vague forms, glimmering in the dark of the night.

"Behind you! Behind you!" gasped a voice, and one of those pairs of boots leaped sidewise into darkness.

Into the phantom silhouette of the other, Rippon fired at the height of the heart.

CHAPTER ELEVEN

The whisper of the moment before was the precursor; the sound of Rippon's own shot was the signal for a moment of pandemonium. All in a trice, a dozen voices seemed to be shouting in unison. An answering gun fired from the corner of the doorway at him, and the bullet ripped along the wall beside his head, tearing through the rotten wood.

Then he was up. He got into the doorway with a single bound and slid like a serpent into the hall—like a serpent, for he landed on all fours—and, flattening out, he opened fire on the vague forms that rushed through the darkness into the dining room. Two bullets he spent on them, but he had a feeling that the first was low and the second too far to the left. Then he rose and charged.

Ordinarily he was a patient, cool man—almost cold. But there was something in the caution of this midnight attack and the murderous stealth of it that maddened him. Not only odds of number but of time and place were to be used against him, it appeared.

So, half maddened, he charged toward the dining room, and at the second step caught his toe in something soft and fell headlong, caroming from wall to wall before he hit the floor again. He was not stunned, but by the time he got to his feet again, he heard the footfalls fleeing over the back porch and away under the trees.

He jumped in turn to the dining room, through the open

doorway, and out onto the porch. There the hunter's instinct told him that the quarry had escaped. Yes, already hoof beats were beginning to rush away from the house. They must have brought the animals up close, leading them at a snail's pace.

The madness still held big Rippon. He leaped into the yard and sprinted to the corral gate. But there was nothing in sight. There was only the invisible and acrid dust still rising and blowing into his face on a gentle wind. He shouted with all his might. The beating of the hoofs was his answer. He shouted again, and heard, as he ended, the creaking of the windmill as it turned back and forth upon its pivot. Then sanity returned to him.

They were gone. They might return, but hardly on this night, for the gray of the dawn was already beginning, and they would not recover in a moment from the panic into which he had thrown them. He did not despise them for that panic. The suddenness of his attack would account for that, together with the ghostly atmosphere of the moldy old house. They would return, with their teeth set, bent on finishing the work that they had begun. But he thought he could count upon a day of peace.

That would be the second day of his vigil, and three more were to follow it. Suddenly he shook his head in despair. Five days! No human being could accomplish that visit to an enemies' land when the enemies were such men as the Barretts.

He went back to the house. Before he got inside, he could hear the groaning of a man inside the place. In the kitchen he paused to light a lantern. From the dining room door he held the lantern high, and by its illumination he saw a man lying prone in the hallway, turned upon his side, and clasping his body with both arms.

A fallen revolver gleamed in hand's reach of the fallen man, therefore, Rippon kept his own weapon in readiness as he approached. But the assailant of that night was too badly hurt, it appeared, to think of self-defense. He lay groveling and groaning, and Rippon leaned over him and shone the lantern full in his face.

He had half expected to find that it was one of Charles Barrett's sons. But it was not. Instead, he saw a round, ruffian face, red hair, and small eyes, now closed with pain. The man might be thirty, or even younger.

"Are you done up, stranger?" Rippon asked.

The latter looked suddenly up at him, his eyes opened now, but still half blinded and disfigured with pain. "I'm done up!" he gasped. "I'm killed. You've killed me, Tom Palding. Damn you, you've murdered me from behind."

The humor implied in this remark did not bring a smile from the lips of Rippon. Instead, he nodded his head sagely. "We'll have a look at you," he said.

He leaned and picked up the body of the stranger in his arms. The latter screamed suddenly with agony and stiffened, but Rippon calmly strode on with the weighty burden and brought it into the bedroom, the one in which the bed stood with the clumsy imitation of a man lying under the tucked-in spread. He laid the sufferer on the bed, got the lantern, and put it on the chest of drawers. He found his wounded man still turning a little from side to side. He was groaning, though there was enough manhood in him to make him keep his teeth locked to suppress the groans. Still they broke through, forcing their way.

Rippon examined him. He knew wounds fairly well. He had seen men badly shot before, and now he traced as clearly as he could the probable course of this bullet through the vitals. It had struck in the small of the back; it came out at the right of the breast.

Probably it had gone through the lungs. If so, the fellow would be dead in half an hour. But perhaps it had glanced from the spring of the ribs and shunned the vitals. In that case, he had a chance of living. There was one hopeful sign, which was that he was not breathing crimson foam, as a man whose lungs had been pierced was apt to do.

Rippon had an odd thought as he looked down at the hurt man. An animal, or an insect, or a viper, might be crushed underfoot, mangled, limbs torn away, and still it would live unless the vitals were macerated. But a human being's life went out at the mere comparative prick of a pin. He thought of that, and then he began to give the sufferer such care as he could.

He washed the wound, front and back—a small puncture in back, purple-rimmed, a horrible, gaping hole in front. He made a bandage with a cold compress to cover both the openings. Then he wrapped up the fellow warmly. The rosy dawn light now slowly seeped through the windows and made the lantern unnecessary.

"Now what'll you have?" he asked.

"A smoke," said the wounded man.

Rippon made him a cigarette, lit it for him, placed it between his lips. The man puffed at it gingerly, but with a deep enjoyment. Deep breathing hurt him too much to allow him to inhale profoundly, and, therefore, he could only smoke with short puffs, but presently the animal look of agony began to abate in his eyes.

"Palding," he murmured.

"Aye?" said Rippon.

"They told me you were a skunk. They lied."

"Thanks," said Rippon. "Who are you, stranger?"

"I'm Bud Caswell of German Creek. They told me you were a skunk. I was a fool to believe them. Damn them, if I live, I'll make things hot for the whole Barrett tribe. Including Jeremy."

"He had nothing to do with this."

"Maybe not, but he's their star. He's their ace."

"Did they pay you big, Bud?"

73

"They paid me twenty dollars down. They were to pay thirty more if the thing went through. Damn them again."

Fifty dollars! Well, the $500 for which he had engaged to take the name of another man and live in a pit of danger was hardly more—considering that he had five days of peril to pass through.

He went back to the kitchen and cooked a breakfast. He made for Caswell black coffee, bacon, flapjacks from the night before, toasted in the frying pan with bacon grease. But Caswell could take nothing but a few swallows of the coffee. He wanted water, much water, and little else. And he cursed the rusty taste of the water from the well.

So Rippon sat beside him for a time and considered. There was still no sign of danger in the breathing of the other. His eye remained fairly clear, but his face was hot and his hands were dry. A fever was undoubtedly coming on, and a fever might carry off the fellow.

As he pondered, he listened to the busy spinning sound and clanking from the windmill near the house—the old red windmill that had fallen down and had been braced again upon tottering legs. The whirring of it sang in his thoughts almost like a human voice. And it seemed to tell him that the life of the Paldings in Tyndal Valley, long intermitted, was now beginning again. When he had untied the lever arm that allowed the fan to straighten into the wind and the wheel to work, he had had no special feeling. Now it seemed to him that it had been important—like the laying of a cornerstone, or the birth of a son to a famous man. Life had resumed its course at the old Palding house—and what would come of it?

"Bud," he said, "how's your head feeling now?"

"Fair. Beginning to ache."

"It's beginning to ache? You're going to have a fever. You'll need nursing. Maybe better nursing than I can give you."

"I ain't gonna live," said Caswell. "I know where the bullet hit me. I can feel the tear of it, where it went inside me. Only, I wanna die a little comfortable. Reach me the water, Tom Palding, like a good fellow." Rippon gave him the tin cup, and Caswell drained it. "That's better," he said. "I seem to be all lined with sand. Deep as the desert. The water, it just soaks in and it's gone. I've got a hot sun eating it up, inside of me."

Rippon resumed his thoughts.

"Palding," said Caswell, "think of what a fool I've been. Fifty dollars, to die. Fifty dollars, and the sneaking hounds ran away and left me, six of 'em."

"Who were they?"

"They were. . . ."

Then suddenly the teeth of Caswell clicked. Rippon looked down at him, and he glared steadily back, in defiance.

"You might as well tell me," said Rippon. "You've already said it was the Barretts."

"I've named nobody," said Caswell. "I'll name nobody. I never passed the word on a partner. Not even on a yellow sneak of a partner."

"Listen to me," said Rippon. "I've got to get you to where you'll have help. You don't mean much to me, Bud. But I'll make a bargain with you. I'll get you into Tyndal, where there are doctors, if you'll promise to tell the names."

There was a deep groan from the other. Then he shook his head, without saying a word, and a look of despair that might be the forerunner of death appeared in his eyes. But, plainly, he was a man willing to die inside his creed.

The manly heart of Rippon was stirred. "Mind you, Bud," he said, "you'll need to keep your teeth set. But I'll try to pull you through. I'll get you to Tyndal if I can, and you won't have to speak a word."

CHAPTER TWELVE

He got Bud Caswell to Tyndal.

It was no easy trip. Under the rack and ruin of the carriage shed he found the remains of an old buckboard. It was hard to call it a wagon, but it had four wheels, and, after Rippon had trussed and bound it with baling wire, it promised to stand for part of the way at least. When the wagon was patched together, a harness had to be improvised for Baldy, and this was managed using the saddle as the center and essential feature of the whole. Then Baldy had to have half an hour's vigorous riding before the fiend that was in him at daybreak every day had been somewhat subdued, and, when all these things had been accomplished, Bud Caswell had to be taken to the buckboard.

That journey was made in the strong arms of Rippon, and, after the first few steps, he could not endure to look down into the agonized face of his burden, set like white iron. But he got Caswell into the buckboard, and well propped and padded with blankets. Two sacks, loosely stuffed with grass, helped to make him easy, but the main help was the bed of pine boughs with which Rippon had filled the bed of the wagon.

Even so, it was to be a painful journey, and they both knew it. Five miles lay ahead before Tyndal would be reached, and the road was rough. To ease the pain of the wounded man, Rippon led Baldy on at a walk. It was two hours before they saw the little town loom suddenly before them around an elbow of the road, and then Rippon called back the cheerful tiding to his passenger. He got no response, however. He stopped the wagon, ran back, and looked at Caswell, as he had done several times during the journey, always to be met with a slightly twisted grin. There was no grin now, however. Caswell had fainted. His forehead was crimson, and his cheeks were white as stone, as though the skin had been painted. At first, Rippon thought the man was dead, but when he laid a hand over the heart, there was a steady pulsation, though a feeble one. He went back to Baldy's head and hurried him on into the village.

A pair of boys came out, whooping with laughter at the sight of the strange vehicle.

"Where's the best doctor, kids?" asked Rippon.

"Doc Power," they answered together. Then they peeked at the motionless figure inside the buckboard and stopped their merriment. They led the way straight down the single street of Tyndal.

It was cut after the universal Western pattern of that day, with false-front second stories rising meager and flat above the street floor. At every corner was a saloon. Wind pools of dust formed above the unpaved street. And loiterers started out from the verandah of the old hotel, from the corners, from before the post office, and formed a sudden crowd around the buckboard and its cargo.

They passed through the business section—a single block—and reached a small house, white painted, with a trim hedge of fir growing around it. Inside a front window appeared a long card, and on it, in tall lettering: *CHESTER POWER, M.D.*

Dr. Power was in the front yard, hoeing weeds. His clothes were like those of any cattleman, but he contrived a professional appearance by wearing a short beard, trimmed to a point, and a big pair of spectacles that were now pushed up on his wet forehead. He was an old man, with white hair and beard, and bristling black eyebrows.

The boys scampered ahead and told him why he was wanted, so he came hurrying out and stepped through the crowd to the wounded man. He laid a hand on his pulse and then looked into his face.

"Take him right into my house, boys," he said. "He may live there and he may die there . . . it'll be a quick turn, either way."

Very readily half a dozen men picked up the hurt man and the bed of evergreen boughs on which he rested. This acted as a stretcher, and they bore him into the doctor's house, down the neatly carpeted hall, and into the spare bedroom. The doctor's wife was already turning back the covers of the bed. Bowed and starved thin by years, she seemed to big Rippon a mere little cricket of a woman. But her compressed lips gave her the appearance of a person capable of action, and her eyes were uncannily bright and quick.

On that bed they laid poor Bud Caswell. They cut away his clothes. Mrs. Power brought a basin of hot water and other essentials. The doctor set about his work calmly, smiling a little. It was not that he despised the pain or the danger of his patient, but he seemed to feel a touch of professional joy in finding a case that filled his hands with occupation and tested his skill at the same time.

The crowd was banished from the house. Perhaps it was out of respect for the mortal danger in which Caswell lay. Perhaps it was merely the bright neatness of the little house, the polished margins of the floors, the thin vases of flowers, here and there— but they went out on tiptoes, creaking down the hallway, closing the door softly behind them. Only when they reached the street did their voices begin again.

Rippon remained behind to assist. He had never seen the probing of a wound. It sickened him to watch the thin, gleaming steel pass into the body of the hurt man where the bullet had made a way before.

The doctor asked him now for this, now for that. And Rippon handed over what was needed, but he felt his face growing cold and his brain dizzy. Caswell stirred and groaned deeply, slowly. Rippon felt a stroke of pain dart through his own flesh.

The doctor was drawing out the probe. "He ought to be dead now," said Dr. Power as he began to dress the wound. "There's no good reason why he shouldn't have died when that slug struck him in the back." He looked suddenly aside at Rippon. "Friend of his?"

"No. Not hardly that."

"You did it, then?"

Rippon nodded.

"Through the back, too," said the doctor meditatively, and began to nod. "Well, it'll be a good thing for you if he gets well. It certainly will. And I'll be able to tell you, inside of an hour or so. What's your name?"

"I'm Tom Palding."

Dr. Power continued to put the dressing on the wound. He did not look up toward Rippon as he heard the name, but merely murmured: "Tom Palding, eh? You've come back, have you? And sort of picked up where you left off, it seems?"

Rippon gritted his teeth. This side of the thing had not occurred to him as a possibility. Now he could see the natural cause of it, however. Tom Palding had gone away under a cloud, suspected, rightly, of the murder of young Barrett. Now, when a man who called himself Tom Palding returned to Tyndal, his first act was to shoot another man through the back.

"I'll go outside and wait there till you know how he'll do," said Rippon.

"Yes, you go out and wait," Dr. Power said. "He should have died when this slug hit him, but I think the ribs may have turned it enough."

Rippon went out through the house, not on tiptoe, but head

down, with a heavy stride. His feet were still sore inside the big boots of Tom Palding, but he forgot the pain as he strode down the little hallway and stepped out onto the verandah. There he sat down to wait.

The front of the house looked west, and the sun was creeping slowly around the corner from the south, dividing the garden into two sectors, one cold with shadow, the other glistening with light. Rippon looked down at the flowers in the dark and the flowers in the light and felt an odd pang of heart. He could not tell why—perhaps it was because there was both beauty and senselessness in those blossoms and the fragile leaves that shuddered and bent under the wind.

He looked across the street. There were gathered a few loitering men. A woman came out from a house opposite, wiping her hands on her apron. She stood, arms akimbo, in the middle of the group, and talked busily with the men. She had a brutal, flat face, and a round red neck, with unkempt hair flying about. She had her greasy hands doubled into fists and planted on her big hips, and presently she turned her head and stared toward Rippon.

Besides men and the woman, there were boys, as a matter of course, assembled in that group. They scurried here and there, from time to time, playing pranks on one another, but they always returned to stand and stare. Sometimes they whispered opinions to one another, and then yelled suddenly with laughter.

These were all small signs and a small picture, perhaps, but the heart of Rippon grew steadily colder. A youngster ran around from the back of the house. As he passed Rippon, he stared at him so hard that he blundered into a flower bed. He ran on to the gate, still looking over his shoulder at the stranger. He crossed the street and began to talk, pointing back toward the house of the doctor.

Suddenly all the talk ended. Everyone turned and stared

steadily, fixedly at Rippon. He understood, then, what had happened. The word had been passed that he was Tom Murderer Palding, and that he had shot a man through the back.

Well, Bud Caswell would rectify that. Bud was man enough to put that story straight. The thought had hardly brought its comfort to Rippon, when he heard an outburst of talk from within the house, talk in a rapid, high-pitched voice that broke off in a groan. Then it began again, a senseless babbling. No, there would be no immediate testimony from Bud Caswell. The man lay delirious on his bed and could not speak in behalf of anyone.

Other people gathered now to the crowd, as to a lodestone. And still, as they talked, canting their heads together, they stared solemnly at the stranger. Rippon began to wish that he were a hundred miles from that town.

Then, up the street, came a little man with a brisk step and a smiling face. Even in the distance, Rippon had an extra sense that told him that brisk little fellow meant to come to him. He was not mistaken. He saw the stranger wave to the group across the street, and then he turned straight in through the doctor's gate.

The instant he did so, the crowd flooded across the street, kicking up a lofty dust cloud that hung like a thunderhead in the windless air of the moment. And along the line of the hedge they pressed, resting their elbows on the yielding upper surface of the evergreens, staring always at one local point, and that point was the face of Rippon. They leered at him, as at some creature already prisoned and confined, helpless and hopeless, and worthy of their malice. By their coming, and by their leering looks, he could gather that the approach of the little man bore no good for him.

"Well?" said Rippon.

"I'm Sheriff Joe Clark," said the stranger, and smiled at him.

CHAPTER THIRTEEN

As for his smile, well, he was always smiling, and, therefore, Rippon discounted the amiable expression. The man had one of those lean faces that naturally wrinkle and pucker in the center of the cheeks, drawing back the corners of the mouth.

"My name is Tom Palding," Rippon said, and waited.

He was beginning to feel uglier than he ever had felt in his life. He looked straight and steadily at the other, and the sheriff looked straight back at him. Horsemen have such an eye, gentle ordinarily, but when they are aroused, cold and still as a reflection in still water. Rippon knew both the eye and the expression of it perfectly well. He knew that behind this man there was a real soul of courage and a nerve of steel.

"That's what I heard," said Sheriff Joe Clark. "That's why I'm here."

"Interested?" suggested Rippon.

"Yes. A lot."

"In me, I suppose."

"Always interested in a killer," said the sheriff, and his puckering cheeks forced him to smile again. He added, and even that unnatural smile went out: "Interested a lot more in murder."

"Murder?" Rippon said.

"Maybe you don't know what I mean," said the sheriff. "But shooting folks in the back . . . that's murder, in this part of the world."

"You mean that I shot Bud Caswell in the back?"

"Well, didn't you?"

"You ask Bud . . . well, you can't ask him, because he's delirious just now."

He hooked a thumb over his shoulder, and the sheriff canted his head a trifle to listen to the faint ravings of the sick man.

"Yeah," said the sheriff, "you'd like me to ask him, I guess."

"Yeah. I would, though."

"But you admit that I can't?"

"I admit that."

"You're under arrest," Joe Clark said. "Anything that you might be used ag'in' you. D'you want to talk?"

"To you?"

"Yes. You might try me. I never crowd a man, Tom Palding. Not even a man like you."

There was enough disgust in the voice and in the words, but there was more in the glance that hastily swept Rippon from head to foot, considering him and finding him unsavory. That was because he wore the name of Tom Palding, of course. Never in his own life had he been regarded by another human with such a glance. He was dressed by that name in a reputation that was none of his own. And it was a skin that he could not cast. According to its pattern, he must have his being and his name in Tyndal and all the valley and all the range of the nearby mountains.

"You want me to tell you what happened, I suppose?" Rippon said.

"I don't ask you. Unless you want to give me the truth. I say, you're under arrest. Maybe you'd better save everything for the judge."

Rippon smiled bitterly. "I'll talk to you a little. I don't mind," he said.

"Go ahead, then."

"I came down here because Charles Barrett wrote me a letter. You know the Barretts?"

"I know 'em. Better citizens never were in Tyndal Valley."

"So you won't believe anything that I tell you, of course."

"You can try me," said the sheriff, the acid coming strongly into his voice and into his sneering eye.

"I'll try you," Rippon said. "I want to see how far an honest man can make a fool of himself. I tell you that Barrett wrote a letter and asked Tom Palding down here into the valley."

"He asked you, did he?" There was surprise in the face of the sheriff.

"He asked. Like a fool, I came. I went to his house. He said that he wanted to buy the Palding ranch for ten thousand dollars."

"Hey!" cried the sheriff. "It never was worth that much."

"He wanted to buy for ten thousand, and I said no."

"You refused it? That was a fool thing to do."

"Maybe, but that's what I did. I hadn't been back for twenty years. Sometimes a house and land means more than money."

"To you, eh?" The sheriff sneered. Disbelief was written all over his face.

"Hear what I have to say," said Rippon. "When I said that I wouldn't sell, he got in his three sons, and with them he got in Jeremy Barrett. He was going to have me butchered on the spot. For the killing of Sam Barrett, twenty years back."

"I know all about that," said the sheriff. "Go on and talk, Palding."

"Well, then," Rippon continued, "I said that I wouldn't sell, anyway."

"Even with guns at your head?" the sheriff said, incredulity in his voice strongly.

"I said that I wouldn't sell."

"And then?"

"They were about to mob me, but Jeremy interfered. He's

nine-tenths honest."

"Jeremy Barrett? He don't know what it means to be crooked."

"Well, he got me away from them. He rode with me back to my house. There we had supper together."

"He ate with you in the Palding house?" the sheriff said.

"That's what he did. Then he went home. I went to sleep in a broken-down bedroom. In the middle of the night, half a dozen or more men walked into the house. I expected them. I'd laid a sort of a trap. I sprang the trap when I heard them, and I shot at a man that I saw in the hall. That man dropped. The others ran. The man that dropped I've brought back here to Tyndal. That's the story . . . the long and short of it."

"What's your proof?" snapped the sheriff.

"For what happened in the Barrett house, you can ask Jeremy Barrett or the girl who cooks there . . . Maisry."

"The half-wit, you mean . . . or pretty nearly half-wit, I suppose," the sheriff said.

"Is Jeremy a half-wit?" asked Rippon. Then he stopped himself short. Certainly the wits of Jeremy were not as acute as those of other men. He had, in a way, put a word into the mouth of the sheriff.

Now Joe Clark answered: "I dunno that your two witnesses would be worth a damn in the minds of jurymen. Not against the words of such men as Charles Barrett and his sons. But this is outside of the law. Is there any good reason why I shouldn't slam you in the jail?"

"Well, maybe no good reason. That's up to you, more or less. You see that I've brought Bud into the town. He would have died, if I'd left him out there."

"A good, smart play on your part," the sheriff responded. "You bring in a man that's out of his head, and that's sure to die before he ever can tell the truth about what happened to him. But the fact that counts with me and with the rest of the world is that you shot that man through the back, partner. Does that percolate into your brain?"

"I know what you mean," said Rippon.

"You'll come along with me," Joe Clark said. His voice was like the chiming of iron now. He went on: "In the old days, when you were a kid, they let you go for murder. They'll not let you go again. I don't think so, anyway. The law has a grip on you, and the law is sure going to use that grip. You march along right ahead of me."

"Is that the finish?"

"That's the finish."

"Well, give the doctor a call, and ask how Bud is doing."

"I'll do that." He raised his voice. "Hey, Doc!"

The doctor came to the screen door, the wires dimming his face as if with evening light.

"Doc," said the sheriff, "how is Caswell doing?"

"He's got one chance in about five," the doctor said calmly. He turned his glance from the sheriff and rested it coldly upon Rippon. "This fellow going along with you?" he asked.

"Well, I'm going to take care of him," the sheriff answered.

"Yeah," drawled the doctor, "and maybe that's a good idea, too."

He waited no longer. He turned his back upon them and went down the hall. Behind the screen, he disappeared before he turned into a doorway, as a fish disappears, swimming down into deep, green water.

"We'll get along," said the sheriff.

"All right," Rippon said.

"You might give me that gun of yours. Some of the boys are watching."

"Here it is." He gave up Tom Palding's revolver. He had a

feeling, as he did so, that he was putting a noose around his neck.

The sheriff put up the heavy revolver, saying simply: "That's a beauty, Tom."

"Yeah, it's a straight shooter," Rippon commented with an equal simplicity.

They went down the path toward the gate, and there Rippon saw that the crowd had suddenly grown. At least the essential portion of it had grown. There had been only two or three men before. Now suddenly there were maybe twenty. Their faces were not pleasant, and all of their glances avoided the sheriff and fastened straight upon the prisoner.

The sheriff pushed the gate open. Rippon walked through it before him, without offering the way to the man of the law, because he knew it would not be expected or accepted.

Suddenly the men of the crowd closed around him. There were faces not six inches away from his—ugly faces, slowly contorting with hatred.

"Joe," sang out someone, "just turn your head a minute, will you?"

"Hey, you fellows," Joe Clark cried, "don't be such fools, will you? This here man belongs to me. You scatter. Get back!"

They did not scatter. Instead, they packed in more closely around the stranger, and their faces were darker than ever with their hatred. Murder was in them. The hunger for killing contorted their mouths and their eyes.

"Hey!" shouted the sheriff again. "In the name of the law . . . and I'll slam the first of you into jail that tries to start anything."

Slowly they gave back reluctantly, as men who know that they are missing an opportunity. They gave back, looking at one another, hoping to find a leader.

So the prisoner and the sheriff walked through them.

CHAPTER FOURTEEN

As he saw his master go by, Baldy whinnied softly, in recognition, and Rippon heard a man bawl out: "Horses ain't fools, but they can't tell a crook from an honest man!"

"Do you hear that?" Rippon said to the sheriff.

"I hear it, well enough," said the sheriff.

"You'll all change your minds, one of these days," Rippon said.

"You're more apt to change your neck before we change our minds about you," said the sheriff harshly.

They were soon up the street in the business block, and, turning near that corner, they reached the jail.

It was a new jail, of the sheriff's own planning, the newest thing in Tyndal, and the pride of the town. It was built of squared stone, the blocks being two feet in diameter. Those ponderous monsters had been chipped out at great expense, and as for the cells, they were arranged with the finest of tool-proof steel for the bars and the door fittings. Rippon had been in jails before—for breaking the peace. He was to go into this one for an attempt at a man's life.

Presently the door opened. He passed through, and the sheriff closed the heavy door with a clank behind him.

Beyond them came a groan of derision and disgust from the crowd that had followed. And the prisoner knew well what it meant. With a leader, they would have taken him instantly from the sheriff and given him the justice of a rope to stretch his neck. With a leader, and one was fairly sure to come soon, they would be apt to rise and attack the jail itself in order to get a victim. This was the expression of casual public opinion. What would it be like when the Barretts began to work behind the scenes?

In the jailer's room, Rippon was stripped of everything he possessed except his clothes and boots. A list was made of the articles taken from him and they were then wrapped in a cloth and put into a drawer in a locker at one end of the room. Then was his history asked for.

"You've had enough history from me, Clark," he said to the sheriff. "You've had too much history, and I'll talk no more. Everything that I say, you'll put down for a lie. I'll save myself the trouble of talking, and yourself the trouble of being wrong. Mind you this . . . whatever you think about me, I'm an honest man."

The sheriff looked him full in the face. "You're Tom Palding?" he said.

"Yes."

"Palding," Joe Clark said, "I've followed you and your record for a good while. I've had reports about you sifting in here, from time to time, and every report that I've heard has been bad . . . one worse than the last. I don't mind a gunman. I almost like 'em, in fact. They have nerve. But a cur that shoots from behind doesn't deserve a court of justice for his trial. A rail and a noosed rope are good enough for him. But that's not all. You've been playing the ponies. You've fixed jockeys, you've worked all sorts of crooked deals to make money. You've marked cards. You've pushed the green. You've done about everything that a sneak would do and an honest man would never do. Now you stand here and tell me that you're an honest man."

Rippon stared back at him. He was wondering what answer he could make, but no answer came readily to mind, and, therefore, he said nothing at all. But he had an interesting idea, as he listened to the sheriff. There is a common opinion that the crook has a vast advantage in making sport of the gullible and soft-hearted world. Rippon began to doubt that was the case. The crook might win for a year or two, but, in the end, public opinion, clad in armor and with a hand of steel, pinched the criminal by the back of the neck and wrung out of him, in pain, all the pleasure of easy money that he had taken from the public.

This was public opinion—the steel claws of public opinion, there before him in the person of the sheriff, sneering as he spoke. There was no more mercy in that man than in a tiger. A good man, doubtless, and a kind man—but for a malefactor, he had nothing but a fierce hatred.

So stood honest Rippon and felt himself judged, and could not fight to gain a better opinion.

He was taken to a corner cell where the heavy blocks of stone that formed the outer wall would confine him upon two sides, and tool-proofed bars of steel would wall him in on the other two sides. The sheriff fitted upon his ankles two fetters. The loose end of the attached chain he fastened to a bolt that was sunk deeply into the wall. The hands of the prisoner, also, were clasped in steel cuffs, united by a short, strong chain.

"Are you satisfied, Sheriff?" asked the prisoner.

"I think that you'll keep quiet here, for a while," said the sheriff.

"If you think that," said Rippon, "then double the guards, because they'll need doubling to keep the crowd off from smashing in the door of the jail."

The sheriff looked curiously upon him. "Are you afraid, Palding?" he asked. "After the number of times you have buncoed poor suckers, and after the number of times that you have trimmed the unlucky fellows who were willing to take you as an honest man, are you afraid now?"

"Go out and talk to Jeremy Barrett and to little Maisry," said the prisoner. "Maybe they'll change your mind for you. Send me in some breakfast. I'm going to go to sleep. I need it."

The sheriff, scanning him now for the first time from head to foot, rested his eyes last of all upon the big, strongly arched nose, and the brown face, and the bright, steady eyes of the prisoner. Then he shook his head and walked away.

Such a man, he thought to himself, *might well be a criminal of a sort . . . a man capable of committing crimes of the greatest violence. But he does not at all look like a fellow who would shoot other men in the back. However, the facts seem clearly enough proved.*

He ordered a breakfast sent in to the prisoner. There was no other man in the jail, and he heard the cook and assistant jailer singing in the little kitchen as the food was prepared. The sheriff listened through the wall to the hissing of the bacon in the pan. Then he walked out into the blinding sun.

There was not a cloud over the lower valley. Only above the heads of the Tyndal Mountains there were dark masses, from some of which fragments broke off and sailed down the length of the valley in dissolving particles, leaden black, at first, and then turning translucent white, and finally the sheerest of films with the sun breaking brightly through them. But all this movement was in the upper air alone. There was no stir in the air close to the ground.

But it was not merely the atmospheric conditions that interested the sheriff. He had other things to take his eye. Among them was the form of young Dick Stanley, loitering on a corner, rolling a cigarette.

Dick should have been on his way to the ranch before this. The sheriff personally knew that the lad was expected. And there was Billy Samuels, on another corner, whistling idly, his back against the wall, a heel raised against it, also. Billy always looked like a half-wit, but the sheriff had deeper and uglier opinions about him.

He walked up to Billy and said: "Billy, what are you doing here?"

"Aw, I'm just standing around," was the answer.

"For what?"

"For fun."

"For trouble, you mean," said the sheriff. "You get out of here and move along home."

Billy looked at him with mildly smiling eyes. "You try to send me home . . . you try to take me home, Sheriff," he said. "That's all."

The sheriff gritted his teeth. It was quite true that he had no right to order peaceful—apparently—citizens to stir on the streets. But he had wit enough to join two together and derive the proper sum. Billy was an outpost, an outlook, to tell when the coast was clear and when the crowd might rise. So was the other lad on the opposite corner. Between them, they were capable of taking observances of all the people who came to the jail and left it.

That was not all. The crowd itself was not far to seek. When the sheriff stepped for a moment into Brown's saloon, he had a glimpse of a long room, blue with smoke, and behind the smoke sat a crowd at cards and drinks. Some, along the walls, neither drank nor played, but merely smoked in quiet content, waiting.

Waiting for what? The sheriff could guess that easily enough.

When he entered, he saw that he knew every man present, either by name or by sight. Some of them he knew by both. And he was a popular man, was the sheriff, on ordinary days.

This was no ordinary day. For proof of it, he saw these familiar faces canted up, the glint of eyes taking stock of him, and then, without a word of greeting, all attention was turned back to the drinks and the cards, or to the fuming smoke that curled upward from the ends of cigarettes, or out of the hot bowls of pipes. He understood clearly. It was not the first time that he had seen a mob rising, both incipient and in action.

Quietly it began, a gathering of people together, and the creation of a heat, like that of bees massed together for the making of wax. So anger and poisonous hatred were gradually distilled in the mind of a mob. So it was being distilled there in Brown's saloon.

He went up the street and around the entire square. In every saloon there was a similar gathering. They sat quietly, drinking very little. And when he entered, there was an air as if his coming had interrupted the speaking of important words, which would be repeated after he had withdrawn.

Something would happen before long. Something would happen that would make that gathering mass of gunpowder-like humanity fume, and flames would spurt out. And it would be strange, after the explosion, if Tom Palding were still in possession of his life.

Upon the shoulder of the sheriff was the responsibility. And he was no shiftless, yellow cur to shrug his shoulders and let the mob murder occur. He was rather a man to fight for the letter of the law, and the whole process of the law.

Should he take the prisoner away, or stay there himself, and strive to fight off the armed mass of the assailants?

CHAPTER FIFTEEN

There was no more honest man in the world than Sheriff Joe Clark. Honesty, in fact, was his distinguishing characteristic. Because, with it, there went an equal hatred for the criminals, the pretenders, the sham of the crooked underworld. And, knowing the faults of the evaders of the law, the enforcement of its power and its rules became to Joe Clark the center and the occupation of his life. He had been a deputy and he had been a member in every posse that had ridden out of Tyndal for many and many a year. It never had occurred to his modesty to run for the office of sheriff. When his friends forced him to undertake a campaign, he refused to make a single stump speech or utter a single promise.

But his friends did the talking for him. They elected him in that county by a majority of less than a single hundred, but after his first term of office there was no need for a campaign or campaign speeches. His own work reëlected him. Totally incorruptible, patient of labor, utterly fearless, the little sheriff with his semi-smile had ridden from one end of the county to the other and routed out the nests of criminals that, before that time, had been settled here and there like parasites, drawing out the honest blood of the community. As he hated all criminals, so he hated above all those who murder by stealth, and in that class he placed his present prisoner, the so-called Tom Palding.

To him, Palding, the murderer, was an offense to the very soul. And yet he saw that for this very man he was about to risk life and limb in order to protect him from the attack of a mob of lynchers. He had not the slightest doubt as to the meaning of the crowds assembled quietly in the saloons. Here and there the ringleaders would appear, some of them men like Henry Clowden, who were fiercely honest themselves and upright in every respect, but who could remember the old vigilante days and regret the passing of the swift and cheap justice of those times. Others would be people who loved mischief of any kind for its own sake. And these men were apt to be noisier and more violent than the better class of citizen. It was always that way. Many bad men sheltered themselves behind the decent impulses of the few good citizens. But what could he, the sheriff, do?

Twice before, the men of Tyndal had tried to take prisoners away from him. In each case, he had foiled the attempts without great difficulty. But, on both occasions, the trials had been made by only a handful. And the prisoners were, in one case, a cattle rustler, and in the other a horse thief.

This affair was entirely different. Twenty years of detestation had been heaped and gathered against the head of Tom Palding. Now it was about to be poured forth. Not only were the men of the town up, in a body, but the citizens from the surrounding countryside had ridden in to Tyndal. The great majority were hardy ranchers and their cowpunchers, men of action pure and simple, men not liable to hesitate if some authoritative voice told them that violence was the proper course in this case.

The sheriff, perspiration pouring down his lean, hard face, pictured himself lying in the jail, a rifle at his shoulder directed toward the door, and the battering-ram in the hands of the crowd, crashing and smashing against that door, making it spring upon its hinges. He could shoot through the door safely above their heads, to be sure. Or else, he could fire straight through at the level of a man's breast.

Which would he do? Bullets fired above their heads would not stop such men as these. And if he fired into the mass, point-blank, he was sure to kill some worthy and law-abiding citizen.

His name, from that moment, would become a detestation and a shame in all the countryside where now he was followed with such respect. It would mean the eventual loss of his office, and the scorn, the hatred, the revenge, of all the county directed toward him.

To kill a good citizen to protect the life of a scoundrel, a murderer by stealth—that was the alternative to permitting the crowd to wash into the jail, haranguing them, threatening them, shooting idly into the air above their heads, struggling with his mere bare hands, finally, against the vast and gentle strength of the crowd that would master him with such a perfect ease. They would smile. Three or four of them would be detailed to hold him, helpless. He could curse and threaten them as much as he pleased. But a hundred men could not possibly be hanged for taking the life of a single criminal.

Was not that life, in any case, forfeit? Would not Tom Palding, if Caswell died, certainly be hanged? There was no question about that.

So the poor sheriff leaned his hand against a hitching rack and miserably pondered the thing that lay before him. He could act the part and allow himself to be made putty in the hands of the mob. Or else, he could take a life, and destroy his own happiness forever in the defense of his duty. Never was a man more hardly pressed. He gripped his narrow breast, because a pain was shooting through his heart. He felt stifled. There seemed not air enough between the mountains for his breathing.

And then, looking up at the glimmering blue-white of the morning sky, he told himself that duty was greater than self-love, ambition, the respect and affection of his countrymen. They had elected him to office. He had sworn to defend the laws, and defend them he would, while life and breath were in him.

Now, in that quiet moment as he leaned against the hitching rack, he reached a conclusion as great and as heroic as any that ever filled the breast of a famous Roman patriot, in those ages when blind worship of the law was the rule and not the exception. There was no poet to enter into the mind of the little sheriff and sing his praises. There was no sculptor to express the agony and the fixed resolve that appeared upon his face.

But when he stepped on again, settling his hat upon his forehead, his mind was as that of a man who had signed to march with a lost cause, a forlorn hope. Destruction was there before him, and the good of his life was gone from him.

A dusty buggy jogged toward him. There was a down-headed mule, gray as a mouse, still grayer with dust, wobbling its ears back and forth as it went along at a trot slower than a man's walk. It swayed a little from side to side. Its lower lip dangled, flopping upward from time to time convulsively. The animal looked as if it was asleep on its feet.

In the seat, holding the reins as tightly as though a dancing thoroughbred were racing along with a rubber-tired sulky, sat a young woman with a broad-brimmed straw hat shading her face, and a linen duster, much patched and greatly too big for her, swallowing her body. She gripped the reins with force, and from her hands a buggy whip projected upward, sometimes dipping toward the tough back of the mule, but never quite descending to its target.

Through the gradual, thin, upward drifting of the dust, the sheriff made out a pretty, childish face beneath the shadow of the hat. It was Maisry, come in from the Barrett place to do her weekly marketing. Poor Maisry. She was a hard-working youngster. He remembered to have thought that before, but now she was going by him like a figure in a dream when suddenly he remembered that his prisoner had mentioned her name.

At that, the sheriff raised his hand. The girl, with a frightened exclamation, jerked in on the reins, and the mule stopped so short that she was slid half out of her seat. Joe Clark went and stood beside her, resting his foot on the hub of the wheel.

"Mister Sheriff . . . Mister Clark, I mean," said Maisry, her eyes growing round, "what have I done? What do you want with me?"

The sheriff looked at her as at blue mountains across a desert. In the desert of dreadful trouble he stood with ruin before him. In the cool, blue distance of innocence and safety was this girl, this child. Yet she had the fear; he had merely the aching foreboding in his heart.

"I only want some talk with you, Maisry," he said.

"Oh," Maisry said, and swallowed, ducking her head a little with the effort of it. "I sort of thought. . . ."

"What did you think, Maisry?"

"Oh, nothing, I guess."

She smiled a little at him, so great was her relief. And he, nodding like a wise old man at an infant, read in her nothing but gentleness, goodness, and a savor of weakness that was not altogether unpleasant. She was only a woman. Some good man would protect and save her, one day, with the iron of his hand.

"Maisry," he said, "we have a man in that jail of mine."

She nodded. Even under the gray of the dust, he thought he could see her color diminish.

"You've seen him, Maisry?"

"Yes."

"Where? At the Barrett house?"

"Yes."

"What happened out there?"

She looked at the slowly stirring, flopping ears of the mule. He had dropped his head until his chin was almost in the dust of the street. "Will it help Tom Palding?" she asked.

"I can't say that," the sheriff said. "But he needs help. Oh, he needs help, all right."

She sat up. She dropped the reins and clasped her hands together. "They wanted to kill him. They would have killed him," she admitted.

The sheriff did not stir. He was unable to as a matter of fact. "Maisry, what are you saying?"

"Mister Barrett, he wanted to buy the Palding ranch, and Mister Palding wouldn't sell."

"Was it ten thousand Barrett offered?"

"Yes."

"Were you in the room?"

"I was in the kitchen. They were in the dining room. And I could hear every word."

The sheriff took out a bandanna and wiped his forehead. His poor brain was beginning to whirl. "Well," he said, "they have enough against him . . . the Barretts. He killed Sam Barrett, a long time back. He murdered Sam Barrett. No wonder that they want his blood."

"He didn't murder Sam Barrett," Maisry said.

The sheriff gaped at her.

"He didn't murder Sam Barrett," she repeated, and her eyes flashed at the sheriff. "He never murdered any man in his life."

"Oh, he's an honest man, is he?" Joe Clark said, smiling a little.

"Oh, yes, on my soul he is," said the girl.

Chapter Sixteen

Like all bachelors, the sheriff was a bit sentimental about women. Like all bachelors, he consoled himself by constructing a series of aphorisms concerning the opposite sex. He was fond of saying: "The nicer the girl, the sillier."

He used to declare, also: "The sweeter the smile, the emptier the head."

Furthermore, the sheriff used to remark, when expanding to a friend: "Young things are always kind of nice . . . puppies, calves, and girls."

Now, as Joe Clark looked into the snapping eyes of poor Maisry, he remembered all three of these habitual remarks of his and felt that they were all justified, again. He was reinforced in his contempt for women; he was reinforced in a weak devotion to them. Like watered wine, his affection for them was rather a color than a genuine taste.

"Look here, Maisry," he said, "it's sort of bold for you to stand up like that against what everybody else feels."

"Everybody?" said the girl.

"Yes. Everybody. The whole town's getting ready to lynch that honest man of yours."

Maisry leaned from the seat and one hand pressed against her heart. "To hang Tom Palding?" she said.

"Well, something like that, I take it. But I'm going to stop them, or else come to the end of my own rope."

"You're going to stop them, are you?" said the girl, and suddenly she looked him over from head to foot.

"I'm not a big man, but I'll do my best," said the sheriff.

There was no use in confiding, to a child like this, the terrible nature of his duty, or what it would mean to his career. It might be that, having checked the crowd with bullets, they would rush on over him and trample him into the ground as a right payment to him for having taken the life of a man in order to protect the criminal life of a hunted dog.

"I'm going on!" Maisry cried with a sudden alteration in her voice.

The sheriff stepped back from the buggy. "What's the matter, Maisry?" he called to her.

Instead of answering, she struck the mule a sudden, hard blow with the whip. The thick skin of the mule saved him from any sensation except one of utter surprise. But the surprise was sufficiently great to make him jump ahead. With his head over his shoulder and both ears flattened, like the ears of a running rabbit, he regarded his transformed driver and got, for a reward, another slash laid along his ribs.

Down the street went the mule. He was not hurt. Nature had provided him with an armor of thick hide and hair that defied such puny strokes as those from Maisry, but astonishment enthralled the mule. He had gone as he pleased with this driver for a year. He never had been forced out of the equivalent of a fast walk. Now he was called upon for a brisk trot, and he trotted. That was not enough. He was forced to break into a gallop.

The sheriff looked after the girl and the buggy as though he were seeing something in a dream. "Why, there's grit in her, after all," he said.

The buggy hit a bump at the crossing of another lane, where the ruts were worn more deeply in the center of the way. Over the tailboard of the buggy flopped a ham and landed into the dust.

He saw Maisry turn her head and, apparently, take stock of the loss, but she did not stop to pick up the parcel. Instead, she flogged the mule afresh. He no longer cantered. He was flying at a full gallop, and the sheriff could not believe his eyes.

He went to the crossing and there picked the ham out of the deep dust. He carried it to the grocery store of Wentworth & Blaize, and he was in a quandary as he walked. He knew that Maisry was a devoted slave to her work, and that she feared Charles Barrett almost like another prophet. But she had allowed a ham to be lost over the end of the buggy, and still she dared to rush on, and not stop to pick up her loss.

What madness had taken hold upon the girl? What utter madness? This exhibition of temper or of decision upon her part was to the sheriff more amazing than twenty similar exhibitions on the part of ordinary men or women. She had been like a lamb. Now she rushed away like a wolf.

When he went into the grocery store, he found Mrs. Wentworth behind the counter. The poor woman was hardly a week from a sickbed, and looked hollow-eyed and haggard.

"Look here, Missus Wentworth," he said. "You oughta be home in bed." He laid the ham on the counter and told from whose rig it had been lost.

"I oughta be," she said to him bitterly, "but you know why I ain't."

He went slowly back onto the street. Yes, he knew why she was called to look after the affairs of the grocery store—her husband and his partner were out with the other men of the town preparing for work to which no woman could put her hand.

When he reached the street, the sheriff saw half a dozen men pour out of the swinging doors of the Molloy saloon with a suddenness that indicated pressure from behind thrusting against them. When they saw him, they stopped short, hesitated, spoke to one another, and then pressed slowly back inside the place. The swinging doors shut, and the street looked as empty, as innocent of harm as ever before. But the sheriff knew. He could tell, by the first bubbling, that the pot was about to boil over. In that saloon, and in others, there were men at the fever point of anger, and soon from many doors armed people would flow out and surge toward the jail.

The sheriff went straight to the door of the jail. He rapped against it.

"Who's there, for the love of pity?" cried a treble, Negro voice inside.

"It's Joe Clark," said the sheriff.

There was a groan from within, and the door was unlocked. Inside, he saw amidst the shadows of the interior the rolling eyes of the cook.

"Why, what's the matter with you, George?" he asked.

"I thought they was coming," said the Negro.

The sheriff frowned. *Was the thing in the air, then? Did everyone in Tyndal know it?*

"Coming? Who? For what?" he snapped.

The Negro hitched a thumb over his shoulder. "You know, Mister Clark. For him. They're all comin' for him."

"So you locked the door against 'em?"

"I wouldn't've kept it locked," George confessed.

"A mob's a rough thing to meet . . . even in a jail. D'you want to be here when they come, George?" asked the sheriff.

"This darky's got some white hair already," said George. "There's something worth more to me than a job, Mister Clark."

"You won't lose your job, George," said the sheriff. "But go on and get out of here." He opened the door a little wider and stood aside.

George stepped into the opening with a sigh of vast relief. There he paused for a moment. "You gonna come along after me, when you've locked that door, sir?" he asked.

"Never mind what I'm going to do," declared the sheriff. "You've got a day off . . . a holiday."

The Negro made a step to go away, but returned instantly, saying in a high, whining voice: "If locks won't hold good for the law, I dunno why men should be busted as well as locks, Mister Clark. You sure better come along with me."

The sheriff smiled at him. There was some affection under that black skin, he perceived. In this time of his agony of spirit, he could appreciate the struggle in the will of the Negro.

"It's all right, George," he assured. "You run along. Don't you worry about what's likely to happen here."

The eyes of George widened until they seemed all white, like the open eyes of a Greek statue. He stepped back into the door of the jail. "Mister Clark," he said in a ghostly and ghastly whisper, "what you mind to do, sir?"

The sheriff lost patience.

"I'm going to stay here, and be damned with that yellow dog yonder in the cell!" he exclaimed. "Now get out of here and don't bother me with your talk any more."

At that moment, from well down the street—the very direction of the Molloy saloon—there was a rumbling outbreak of voices, and suddenly the clangor of two or three revolvers barking in the air. Those sounds were answered by a whooping yell from the opposite direction.

George gripped the side of the door and turned yellow. His head strained over his shoulder and he shook in every limb.

"George, d'you hear me? Get out of here!" The sheriff laid his hand upon the burly shoulder of the Negro and tried to thrust him out. The last moment had begun and he knew it as well as the cook did.

George stepped resolutely inside the jail. "I'm gonna stay, Mister Clark," he said. "I reckon that I'll stay here. You've given me a soft life here for quite a spell, and I guess that I gotta die sometime." He turned, and shuffled off down the corridor, between the cells.

The sheriff looked after him, bewildered, but then he understood. It was duty, the goddess of his own choice, now working in the soul of George. Even in the Negro there was the quality out of which martyrs are made. So, staring for one moment, he found his own resolution tempered, and turned to steel. It was well enough to do the right thing, standing firmly alone. But how much easier to do it with a companion.

He turned slowly back, caught hold of the edge of the door, and threw it shut. It closed with a heavy bang. There was a steel lining in the door, and the weight of this caused a clangor like the report of a gun to reverberate among the steel bars that rose like a thin forest within the cell room.

That echo found a space in the heart of the sheriff through which it rolled with a sickening meaning. By closing the door he had shut himself away from the men of the outer world and their ways, and their affection. He had enlisted himself upon the other side, and on that side was nothing more than duty, a pale, cold comforter in such a time as this.

CHAPTER SEVENTEEN

He walked down the aisle of the cells. As he went, he glanced from side to side. There once had sat Hank Wallis, the man-killer from the Tyndal Mountains. Dingy of skin and mind, his lank hair falling over his eyes, he had looked up like a beast when the sheriff went by. His jaws were locked. His meditations sour and sweet had filled his mind to the last moment, when the hangman had turned him off. And even as he had walked up to the platform from which the door would be sprung, there had been a faint smile flickering on the lips of Hank Wallis and his eyes had been looking absently into the distance. What had he been savoring, at that moment? The delight of some brutal or profitable crime? Or the memory of some great ride, or a glorious fight on equal terms with his peers?

Hank Wallis was gone.

In the opposite cell, Jerry Overton, of Cramerton, had smoked his cigarettes and chatted and joked with visitors to the last, before he, too, went to the hangman. Old Silver Joe Murphy had been in the next cell, wise and calm, willing to speak of his cunning expedients during a long life of safe-cracking and cattle lifting. No harm had come to Joe from the law. But in order to escape, he had had to talk too much, and the very day of his release from jail, he had been shot down by a horseman, who then dashed out of Tyndal into the mountains.

It was Tucker Breck, of the old Breck family, a wild tribe of mountaineers, inculpated by the confessions of Joe Murphy.

And the sheriff had followed him for ten mortal weeks, letting all other business pass, refusing to leave that trail until, like a bloodhound, he came upon the murderer surrounded by five of his kin.

It had been the great day, the great moment, of the sheriff's life. He had walked into the crossroads saloon without a gun in his hand, and, touching Tucker Breck on the shoulder, he told the man to follow him. And Breck had come.

The five others had drawn guns like a flash, but they hesitated to use them. Already, the sheriff's back was turned confidently upon them, and the prisoner was approaching the door. Out that door they went, and the sheriff mounted his prisoner and put irons on his hands. Then they rode quietly away.

It was a great triumph not only because it had allowed the sheriff to show what he was made of, but, also, it had enabled him to learn how he impressed the men of the mountains, where manhood was the wildest. They had been stilled and overawed by his presence as a bird is stilled and overawed by the eye of a great snake. It was partly the law that worked upon them; it was partly the fear that he inspired.

Well, in yonder cell had sat Breck, until his time of trial, his conviction, his death.

Other famous men had occupied those cells. It was not an old jail, but already it was rich in tradition and in history, in profane comments upon the law, and in ringing death statements, defiances, pitiful, cringing appeals, broken-hearted confessions.

Through a world of tears and rage, weakness and god-like strength, the sheriff walked back to the end cell, and there he found Rippon sitting. The sheriff paused at the bars and looked through for a moment. The chained hands of Rippon rose slowly; he puffed at a cigarette; he lowered his hands again. Calmly he returned the gaze of Joe Clark as a snarling yell tore the air outside the jail. The throats of twenty men were strained in that great savage cry.

"You come to say good bye, Clark?" asked Rippon.

The sheriff blinked. From the reputed past history of this man, he had not expected to find such iron nerve in him when the crisis came. "You hear it?" asked Clark, raising one forefinger.

"Oh, I hear it, all right."

"You know what it means?" insisted the sheriff.

"I know that, too. I watched a crowd, once, chewing up a poor chap. That was up in Yellow Springs, in the old days. Oh, twelve years back. It left a mark on me, though. It left a good deal of a mark, I'll tell you. Good bye, Clark. You've treated me pretty good."

"I'm to go, am I?" asked the sheriff.

"Unless you want to stay here and be stewed in the same fire with me," said the prisoner.

"Tell me, man," said Joe Clark. "You're shaking in your boots. Tell me true."

"Me? Not a bit. Look at my hands. No, I'm not shaking."

"You have nerve," commented the sheriff.

"Well, you better mosey along, Clark. Start moving, and you'll save your face. Nobody'll blame you for finding work outside the jail on a day like this."

The sheriff nodded. "Nobody'd blame me. Only me, I'd blame myself. I'm going to stay."

Rippon rose slowly to his feet. "Hold on, Clark!" he said huskily.

"I don't want no damned chatter about it," snarled the sheriff. "I'm going to stay here. My duty keeps me here, not you, Tom Palding."

"Well, here you stay, then," Rippon said. "And here you'll be ended. If you lift a hand to help me, they'll rip you to pieces. I know crowds. Listen to that one, and you'll know that it's a beauty. Listen to it, humming like a tight wire. Hear the babble and the yipping, too. That comes from the fellows who've had too much to drink. Oh, I know crowds. I know the whole keyboard of 'em, and the tune that piano is playing is 'Murder' in any man's language. Sheriff, if you love your hide, get out of the place, will you?"

It was a great trial and a shock to the sheriff to hear this speech from his prisoner. It showed, beyond the slightest doubt, that the nerve of this man called Tom Palding was better than the finest steel. People who shoot their enemies through the back are not supposed to possess such nerve. In addition, it indicated that in the prisoner there was a decent regard for the welfare of his fellow humans—even for the sheriff who had arrested him.

The sheriff was thrown into a quandary. For one thing, he was not accustomed to complicated crimes and complicated psychologies. He dealt with the results of gunfights or knife battles, with horse and cattle theft, with safe-cracking and claim-jumping. Nineteen times out of twenty the accused was guilty, and the accused was a criminal of long standing. Now, as Joe Clark tried to fit all that he knew about Tom Palding upon the shoulders of Rippon, his old theories about the simplicity of the law cracked to bits. He was bewildered and ill at ease. Of one thing only he was sure—and this was that the prisoner was distinctly worth saving. He had remained there merely from a spiritual sense of duty. Now he found that there was a human cause, also.

Straightway, the sheriff unlocked the door of the cell, entered it, and unlocked the fetters that weighted down the prisoner.

Rippon regarded him with a curious eye. "What's the idea, chief?" he asked. "Are we to make a break for it?"

"Make a break for it?" the sheriff snarled.

He held up his hand to invite attention to the sea of noise that was closing in around the jail. In fact, it was like the clashing of waves. High voices shouted orders—imprecations. Others echoed the same sounds from a distance.

"Break through that?" said the sheriff. "Break through a quarter of a mile of burning oil, but not through those angry men. They'd burn us to the bone in two steps. But if I'd known . . . if I'd guessed. . . ." He finished unlocking the fetters and stood back from the prisoner, eying Rippon with what seemed a personal hatred.

"How could I tell that you had decency in you, Palding?" he demanded. "How could I tell that you were a white man? If I'd guessed that, I would have clapped you on a horse and off with you before the crowd rose. And now I'm going to do what I can for you. That cell door is open. That is to say, there's no key in the lock. In yonder room, you'll find the guns that were taken off you. You can get those guns, man, and in the pinch you can fight for your life. The cook, yonder . . . that fellow George . . . he's scared to death, but he's a good Negro, and good Negroes are liable to surprise you a lot when the pinch comes. He may be a lot of help, and he may be as limp as a rag. Now, Palding, I think you have it straight. You're free to fight for your life. It may do some good for them to know that I have two men in here with me, armed and ready to hit back when they come. You're free to fight for your life. I can only say that, for my part I'm going to shoot to scare the crowd, and not to kill."

"Sheriff," said Rippon, "I'll give you my oath never to aim higher than a knee or closer than a shoulder. A riot gun with fine bird shot in it . . . that would be the best way of hosing down the streets and washing that crowd away. Aye, or pepper and salt would do the business, too."

"You don't know Tyndal men," answered the sheriff. "You've been away for twenty years, and you've forgotten what the Tyndal men are like. Bird shot or pepper salt would never turn them. They've got hides that would blunt the edge of a knife, and they've got enough nerve in them to climb up the blue wall of heaven and kick in the golden gates. Now, Palding, you're a free man, so far as this jail is concerned. You're a free man to fight for your life. I won't even ask you to stay here, if you can get out. If you can worm or squeeze or work or fly out of this jail, you're free to go."

"I'll come again when you ask for me," said the prisoner.

At this, the sheriff smiled sardonically, but the eyes of Rippon held so steadily upon his that Sheriff Joe Clark turned upon his heel and walked hastily away.

His head was spinning worse than ever. He actually found himself on the point of believing that this man, if he succeeded in escaping, would surely return at bidding to the sheriff who had given him the chance to escape.

He kicked open the door to the room in which the guns were kept. He opened the locker and laid upon the central table the guns of Rippon. Then he went back to the front door of the jail. It was high time, for the tide of anger that had been sweeping about the building had at last gathered itself into a strong wave, and that wave had reached the front door of the jail. Strong hands were beating against it, and voices shouted loudly.

"Hello!" cried the sheriff from within.

"Shut up, some of you!" he heard a bull-voiced fellow roar on the farther side of the doorway.

"Shut up, boys, and let Will Bascom speak," said several hastily.

So a silence came, and the parley was possible.

Chapter Eighteen

There were still voices in the distance that interfered for a moment, and particularly one huge-throated yokel who was bellowing for Charlie Barrett because he said that this was particularly the Barretts' business.

But presently the silence was sufficient.

"Is that you in there, Sheriff?"

"This is Joe Clark," said the sheriff. "Are you Will Bascom?"

"Yes. I've come along here with the whole county behind me, Joe."

"I'm mighty sorry that you're leading 'em down the wrong road," said the sheriff.

"You're only one man," said Bascom. "We outvote you a hundred to one. There's a hundred men out here, Joe, and they all say that you've got to open that door to us."

"Will," said the sheriff, "I've got more than a hundred men on my side. I've got the law."

"Now, don't you go ahead and be a fool, Joe," said Will Bascom. "You've done a fine job around here. We all think a lot of you. But if you make trouble here today, it's gonna undo all that you've done before in the way of building yourself a reputation."

Rippon, listening and watching like a hawk, saw the head of the sheriff twitch back a little, a sure sign that the last speech had told heavily.

"On my job," said the sheriff, "I've rode a good many

thousand miles . . . always for the lawkeepers and the decent men in this country. You know that, Will."

"I know that, Joe. There's not a man in the county that doesn't know what you've done. There's not a man that doesn't respect you and like you for it. But you're our sheriff. You belong to us. You've got to do what we tell you to do. I tell you, that's the way of a democracy. Folks elect other folks to represent them. You represent us. Well, now we come to you and tell you that today you can stop representing us. Inside there, you've got a danged, sneaking murderer. We want him. We're going to have him. He sneaked through the fingers of the law once before. This time we're going to make sure of him."

This was the most logical way of presenting the case for the crowd. At least they appeared to approve of it heartily, for there was instantly a great roar in which every throat joined.

The sheriff waited until the roar died down, and Rippon half expected to see his hand turn the key that secured the door.

"Will Bascom," said the sheriff, "I'll tell you that I represent something bigger and greater than all the people in Tyndal County."

"Hold on, Joe. Don't you go to talking like a fool," said Bascom.

"I'm not talking like a fool. I'm telling you the truth, too. I represent the people of Tyndal County, but I represent the law, too. You didn't make that law. The rest of the people didn't make it. God Almighty made it, and while I'm sheriff of this county, I'm gonna enforce it."

The speech was apparently distinctly heard by the entire group outside, and their answer to it was a single sound, like the growl of a dog with a hundred throats.

"Clark," said Will Bascom, "this'll be the blackest day of your life, if you resist us. You can't. You're only one man against more'n a hundred."

"You're wrong," said the sheriff. "I've got two to help me. I've taken the irons off Tom Palding and he's ready to fight for his life. And I've got George with me and he's going to be man enough for any of you."

Another growl from many throats answered this speech.

"What are three against a hundred?" shouted Bascom. "And you mean to tell us that you've put guns in the hands of Tom Palding?"

"That's what I've done."

"Then you're the rottenest excuse for a sheriff that we've ever had in this county!" thundered Bascom. "We're done with you, and be danged to you."

"We're done with him," clamored others. "We've talked enough. Get the door down and let's have Palding out!"

The next moment, there was a rush of steps and a heavy shock against the door of the jail.

An ordinary door would have gone down at the very first stroke. Even that steel-framed and steel-lined door of the sheriff's invention groaned, and sprang a little in the center.

A shout of triumph came from the crowd as they saw the mischief actually begun and under way. The shout became an indescribable yell. And Rippon well knew the sound. He had heard it before. He knew that it meant the end of reason and sense in that throng, and the beginning of sheer, blind, ravening hysteria. They were no longer men, out yonder. They were beasts, and they wanted to have their teeth in his throat. He heard a movement beside him. And, turning, he saw the Negro, with rolling eyes and shaking body.

"George," said Rippon, "I'm mighty sorry that you're in this mess. It's no business of yours."

"Mister Palding," said George, "it's the waitin' for the end that I can't stand so good. If only they would finish us quick. It's the waitin' and the poundin' that I can't stand so good."

114

Rippon smiled, but he put a hand on the shoulder of the cook of the jail. "No man's down and lost until he's counted out," he said. "And a good many fellows have had a gun laid alongside their heads and yet lived to talk about it afterward. Don't you give up hope, George. Anyway, those people won't bother you if you don't bother them."

On the heels of this speech, the battering-ram dashed against the front door of the jail again with a crash like that made by a falling wall. The door sprang so far that daylight appeared in a blinding streak, and the crowd roared again exultantly.

"It won't stand the pounding." said the sheriff. "It's guns, now, Palding. Shoot, but for mercy's sake don't shoot to kill. I'll wait till you open up on the mob from the window on the left. I'll take the opposite window."

Rippon went to the appointed place.

As in many structures far more pretentious than this Tyndal jail, the front door was recessed a little into the face of the wall, and the windows on either side of it looked out at an angle. Those windows were heavily barred, and, furthermore, they were at such a height that the battering-ram could not be used with effect against them, otherwise, a few strokes would have swept the bars away, beating them out of their sockets.

But it made an ideal look-out for Rippon, and, if worst came to worst, a perfect place from which to open fire, pointblank, upon the assailants.

Rippon, revolver in hand, poised, watched the bearers of the ram recede, he saw them come again, watched their contorted faces. Twenty of them were wielding the ram. It was the trunk of a tree well over a foot in diameter and thirty feet in length. Along its sides the carriers were crowded, holding to the bare, round trunk, or to the stumps of the branches which had been cut away. Back they surged, then came with a rush that carried them up the steps, and the bottom of the stump thudded heavily against the door.

Rippon, his gun ready, saw that charge go by him. Perhaps this was the stroke that would beat in the door and let the flood loose in the jail. One bullet would probably stop the charge—for the moment, at least. So he took aim at one straining pair of legs, and then at another and another—but he could not pull the trigger. Something in him revolted too strongly against the act, for they were human beings, after all, though maddened now by mob rage.

The blow went home—the door still stood. But now it was obviously bending in the center, and the bolts could not endure such punishment much longer.

Rippon looked wildly about him, as a desperate man will do, when there is no escape.

He was in a small storeroom off that in which the guns were kept. Two or three lanterns hung on the wall. There were lariats, horse furniture, some old clothes, some boxes of tinned goods, a five-gallon can of kerosene for replenishing the oil in the lanterns and lamps in the jail. Something he remembered then of what the sheriff had said of running through fire, and the next second he had acted.

He hefted the oil can and found it nearly full. Then he opened the spout and ran two gallons into a pail. The battering-ram was coming with a rush for another stroke at the door as Rippon stood up, pail in hand. He dashed the contents through the bars of the window and into the faces of the log bearers.

With a yell they dropped the burden. Into their eyes, into their gaping mouths as they yelled the stinging, abhorrent stuff had flown. Some of them were temporarily blinded. All shrank back from the oil that dripped upon the stone steps of the building and ran down to form in little pools at the bottom of them. But they were halted only for an instant.

This check brought their fury up to the screaming point. And these were, as the sheriff had said, the hardiest of the hardy—stalwart cowpunchers from the mountains, timber men, and ranchers. A mere cold shower of kerosene could not be expected to delay them for more than a moment. The few whose eyes were tormenting them stood about on the outskirts, stamping their feet and cursing. But others came in a swarm and picked up the log again. All the hands that could get a grip seized it and swayed it lightly. Then they came with a shout, while half a dozen men with repeating rifles covered the window through which the oil had been flung. They could cover the window, but they could not stop Rippon.

He had taken a bit of rag waste, soaked it with oil, and twisted the rag into a knot. Now he scratched a match and touched the flame to the rag. It was instantly a mass of bursting flame that seared his fingers, and he, still on his knees, flung the burning rag over the sill of the window, between the bars. It fell upon the oil-dripping steps right under the feet of the assailants and instantly the steps were a blue welter of fire. That flame ran to the pools of standing oil and there shot up small columns of fire.

The effect was like the hurling of a powerful bomb. The log fell. Off of those burning stairs the bearers of the battering-ram sprang, leaping high as dancers. And that was not all. Two or three of the carriers had been splashed by the throwing of the oil, and the flames instantly caught upon their clothes!

CHAPTER NINETEEN

The yells of those unlucky fellows darted through the brain of Rippon like needles and filled him with horror. Would not bullets have been more merciful?

No, yonder they were, rolling in the street, and the thick dust instantly put out the flames. They were singed, but not badly burned. This check did not depress, it simply maddened the crowd, and the voice of it rose with a booming shout. Oh, they meant business now.

George came into the room from which Rippon had performed the exploit. He was shaking his head like one who has just seen a horror, and his face was dusty with fear. "Now they'll kill us all, sure!" said George.

Rifles opened upon the window of Rippon. Under cover of it, men ran forward and threw dust upon the flames that still rolled and licked along the jail steps and at their foot. Then in came the crowd again. Their yelling had ceased. They had teeth set and their eyes were glowering, and when they caught up the log it was plain that they meant to dash the door to pieces with the very next stroke.

Rippon, standing well back from the window, gave the Negro more oil-dampened, wadded rags to hold, and as the group went by, grunting with the weight of the log, savagely eager, their heads down, he spun the oil in the bucket and flung the last three gallons over the group, instantly following it with three fireballs that fell among the rioters.

The steps were blazing from one end to the other, in no time. And half a dozen of the men were in flames. Some of them had been well soaked. And one man seemed to Rippon to be running on wings of fire as he fled back for the street.

They knew the cure, now. Instantly they were rolling in the dust of the street, but, for all that, some were badly seared by the fire. Three or four went hurrying off to get better remedies for their hurts, clapping their hands, as they went, to various parts of their clothes where the smoldering fires were reawakening and stinging them like hornets.

There was a fresh outburst of rifle play. The whole front of the jail was swept with bullets, and the yelling of the crowd amazed Rippon with its intense rage and malice.

Twice they had been turned back, and fire had been used for it.

"Burn them . . . damn 'em! . . . burn them when we get them into our hands!" was the cry.

Fire for the prisoner, and for the sheriff along with him, and the Negro would make a roast, as well.

The sheriff came into Rippon's room. "If there's enough oil we may stave them off for a while," said Joe Clark. "Is there any more, George?"

The Negro swished the contents of the oil tin mournfully. There was not a cupful remaining. And in all the jail there was only what could be collected from the half-filled lamps and lanterns. It was very little—hardly enough to stop the next strong attack.

"It has to be bullets," said the sheriff. "Heaven forgive me, Palding, but I can't open up on them. It's my duty to keep them away from that door, but I can't shoot, and they know it."

"Joe Clark! Joe Clark!" yelled a voice close by, around the corner of the jail.

"That's Charles Barrett," said the sheriff. "I know that he'd be in the thick of the thing." He called back: "Aye, Barrett! What do you want? It's a mighty yellow business that you've mixed into today, Barrett!"

"It's right and justice that I've mixed into," said Barrett. "We're going to have him, man, in spite of the fire, and you! But here's the last offer we make. The men are pretty hot, Clark. They're talking of giving all three of you what you've been trying to give them. They're pretty hot. I'm trying to hold 'em, but I can't hold 'em long. Open that door, and we'll take only one of you . . . the one we want . . . Tom Palding. If we have to charge in again, it'll be all three that come away with us."

"Not one'll come!" spoke up another infuriated voice. "We'll douse them with oil and let the sheriff stew with the other two!"

"Do you hear, Clark?" demanded the rancher.

"I hear every word," said Clark. "It's a hard thing to believe that Charlie Barrett is working with a mob. But I hear what you say and my answer is just this. You may all go to blazes!"

His voice rang out clearly, and reached all the men who were massed in front of the jail. It reached, furthermore, to the numbers of women and children and the aged who filled doors and windows and clambered upon roofs in order to have a better view of the attack upon the jail. From the men came a shout like a battle cry. From the spectators a shriller and more lasting cry that tingled like painful music in the ears of Rippon.

But, after all, was the shout of the spectators anything more than a thrilling interest? It was not a cry for blood. It was rather like the whoop that goes up at the beginning of a horse race.

There was now a fresh outburst of rifle fire, and the bearers of the battering-ram came on with a rush.

Rippon took his rifle, and, dragging the table to a corner where it was outside of the angle of the rifle bullets that whirred across the room, he leveled the rifle toward the assailants.

The sheriff, suddenly bowing his head, went hastily from the room. He could not endure the sight of a lawbreaker, as he supposed his prisoner to be, firing upon citizens of the town, no matter how criminal the nature of their procedure in attacking the jail.

Old George, with a groan of terror, threw up his hands to invoke the help of that heaven that ordained and permitted such things to be.

But Rippon, in the meantime, had no intention of taking a life if he could avoid it. He merely wanted to turn the charge of those men, who came on with murder in their faces. His own position was not quite secure. A bullet ripped open the side of his trousers. Another clipped the coat under the pit of his left arm, which was closest to the stream of bullets. He could hardly be seen, so far back was he among the shadows of the room, but he was still on the edge of the blind currents of danger.

He picked out the first man, and, leveling his rifle with consummate nicety and skill, he knocked the felt hat from the tawny head of the rioter.

The fellow, with a dazed look, jumped aside and clapped his hands to his head as though he were surprised to find that important item still on his shoulders.

A little farther back was a huge fellow with a face sunblackened. His lofty sombrero was tilted on the rear of his head, and this hat the marksman next knocked off.

That was not all the bullet did. Speeding onward and down in its slanting course, it slashed open the hip of the last carrier on the right-hand side. He whooped like a mad Indian and leaped away. So did the other from whose head the hat had been knocked. The whole party fell into confusion. Some urged forward. But others gave up the attempt, and in a sudden panic the log was dropped and the group bolted.

Rippon, watching them flee, smiled grimly to himself. If he had been shooting in deadly earnest how many of them might he have drilled through with a single bullet? How many might he have picked off both in the going and the coming?

They yelled as they ran. They threw out their arms before them; they looked wildly over their shoulders. They bolted until they were quite out of sight.

Well, perhaps they were fully as brave and as hardy as the sheriff declared, but all men, in a mob, became as weak, as savage, as fierce, as cowardly as the most inferior member of the group. So it was with these men.

Three times, now, Rippon had turned them back, single-handed. He had not really harmed one of them. He had sent a few away to nurse singed places and scratches, but he had not seriously wounded a single one.

Three times he had managed—by what seemed a miracle to him—to turn back the headlong rushes of that mass of well-armed and courageous fighting men. He knew that he was near the end of his resources.

The sheriff now came in, calmly smoking a cigarette. He leaned in the doorway, and nodded at Rippon. "Palding," he said, "I didn't know that it could be done. I didn't dream that it could be done . . . and you've done it."

"If you'd opened up from the other side . . . ," suggested Rippon.

The sheriff shook his head. "I wanted to," he said. "But I couldn't. I've had fifty fights with thugs and crooks. But I can't shoot at those people. They're not lawbreakers really. They're just mad, Palding. Mad, as you must have been on the day when you killed Sam Barrett . . . because the man that you are now would never have done such a thing."

The truth came swelling in the throat of Rippon and almost reached his lips, but he repressed it. There was no use striving to say what could never be believed. It would be considered a mere weakening at the last moment.

Besides, his tongue was stopped by the memory of the contract that he had made with worthless Tom Palding. For five days he was to wear that name in Tyndal Valley. Well, the second day was not yet over—and he would not speak—not even when they had the rope around his neck or had flung on him the oil that finally was to burn out his life. The thought made him pant and his nostrils expanded as he drew in deeper breaths.

"Tell me something, Clark," he asked.

"What is it, old son?" The voice of Clark was almost affectionate. He looked with a touch of admiring awe upon his prisoner who he had so bitterly despised.

"Will they come again?"

"They'll come again, and still again." said the sheriff. "And one of those two times, you'll have to shoot to kill. They mean business, now. You hear it?" He held up his hand.

"I don't hear a thing," said Rippon.

For a sudden hush had come over the crowd, and even the distant spectators were caught in the spell of it.

"That's what I mean," said the sheriff. "A talking man is like a smoking fire . . . he seems bigger than he is. But now these folks are going to raise a dust."

CHAPTER TWENTY

With the mule galloping all the way, Maisry went home in the buggy, and even his gallop was not fast enough to please her. Half rising from her seat, she slashed the poor animal again and again, until it shook its head in a futile protest. Many an arrear of rightful punishment came to the mule on that trip home. What drove Maisry was an almost blind fear.

She knew that the sheriff was a man of might in the Tyndal Valley. If he were frightened, then it was high time for everyone to have fear. He said that the town was rising. The sheriff's force was not enough to turn the tide. Then what force remained?

Charles Barrett was a wise and a powerful man, but, alas, his force would be used against that unlucky fellow, Tom Palding.

There remained Jeremy. She felt, sometimes, that Jeremy could meet a hundred men and with the single force of his arm defeat and destroy them. She was sure that twenty would be as nothing to him. So she sped out to the ranch, and found Jeremy working with a great cross-cut saw, meant to be manned by two strong pairs of arms. But Jeremy worked it alone. The huge steel blade, flashing back and forth, rising and falling a little as the curve of its keen edge bit into the green log, was a mere nothing to him. He whistled and he sang. Sometimes with one hand he whipped the great saw back and forth. Sometimes with the other he moved it. But he did not change hands because his arms were weary. How could they be tired?

He had thrown off his outer shirt. He was clad in a thinly woven undershirt, such as an athlete uses. His arms were bare to the shoulders, and the drawing and pushing at the saw made the tangles of power appear from wrist to neck in an amazing, smooth flow of ripples. He waved one hand when he saw her drive in, but he continued his labor.

He was always at labor, it seemed to Maisry. In the early dawn they harnessed him to some task, and his enormous cheerfulness kept him at the thing until dusk. In the half of this day, he had done far more work than two pairs of skilled sawyers would have accomplished in a full day's shift. And still he was untired, fresh, and turning toward her that special smile that appeared for Maisry and for no other person.

She pulled up the mule with a jerk, close to him, and then he saw the trouble in her face and sprang to her. She tried to climb from the buggy, but he extended his tremendous hands and picked her out gingerly, daintily and set her down on the road before him.

He was not so very tall. He was not so tall, for instance, as that fellow with the arched nose, and the brown face, and the keen eyes. But there was something about Jeremy that always made the girl look up, as if to the sky.

"Now, Maisry, what's happened?"

She could not talk, for an instant. She put both her hands on the base of her throat, where the pain was choking her. "They're killing him," she said.

"Who, Maisry?"

"Tom Palding."

"What?"

"Yes. They're killing him."

Suddenly he shrugged his thick shoulders. "Well, with Charlie and all the rest against him, he couldn't be likely to hold out long, could he? I'm sorry. I liked him. He had the straightest eye that I ever saw."

"Oh, yes," said the girl. "He has the straightest eye. He's a gentleman, too. There's pity in him. He understands, Jeremy. Oh, how swiftly he understands and sees the hearts of things and people."

"You like him pretty well, Maisry," he said.

"Yes. I like him. And they're killing him."

"Who is?"

"Oh, all the people in Tyndal. All the people in the town are killing him. They're gathering and humming like wasps. I never heard such a sound."

"And they've got him?"

"No, but you've heard, Jeremy? You've heard that he's in the jail now?"

"In the jail? Maisry! Who put him there?"

"Why, the sheriff did. They attacked the old Palding house, last night. A lot of them did. I think Harry and Jim were with them. They attacked the house. They got into it in the middle of the night, and there they found that Tom Palding was ready for them."

"How many were there?"

"Eight or ten, I don't know. . . ."

"Eight or ten . . . then, of course, they swamped him . . . eight or ten of the sort of men that the Barretts have." He always spoke of his family in a detached manner, like this, as though he were similar in name rather than in blood.

"No, no," said Maisry. She tilted up her face, and her eyes were shining. "Oh, Jeremy, how I should have loved to see it. You would have loved it, too."

"You mean that he fought 'em away? You mean that, Maisry?"

"Why, there were ten or a dozen of them, and they were in the house, and he was waiting there in the terrible dark of the night, Jeremy . . . think of it."

"Aye, I'm thinking of it."

"And then he leaped in among them. He must have been like a tiger. They were afraid. All those men were afraid. I know that he shouted. They told me that. I know that he ran outside, chasing them, and they all ran away like dogs when a wolf comes out of its cave. And so he went back and took care of the man he had struck down."

"He knocked down somebody?"

"Yes. With a bullet. That Bud Caswell. He was hurt, and what did Tom Palding do then?"

Jeremy Barrett began to rub his chin thoughtfully with his knuckles. "Well, I don't know. What did he do then, Maisry?" he asked. He was looking down earnestly at her, as though there were something new in her, which he descried dimly and at a great distance. But she was accustomed to the appearance of a dawning idea in the mind of Jeremy.

"He tied up the wound, and he loaded the man onto a wagon that he put together, and, at a walk, he took him all the way into Tyndal, and brought him to the doctor there."

"That was a pretty good thing to do," said Jeremy. And suddenly he flushed just a little for some hidden reason.

"And while he was there at the doctor's, waiting to learn whether the man would live or die . . . while he was waiting there, the sheriff came and arrested him. For the attack on Bud Caswell. And none of the Barretts would tell the truth . . . that poor Tom Palding was only defending his life . . . and now that Tom is in the jail, the town wants to take him out and lynch him. Oh, but I could hear the whisper of it, everywhere, and the men went around looking like dogs about to bite. I never saw such faces. It's a dreadful thing, Jeremy."

He took her hands away from her throat as though they prevented him from seeing her behind a mask, as it were. "Now, you look here, Maisry," he said. "What do you think that I ought to do?"

"Oh, I know what you'll do, Jeremy," she said.

"Do you?"

"Yes."

"Tell me what I'll do?"

"You'll go and drive the men away and save Tom Palding. Of course that's what you'll do."

The flush grew deeper on the face of Jeremy. "You like him pretty much," he repeated.

"Yes. I hardly ever saw anybody I ever liked so well. He looked right into me, and seemed to understand. You'd never be sad or lonely, with a man like that to talk to."

"You like him pretty much," said Jeremy, and he began to frown a little. "What could I do, against the whole town? There's too many of them there. Charlie Barrett's there, too. He'll be the brains of everything. He'll have his own way."

"Jeremy! Aren't you going to try?"

He looked wistfully upon her face. There was nearly always trouble—worry in her eyes—but there was an agony in them now.

"Would you want me to, Maisry?" he asked.

"Oh, yes. Who else could help him? Who has the strength to stand against them all? Only you, Jeremy, in the whole wide world. Do something, do something, dear Jeremy."

He started. His thickly fleshed forehead wrinkled with pain. When it puckered like this into folds, he had more the enduring and wise look of a lion than ever.

"Well, suppose that I do?" he said to himself, looking beyond her. Then he sighed.

"Will you go, Jeremy?" she pleaded. "Oh, quickly, quickly! Take your black horse. The new one. The one that Charles Barrett gave to you. He's the strongest and the fastest. He'll gallop you all the way to Tyndal."

"Yes. He can take a gallop and hold it with me all the way. I suppose that I'll go, Maisry. If it'll make you happy?"

She slipped suddenly between his arms and threw her own arms around his neck. "Jeremy, dear," she said. She raised her bright face to him, with all the unhappiness, the fear, the pain gone from it.

He could have kissed her. He knew that she expected him to, and never yet had his lips touched hers. But he only leaned a little above her and took her arms from around his neck.

"I'm going to go into town and do my best," said Jeremy.

"You'll win," she said. "I can see you scatter them like sparks above a big bonfire. Oh, I laugh when I think of how you'll throw them aside. Jeremy, there's no man in the world but you who could do it. There's no man in the world as wonderful as you are!"

A gleam came into his eye and passed out from it again. He smiled a little, and it seemed to the girl that the smile was sad.

"Well, I'll ride on in," he said quietly, and went to get his horse.

He took the black that she had recommended. It had a special value to him now that she had praised it. He had never known that she so much as cast a glance at horses before this day. He threw the saddle on it, and jerked up the cinches until the black drew in his stomach, with a grunt. Then Jeremy mounted and rode past the house.

The girl was waiting at the open kitchen door, her hands clasped at the base of her throat in the way he knew so well. Jeremy waved to her and she kissed both her hands to him. Then he took the way for Tyndal.

CHAPTER TWENTY-ONE

All the way to Tyndal, as Jeremy had promised, galloped the black gelding. Sweat sprang out on the shining velvet of his shoulders—of his loins. Drops formed and trickled down. The wet appeared behind the saddle, across his hips; the back of his neck was dripping. Then from head to tail, and even halfway up his short ears, he was immersed in perspiration. Foam worked up white as snow under the chafing of the saddle flaps. Where the reins touched the neck was a broad lather. Where the stifles and the elbows played, appeared white patches, and brittle spume blew back from the mouth of the big horse. All the way to Tyndal he galloped, his ears pricking, at first, and his head high. Then the ears declined, and the head stretched out in a straight line. He was working with all his might and the last of his strength when he smote the deep dust of Tyndal's main street and finally turned into the rude square that contained the jail.

It was not really a square, but the jail was the only building in that one block that belonged to the town of Tyndal itself. A rough sea of shrubbery extended behind it to the next street, and all around the block, with its one building, extended the houses of the citizens, with a few shops, here and there. People said that this square would become the business center of Tyndal, if only the jail could be removed to a less offensively public location.

But the picture was so arranged that when Jeremy Barrett arrived he could see the whole thing at a glance. He saw the fighting mob ready in front of the jail. He saw the oil-and-fire-blackened sand and dust that had been thrown upon the steps of the building. He saw the houses around the square, and particularly those facing the jail, jammed with people, and even the roofs occupied.

He flung himself from the saddle. A man from half of whose head the hair had been burned stood leaning against a hitching rack and cursing with every breath he drew. His clothes were scorched. He had a bandage around his forehead, and another rag tying up one wrist and hand.

"What's up, stranger?" said Jeremy Barrett.

"I ain't no stranger to you. I'm Dod Wilkins, Jeremy."

"I'd never would've known you, Dod."

"Who would? Whoever will be able to know me again? The brutes have burned me to crisp."

"How did that happen?"

"It's Tom Palding. I thought he was a yellow cur. He ain't. He's a monster. He's keeping that crowd off with oil and fire. Whoever thought of such a thing? It must be Palding, there behind that window on the right of the door. He turned back the last rush with rifle bullets. It must be him. The sheriff wouldn't fire on law-obeyin' citizens. He knocked off two hats, and then sliced a bullet through Lon Meyers's leg. Just like a knife cut. But the next time they charge that door, he's certainly going to shoot to kill. Look at it."

The front door of the jail had stood up with the honest strength of iron and steel and oak, but the terrific battering was more than it was meant to withstand. Now it was plainly seen to be buckling in the center. A rim gaped there where the lips of the door panels failed to meet, and the huge black arm of the bolt appeared in view. Another stroke or two of the battering-ram would certainly break in that door.

"That door's almost down," commented Jeremy calmly. "They'll knock it wide open the next lick. But are they going to run through bullets to do it? That's what I doubt. They'll wanna save their hides, I guess."

"We're going to have him out," said Dod Wilkins. "I've done my share. You can see that I have. But if nobody else'll help, I'll go back there and grab a hold on the log again. They've played the deuce with us, and we're going to roast every last man of 'em. Look! There they go now!"

The welter of angry, shouting men in front of the jail now formed into some order. A central section spilled outward toward the fallen log. Another wing on either side took up its station with rifles to command the windows of the jail.

But how could they command them any more effectively than they had on the occasion of the last charge? And last time, the prisoner within—or was it the sheriff?—had used his rifle with calm and telling effect.

This time he would certainly shoot to kill. Well, death was a grim price to pay, but where there were so many, each man hoped that some other would pay the penalty and that he himself might escape. And they were mad with the thirst for blood now.

"How many times have they rushed that door?" asked Jeremy.

"Three times," said Dod Wilkins.

"And every time they've been turned back?"

"Aye, every time. Otherwise, they would have smashed that door in long ago."

"You were in it. You saw it with your own eyes," said Jeremy. "But it's hard to believe. Who's in the jail besides that Tom Palding?"

"The sheriff and the Negro cook, George. He's the roustabout for the jail."

"Are they fighting?"

"Only one hand has throwed the oil and fire. Only one rifle has been shooting. It's Palding. We'll burn him in his own oil, damn him! We'll make an example of him. We'll teach him what fire means, and how it eats." Dod Wilkins had worked himself up to such a fury that he was fairly dancing, first on one foot and then on the other.

The hardest men in the county, Jeremy thought, *are out there, and they've been turned back three times. Now they'll have to walk over me before they jump the jail again.* So thinking, he ran straight out toward the selected group of the bravest and the hardiest who were making toward the fallen battering-ram.

As he came among them, he was instantly recognized. He was famous throughout the valley for his courage and his curious might of hand, and they had no doubt as to what brought him here. Was he not a Barrett?

He saw his cousins, Charles Barrett and Harry, and two or three others. They were willing to risk their lives in this final attempt at a good, filling revenge. He was glad that they were willing to take such chances. Before today, he had put them down as a canny lot, making much and spending little.

The group swayed apart, a little, at the coming of Jeremy Barrett. This man who had the strength of four would be invaluable to manage the ponderous weight of the head of the log— incidentally it was a post of honor in which his thick body would be able to stop a few rifle bullets conveniently. With one accord that little mob was willing to yield to Jeremy Barrett the post of honor.

Straight to that point went Jeremy, and encountered Charles Barrett on the way.

"Jeremy," said his cousin, "have you seen the light? Have you got the right sense in you about this now?"

"Oh, I've seen the light," said Jeremy. "I see what you're driving at. You tried to murder Palding last night. And now you're going to push the thing through with a mob in town. You're the worst man I ever knew of, Cousin Charles. I'd rather know a snake than to know you."

"Push him away!" shouted Charles Barrett in a voice that barked like the voice of an angry dog. "Get away with him! Damn him, he's a fool . . . he's a half-wit, and you all know it. Get him away . . . knock him on his crazy head!"

The crowd waited. There were many of them, and they had many strong hands. But they could not use guns against a man like Jeremy, and to tackle him with bare hands would be like coming to grips with a gorilla. Besides, they could not really believe that one Barrett was standing out against all the other Barretts in this matter. For twenty years the hatred of the clan for Tom Palding had been a known thing throughout the valley.

There was a short interval. Jeremy tried to use it. He raised one heavy arm high above his head and commanded silence. He was still wearing the jersey only, and the sight of the muscles in that raised arm effectually put a brake upon the headlong enthusiasm of the crowd.

If Jeremy had been one whit of an orator, he could have stopped the uprising then and there, but words came slowly to him. He only said: "Boys, you're following a wrong steer, just now. Palding's not done what you thought. They raided him last night. It was self-defense. . . ."

"He's a fool!" shouted Charles Barrett. "He's a half-wit. Knock him down and get away with him! Go on to the log. Don't listen to the fool!"

And Harry Barrett yelled: "We want Tom Murderer Palding! We want him now, and we want him bad!"

Jeremy shouted something that was lost in the rising roar of the crowd. They lurched toward Jeremy. Those immediately in front of him halted, their brows lowering, their hands gripped hard. But they dared not come to grips with the big man. Those to the right and left went ahead more easily, however. He was outflanked on either side, and Jeremy bounded back to keep his enemies in front. They were his enemies now.

He had given his promise to Maisry that he would do what he could. Well, what could he do now, except to match the strength of his hands against all of them? He could not draw a gun on them. They would blow him full of holes, and his gesture would be useless. It had to be hand to hand, and no other way.

"Keep back, will you?" he shouted. "The first of you that I put a grip on is going to be hurt!"

"Get him . . . pull him down . . . crack him over the head!" barked Charles Barrett, and shouldered his way forward, as if to set the example of an attack.

That instant the rifles opened from the left of the crowd, to sweep the window behind which Palding was posted. And at this sign of the coming battle, it seemed that the mass of men gathered courage. Half a dozen of them leaped straight at Jeremy Barrett, their hands outstretched to grapple with him.

He struck with his fist at one bent head, and the man fell on his face and skidded in the dust. He struck right and left, but the tangle swept in on him and the fight became a whirl of blindness in a smoke of the rising dust.

CHAPTER TWENTY-TWO

Yonder from the jail, the sheriff, George, and Rippon had watched and heard.

It had seemed, from the first, a futile thing on the part of big Jeremy to attempt to outface so many angry men. Only for an instant, when he raised his muscular arm to halt them and the crowd winced back a little, there had been a gleam of hope. It was lost immediately afterward.

Before the rush began, the sheriff said quietly: "Palding, there's only one way here. We've gotta help Jeremy while he tries to help you. Heaven knows how you've made a friend of a Barrett, but there he is. We might make a flying wedge and cut through them. I don't think we can, but it's our last chance on earth, unless we shoot to kill."

"Aye," Rippon said with an equal calm. "It's our last chance."

They paid no attention to George, as they ran for the door of the jail and thrust back the bolt that held the panels together. But George was there behind them, a very badly frightened Negro, still clinging to his duty and his master with a pitiful, blind determination.

Then, as they worked the heavy bolt back—it had been partially jammed against the panels by the battering blows received from without—they heard the yell of the crowd rise, sudden and shrill, and knew that the living wave was breaking upon Jeremy Barrett.

He might be down before they could get to his aid, but, in

any case, this was the last chance. Desperately they flung back the panels and Rippon bounded down the steps. Behind him came the sheriff, a little to one side, and George, lagging slightly, upon the other. None of them had drawn a gun. It was to be the world of bare hands, or defeat. And straight at the tangle of dust-veiled forms the trio charged.

They found Jeremy half pulled to the ground by half a dozen pairs of grappling hands. Their rush knocked away the assailants. Rippon, striding past Jeremy Barrett, gave him one wild glance over his shoulder, and it was answered. Side-by-side they charged forward into the human mass.

Nothing in the world could have been more unexpected than that sortie, from the viewpoint of the crowd. The blind content and belief in numbers prevailed in every heart. The three times they had been foiled had merely maddened the mountain men all the more. The coming of famous Jeremy Barrett himself had seemed a trifle. But this charge of the three from the jail was another matter. It was a dash of cold water in the face. The lack of numbers in that charge hardly was noticed; it was merely understood that the attackers were being attacked.

They gave back. The hardiest men, to be sure, charged back, but they came scattering, and they were met by the crushing strokes of Jeremy and the iron-hard fists of Rippon. He had not Jeremy's force, but he had skill, the speed of a striking snake, and the desperate coolness of a man who knows that he must not miss in a single step—a single blow. One stumble and the end would come.

Perhaps the sheriff helped more than all else. The conviction that they were in the right melted from them as they saw the lean, grim face of Joe Clark at the shoulder of big Rippon. The very Negro had wonderful weight. In the place of courage, hysteria had come upon him. He bounded and screamed like a monkey among the branches of a tree. He struck wildly to the right and left, and men gave way before him as before a madman.

Right through the heart of the crowd went the quartet. It was not all easy going. The bravest turned and fought and went down under single strokes.

Les Hampton, of the Timberline Ranch, actually got to grips with Rippon, and fairly matched him in strength and desperate valor. But Jeremy struck him behind the ear and Hampton collapsed in the dust, to be trampled by the following crowd.

Two men rushed at Jeremy, and flung their arms around him. His own power was neutralized by the entwining force of their embrace.

Rippon drove his fist into the small of the ribs of one, and, as the man gasped and fell, Jeremy hurled the other lightly away from him.

They were through the central mob, which had been prepared to pick up the log and resume the battering attack upon the door of the jail. There still remained, however, the sections to the right and left, and these fellows were swarming in to join the fight.

There was still no real belief that the four could get away. There was only amazement, stark bewilderment. The crowd seemed to lack a leader, except the screeching, throat-tearing voice of Charles Barrett that was calling to everyone immediately to block the way to the horses.

For, on the opposite side of the street, a whole mass of saddle horses had been left by the out-of-town riders who had been summoned in hastily for this occasion. Some were tethered to the hitching hacks, in front of the grocery store. Some were merely standing with thrown reins, patient, regardless of the yelling and the tumult before the jail. All that concerned them was that they were not, for the moment, jogging across the long, white-hot outer trails beyond Tyndal.

Without a word spoken, the four knew that the horses were the goal toward which they must strike. They pressed on with might and main.

Bare hands were not all that were used against them now. Clubbed rifles began to swing. Jeremy caught one in mid-stroke. He tore it from the hands that wielded it, and, swinging it like a club, strode forward, and the crowd, yelling, divided before him.

They swung back in, like an eddy, upon his flanks and rear. There he was guarded by George and by the little sheriff. Rippon, on his right, took care of that side. But Jeremy was the supreme force that worked a way to the first horses. All around them the crowd was yelling, twisting, striving to get in closer.

"Get on and run for it!" yelled Rippon to Jeremy.

The giant, in reply, gripped the man he had brought this far in the rescue and flung him bodily into a saddle. At the same time, George was struck with a gun barrel and went down with a streak of red across the crown of his head. The dust and the trampling feet closed over him.

A whole wedge of men drove in on the sheriff. He flourished a gun in their faces, but they seemed to know that he would not shoot. They bore him down, they mastered him. Several—some with bruised faces that had felt the fists of the sortie party— dragged Joe Clark out of the mêlée and pinned him against the wall of the grocery store, a helpless man.

The same wave of attack had entangled big Jeremy, as his attention was given to throwing Rippon into the saddle. He turned and struck hard, short, bone-breaking blows, but he could not quite shake off these assailants.

And that, Rippon, from the comparatively safe tower of the saddle height, looked down and saw. He saw, also, a long lane before him and no hand near to touch his gathered reins. He could shoot down that lane between the horses. In a few seconds he could be free.

But Jeremy would be left behind him, and such blows as Jeremy had struck this day would be remembered by many a man whose nose had been flattened, mouth cut, cheek bones laid bare, or teeth battered in. It would go hard with Jeremy if they had their way with him in revenge.

From the pommel of the saddle hung a long, heavy quirt with a loaded handle. Rippon caught it off, and, grasping the lashes, he swung that quirt like a flexible club. The leather-bound head of it would hardly crack skulls, but it was a stroke no wise man would stay to encounter.

A circle spilled back around him. Someone, snatching out a revolver, fired at the hunted man. They had not dared to shoot when the sheriff was so close to the fugitive from mob violence, but now they had Rippon off by himself, and they wanted nothing but his life—and quickly.

The bullet flew wild. Instead of striking Rippon, it slashed the back of the big bay on which he sat, and that hornet sting and knife cut drove the powerful range horse mad. He began to squeal like a dying pig. With arched back, head down, he began to buck and kick. From those flying heels the foremost of the crowd gave back. Rippon, driving home his spurs fiercely, drove the brute straight at the knot in the center of which Jeremy was fighting.

He was like a giant among pygmies. He picked off man by man and flung him away. Some he stunned with short-arm punches. Now he raised his fist and brought it down like a leaden hammer upon the nearest head or neck. But though he knocked them away, they rose and came in again. They were like so many bulldogs around a bear. They might be half stunned and flung aside, but they came closing in again, true to their tough breed.

Jeremy was bare to the waist now. His shirt had been torn to shreds. Red—not all his own—streaked and stained his body. His long hair blew in the wind like the mane of a lion. And lion-like his eyes were flashing. Such a picture of a man, Rippon never had seen, and never would he forget it. As Jeremy fought, the joy of the battle overmastered him. His throat opened. Out poured a great shouting that was like a wordless song.

But he was far spent. Clinging arms clogged his strength. The weight of many bodies dragged at him when Rippon in excitement charged down on the group.

A warning yell rose from the crowd behind. Two bullets in quick succession hummed close by his ear. Then the swing of Rippon's quirt reached the first man beside big Jeremy and brought him down.

Two others turned, yelling at the sight of the horse. And the bay, like a trained warrior, reared, and struck out with its fore-hoofs. Down went those men. It seemed to Rippon, sickening him to the heart, that he saw the heavily shod forehoof strike once full upon the upturned face.

Before he could look again to make sure, he saw Jeremy, having shaken off the last of his immediate foes, bounding into the saddle on the back of a big gray horse.

Swinging the quirt, shouting like a madman, Rippon drove on. Another bullet opened the breast of his shirt like a knife stroke as he turned the bay sharply to the right and headed down a narrow lane. The lane took an elbow turn. Around it, before him, swept Jeremy, jockeying his gray to greater speed. Rippon followed him, and suddenly the uproar that had been splitting their brains was lodged far away, hardly louder than a remembered voice in the ear of the mind.

CHAPTER TWENTY-THREE

The road in front of the jail looked like a battle scene now. From the steps clear to the hitching rack in front of the grocery store there was a scattered litter of fallen men. A few had been actually stunned by the heavy blows of Rippon and Jeremy Barrett, but most of them were unconscious from kicks that they had received from the trampling feet of the crowd. They were picking themselves up here and there, and staggering forward with bulldog determination to join in the fight, if fight still existed.

Where the last stand had been made and where Jeremy and Rippon had managed to mount, there were more hurt men than in all the rest of the street. The hoofs of the horse had stretched out four, who were now groaning from those club-like strokes. Others were down from the fists of Jeremy and the loaded quirt of Rippon.

But the majority of the crowd, fierce as hunting hounds, was throwing itself on horseback when Dr. Chester Power appeared on the scene, running with all the speed of his long legs, and throwing up his arms. He made a scarecrow figure that caused the first riders to swerve aside and wait a moment for the news.

Was Bud Caswell dead? Then the fugitive was honestly and lawfully to be hunted down. But what was this that the doctor shouted?

"Caswell is better! Caswell is going to live!" He reached Charles Barrett and clutched the reins of his horse. In the face of Barrett he shook his long finger. "Barrett," he shouted, "Caswell is going to live, and he swears that if a hair on Tom Palding's head is harmed, he'll tell such things that twenty men will go to jail for it! Call off your men, if you're wise!"

Those who heard this loudly shouted speech reined in their horses on the spot. A few already had galloped on, but when they missed the expected roar of hoofs behind them, they looked on one another, remembered what two men they were chasing, and suddenly stopped the hunt.

Those worthies who were holding the sheriff suddenly loosed him. George was lifted almost tenderly from the dust, and carried into the grocery store. There, stretched out on a counter, he presently began to groan and revive, rolling his eyes wildly from side to side, and nursing his wounded head.

The Barretts had drawn to a head around Charles, the leader of the family.

It was an excessively grim day for Charles Barrett. Two great purposes that he had in mind would have been pushed forward if he had been able to lead on the mob to the murder of the supposed Palding. One of those purposes he conceived would have been fully accomplished. Now he had failed utterly in both.

He looked savagely about him, to the right and left among his special party and among the villagers and the men from the rest of the outlying territory of Tyndal. Hardly a one of them but showed torn or burned clothing, or battered faces. It was an incredible thing that so many stout men could have been gathered together and then have failed in their purpose.

"The fellow has it in for me," said Charles Barrett. Then, with a savage word right and left to his clansmen, he put his horse to a canter and started from the town.

As he went, his going was not unmarked, and the casual gait that proved that he was not pursuing the fugitive. And some of the townsmen and others who remained behind raised a great shout of anger and derision. He had been the main force in spurring them on toward this ignoble work; they could not help venting some of their anger and hatred toward him.

As he heard the snarling jeers, Barrett rose in his stirrups suddenly and threw a wild look behind him. But he did not return. He sank back again into the saddle and locked his jaws like the bulldog he was.

Already he was beginning to turn in his mind other alternative schemes. Out of one of them he would win a victory, he swore.

In the meantime, the sheriff had been released, and those who had been so proud of holding him were now apologizing profusely. As for the sheriff, he was not ordinarily a very politic man, but he was so thoroughly used to violence and the ways of crime that he was hardly shocked by the outburst of this day.

Among that bruised and baffled and unhappy crew, he picked out half a dozen of the most important men of the town and ranchers adjoining it. They came suddenly, when he called. Arrest was what they expected, and arrest was what they deserved. They knew it, and their hearts were sore, but every one of them was a man of such a position that he could not afford to go scampering off on horseback. Gloweringly they came up to the sheriff. He waited until the last one had arrived, and then he talked to them quietly.

"Friends," said the sheriff, "you've all got together to raise the dickens, today. You think that you've had bad luck because you've failed. And a lot of you wish that I were dead. Well, you're wrong. I've helped to keep you from a murder. A murder it would have been, especially since the doctor says that Bud Caswell is going to live. Now, I'll tell you what. I could put a lot of you in jail. I could put that whole mob in jail, and whether I got any convictions or not, by the time you had got through paying lawyer bills, you would be a sick lot, and sick of jail especially. I think that I could get convictions, at that. But I don't want to do it.

"You've tackled my jail, you've promised to roast me alive, but I've known every one of you fellows in other times, and I hate to think that you would be the way you've been today except for getting a little crazy. That's the way I'm going to think of it. The jail has lost a good steel door that needs to be straightened out and rebraced. It has lost also some plaster where bullets chipped in through the windows, and one can of oil is gone."

He paused here with the grimmest of smiles, and one or two of the listeners could not help smiling, also.

"Replace the stuff the jail has lost," said Joe Clark, "plaster up the bullet holes, and send in another can of oil. Then I'll forget everything. You've kicked and hammered me a good deal. But some of you got about as much as I did. If any of you think that you're getting off cheap, there's a Negro in that store who did his duty, today, without being paid or asked for it. You might remember him a little. That's all I have to say. Let's turn our backs on this day and forget about it."

There were six of those eminent citizens gathered before the sheriff. When they understood the humanity and broad common sense of the official, each one of them could not help remembering certain earlier moments in the day when the mob had been howling in front of the jail. The anger was gone from them, and their minds were sorer with shame than their bodies were with bruises. They came up to the sheriff and shook hands with him, one by one.

Bascom was the leader. "Joe," he said, "I never guessed before what a really fine man you are and what a fool I am. I know now. You're sheriff forever, so far as we're concerned, and the next cur that tries to raise a mob in Tyndal, we'll bring him to you personal, riding on a rail in a suit of tar and feathers."

That was the general opinion. When they turned to go away, the sheriff could look after them with a good deal of satisfaction. He suddenly felt that he had been snatched from ruin, this day, and given something more than a reward of money or of fame.

The doctor came up to him with a smile and a proffered hand that the sheriff accepted. There was not a cleaner hand or a purer heart in the valley than the doctor possessed.

"Joe," Doc Power said, "you've done a good job, a grand job. People are going to remember you more for this than for all the men that you've hunted down. I've never been any great admirer of yours, Clark, before today. I like the healing of wounds better than the giving of 'em. But now I see that you stand for the law first and the truth second, and the hangman only third. I'm a late friend, but you won't find me a cold one. Where's Jeremy Barrett that helped to break up the mob?"

"He's gone with Tom Palding," said the sheriff. "I've known you weren't on my side, Power. I'm glad to have you, late rather than never."

"About Palding," said the doctor, "it seems that we've been pretty wrong, these twenty years. Bud Caswell is lying in my house, yonder, just around the corner from death. A dead man he'd surely be if it hadn't been for the humanity and good treatment that he got from Tom Palding . . . and got after he'd gone to murder Palding in the middle of the night."

"The deuce," the sheriff said under his breath.

"I have Caswell's word for it. I could name some names that would make your hair stand on end, but there's been enough trouble out of this business. There's been plenty of trouble, I take it."

"More than plenty," said the sheriff. "I hope that this day dies and every bad thing that started it."

"I hope the same," said the doctor. "Tell me only one thing. What do you think about Tom Palding?"

The sheriff slowly rubbed his hard chin. "I'm beat by him," he said. "There's a murder and twenty years of meanness charged up to him, but he comes back here and plays as straight a line as ever I saw. I've seen cool men, but never a cooler man than Tom Palding in the jail, yonder, when they were talking burning, here in the street. I've seen keen fighters, but never a fairer one than Palding. He could have stopped every charge of that battering-ram with a few bullets from his rifle. He had my permission to use it. But he refused. He simply fired three times, and scared them off. He went out and fought hand to hand, rather than kill a man. If that's not clean, I've never seen cleanness in a man."

"It's clean," agreed the other. "It's as clean as ever I heard. And the older I live, Joe Clark, the more convinced I am that a man can be a fool when he's young, middle-aged, and ready to die. I think we've been fools about Tom Palding. Now let's welcome him home."

The sheriff said: "You've got the very idea that's in my mind. But the strongest family in the valley will hate that idea mighty bad."

"The Barretts?"

"Yes, the Barretts."

"Well, they ain't kings over us. Start the idea working, and we'll all fall in line."

The sheriff wandered slowly back toward the battered door of his jail. He went slowly, because he wanted to taste again the sweetness of the victory that overmastered the aching of his various bruises. And, as he went up the steps one by one, he was telling himself that duty was the greatest god, after all, and a kind one in the end.

CHAPTER TWENTY-FOUR

Jeremy Barrett and Rippon were riding idly out along the road toward the Palding place. They went at ease, because not a rider had pursued them past the edge of the town. They went comfortably, because a smooth pace was better for the various pains that troubled their anatomy. They had been badly pounded from head to foot. Jeremy Barrett, padded and cushioned with muscle as he was, could endure it better than his leaner, more bony companion.

On the other hand, Rippon possessed an infinitely calm philosophy that supported him, and had supported him before. He was too familiar with bangs and blows and bruises to be greatly discommoded by what he had experienced on this day. Neither had the cloud of danger lingered in his mind as an aftereffect of shock to the nerves. He had been through a thousand dangers before in his life. Who could say, for instance, that the terror of that jail experience was a more mortal peril than the march across the heat of the desert? He discarded all thought of the past as of a nightmare, and he whistled as he rode along.

Jeremy Barrett looked upon him with an affectionate and yet a rather wondering eye. For Jeremy rarely sang or whistled, except that musical, leonine roaring, when he was involved in a battle that taxed his glorious strength to the utmost.

So Jeremy looked at Rippon, and Rippon, even while he whistled, smiled with his eyes at his big companion. They understood one another. Rippon had offered no thanks. What were the words fit to express gratitude to a man who had saved one's life? Not a syllable of thanks passed between them, but there was that faintly smiling look as they glanced at one another. And it was sufficient.

As for the trouble in Tyndal, it was not likely that there would be any echoes of it to bother them. In a moment or two the crowd would get its wits back, the sheriff would be set free, and the Barretts would probably receive a thorough cursing for their part in inspiring the riot. All of this was reasonably self-evident. Crowd tempers boil so suddenly and so hot that they soon exhaust their fires. Tyndal's mob was apt to be as dead as ashes, now, and the second great menace had passed from over the head of Rippon.

But still the second day was not ended. How much had been crowded into it since the moonlight through the unshuttered window had showed him the man in the hall. And now it was only the latter part of the afternoon. All the fields shimmered with wind and sunlight—a gentle wind, and a strong, slanting sun. The cattle were leaving the shade of the trees and wandering out to graze again lazily, carelessly—not like the wild-eyed desert cows that hunt for forage as a wolf hunts for meat. And the small streams continually crossed the road in swift rivulets and mere trickles that could make a mud pool, and no more.

"It's a pretty good place, this valley," said Rippon.

"Yeah. It's a pretty good place. It's a green sort of a place," said Jeremy. "You don't get rich here. But you get plenty. You get enough exercise to keep you hard. And that's a good thing, too."

"Yeah. Those fellows were a hard lot," Rippon said meditatively. He hooked the reins over one arm and began to roll a cigarette.

The horse, feeling apparently that this was a golden opportunity to shed its new rider, bucked sidewise, twisting tail and nose close together. It got a severe rake of the spur for a reward, and, being a sensible beast, after all, realized that the iron grip of those legs would not be easily dislodged.

The rider, without tightening rein, produced his sack of makings and his packet of thin wheat-straw papers and made a cigarette swiftly, dexterously avoiding the spilling of any of the light, dry tobacco. Big Jeremy watched this procedure with attention, but from the corner of his eye.

"Now and then you ride a horse," he suggested as the cigarette was lit.

"Mostly now," Rippon responded.

"Punching a lot, maybe?"

"Oh, I've worked on my feet, too. I've done everything from picking watermelons to pounding a drill. I'm a workingman, Jeremy."

A rabbit, at this moment, jumped up from behind a rock and stood an instant on its hind legs, foolishly making sure that danger was near.

In that instant, Jeremy Barrett slid from its long holster the rifle that ran down under his right knee. The owner of this horse, apparently, had gone into action in the mob armed with a revolver only, and his loaded Winchester had been left with his horse. In the grip of Barrett, it was as light as a toy, and, whipping it to the shoulder, he took aim.

The rabbit bounded away at that moment, spy-hopped, and as it landed, the gun spoke. The little fugitive dodged into a tuft of grass and remained there a moment.

"I pulled to the left," said Jeremy.

"You would have got a man, though," said Rippon.

The rifle was half back in its holster when the rabbit scurried out of the grass tuft again. Jeremy, without a word, handed the gun to his companion.

There was no doubting the mute challenge, and Rippon, catching up the rifle, found the fleeing, dodging rabbit in the sights and followed it for three jumps. Then he fired, low and ahead. The rabbit tumbled head over heels and lay still.

"There's supper," said Rippon, handing back the gun. He dismounted, climbed the fence, got the rabbit, and with a few deft strokes of his knife cleaned it. He swathed it in some tall-growing grass and brought it back to the horse, where he dropped it into the saddlebag.

"Now and then you shoot a gun," commented Jeremy.

"That was pretty much luck, Jeremy," said Rippon. "You know how it is. Sometimes you catch a thing in the sights."

"All right," said Jeremy. "But I reckon that you catch 'em pretty often. Some gents always have a killing in the crook of their forefinger. They can't miss. You can't call that luck, though. It's more than luck, I'd say. It sticks to the man that has it, till his nerve breaks."

"You'll get me self-conscious, Jeremy. I'll be doing no more shooting while you're around."

"Tell me a thing, Tom. Are you really here for good . . . here in Tyndal Valley, I mean?"

"Maybe not for good. I dunno. I'm just getting the feel of the place again, and it feels sort of rough, somehow." He chuckled, and Jeremy Barrett smiled with him. "This time," broke in Rippon, "the fact is that I'm not likely to stay on beyond three days more. If I can stand the water for five days, maybe I'll come back for a long swim."

"Five days," said Jeremy, nodding. "I guessed it wouldn't be much longer than that."

"What made you guess that?"

"Well, the other night when you got home to the old house, you didn't seem one thing or the other."

"One thing or the other what?"

"Sad or happy. Not much, I mean. All at once I said to myself that this was only a game to you."

Rippon did not look at his companion as he heard this. He did not dare, for fear that confession might be in his face. And he was amazed and startled to see that there was a great power of penetration hidden under the exterior simplicity of Jeremy.

They got back to the ranch house again, and Rippon looked at it not as a friend, but as an enemy. So much danger already had lurked there for him, and so much danger was sure to come on him again while he was in the place, that he could not help a faint shudder that came with a running chill up his back.

Then Jeremy was saying that he would be riding on home. "Unless you need me here," he said.

"I need you, Jeremy," said Rippon. "And I always will need you, one way or another, but I've got to paddle my own canoe through this bit of white water."

Jeremy watched him curiously.

"What are you thinking of, Jeremy?"

"Something that I've got to tell you. I dunno that I would've heard what was happening to you there in the town . . . I dunno that I would've gone in to help, if it hadn't been for another friend of yours that started me along."

"Who was that? I have no friends in Tyndal Valley, Jeremy, Nothing but enemies."

"Well, you wouldn't've noticed her," said Jeremy. "Mostly people don't. I mean . . . Maisry."

"Oh, the girl at the Barrett place?"

"She came driving out from town. She came making her mule whoop it up. She told me what was happening to you, or likely to happen to you, and so I went right in. I had to tell you about it. She deserves a friendly thought from you, maybe."

"Aye, I've thought of her. I noticed her, all right. I never saw anybody like her before." Then he saw that a dull red was spreading over the face of Jeremy. Rippon had dismounted. He went to the head of Barrett's horse and laid a hand on the reins.

"Look here, Jeremy," he said. "Is she your girl?"

Jeremy, breathing hard, answered: "No, she's not my girl. Not quite. Up to yesterday she was . . . kind of. I guess she's not, today. Well, so long, Tom. If you want, I'll go into town, later on, and fetch out your horse and rig for you. It still may be a bad place for you to hang around . . . Tyndal."

"I'm going back in myself," said Rippon. "I'll return this outfit and get my own. I've got to paddle my own canoe through the rapids, Jerry. Now, about that other thing. . . ."

"You don't have to say anything about it," Jeremy Barrett said. "If there's white water ahead of me . . . I'll have to go through it alone."

"Jeremy."

"Aye."

"This girl means a lot to you?"

"Yeah," said Jeremy. "She kind of does mean a lot."

"Then I'll never . . . ," said Rippon.

But Jeremy raised his hand and shook his head, smiling a little. "I'm not that kind," Jeremy said. "So long."

CHAPTER TWENTY-FIVE

But Rippon made no attempt to speak again. He merely stood there at the head of his bay horse and watched Jeremy cantering off down the road, the horse traveling with the cow pony's rocking lope. He knew that there was nothing he could have said that would help. The quiet manliness of Jeremy touched his very heart. He could tell that there was much trouble, there, inside the big man, but he vowed silently that if Barrett were concerned on account of him and Maisry, he would have his concern in vain. She was a strange girl, a new type, an odd thing, but Rippon would put her out of his mind.

He made the silent resolution. He nodded his head to give it sanction and register it. And then, suddenly, he found that there was an odd feeling of hollowness in his heart. He could not understand that feeling, for a moment, until he traced it back to the face of Maisry.

Suddenly stricken, he looked straight up at the sky and took a big breath. He was glad, then, that Jeremy had not allowed him to make a promise. And yet he detested himself for even the willingness to wish misfortune to his friend in any way. And the bigness of Jeremy's heart, he saw, was as great as his body. Otherwise, there was no need to tell how the girl had rushed out from the town to enlist his help.

Why had she done it? From what Jeremy said, Rippon could infer that there was something more than a mere sense of pity and humanity in her. He thought of his ugly face and ungraceful ways, and shook his head with wonder. What could be in him that had touched her in the slightest degree? But if the miracle had happened . . . ?

His heart leaped. A spinning, dizzy mist passed before his eyes for a moment. And then he remounted the bay horse. He could not go into the dimness of the shadow beneath the trees and sit in the wrecked old house. He had to be out in the open, with this new idea possessing him. He felt, too, that to be where the sun would shine and the wind blow on him would make him stronger in the fight that lay ahead. That fight was to be true to Jeremy and renounce the stinging hope that had risen in his breast.

So he rode the bay gelding across the fields of the old Palding place. He tried to put his mind upon the ground over which the horse was stepping. Plainly it was not worth the $10,000 that Charles Barrett had offered for it, but then there might be reasons in the mind of Barrett, outside of the mere value of the land. The sentimental reason, for one thing, of wishing to round out his land. Or the desire to expunge the hateful name of Palding from the list of the landowners in Tyndal Valley. Either reason was strong enough for a Barrett to act upon. It was only odd that a close-fisted man, such as Charles Barrett apparently was, should have been willing to overpay so much. The tightest of bargains one would ordinarily have expected from him.

It was poor soil. Everywhere the rocks were outcropping. The grass grew scantily, except where the surface soil had gathered in deeper pockets. And as one looked across the big fields, one could see more flashing of stones than the glitter of grass.

Yet there was a beauty about the ranch, also. A number of sloughs, some of them running water at this time of the year, crossed and re-crossed the land, making it difficult to get from field to field. Rickety bridges had been built. The first one he crossed gave with a slow and sickening stagger under the weight of horse and man. But the sloughs and creeks were lined with a heavy growth of trees and brush that made great natural fences, enclosing the sections of the ranch. Sometimes, it was almost like riding through a forest.

He came to the farthest limit of the ranch, according to the map that Palding had taught him, and there he found a creek that ran in a wider, more shallow basin. The bottom was covered with a fine, compact sand, and the water, which was a mere sparkling trickle, meandered from side to side.

This was a roadway that offered easier going to the horse than the rough rocks of the fields, where the shod hoofs were continually slipping on stones that were only filmed over with shallow-rooted grass. So he rode down the bank and pursued his way along the water.

It was like a dusky green tunnel, very dim now that the sun was so far westering. Small wild things had come into the brush to enjoy the coolness, to wait for the real dusk. Here and there, he heard scampering among the brush as they hurried away. The creaking of the saddle leathers sounded strangely loud. When the horse snorted, a great echo seemed to fly before them, and behind. It was like passing down a great, irregular corridor. For the trees grew thick and tall. Their long arms crossed and re-crossed above the head of Rippon, and on either hand the shrubbery filled up the interstices.

He was beginning to think that he had gone far enough, and that he would be reasonably close to the limits of the ranch if he took the first opening to the left, when his way was stopped by the clang of a rifle and the whir of a bullet. It literally clipped the hair from the right side of his head.

The horse spun about as though at a signal. It started back with a short squeal of fear. Another shot sang by the ear of Rippon, but now the horse was turning the next bend of the creek bottom, and this had the effect of a dodging side slant. Perhaps that was what made the marksman miss his second shot.

Rippon, driving the horse up to the right, through the first break in the wall of green, found himself trembling from head to foot. It was not fear that possessed him. It was a huge rage. He had been waylaid in the dark of the night in the house. They had attempted to murder him by mob fury and numbers when he was in the jail after taking one of the first group of murderers to the doctor's care. And now, in an obscure corner of the ranch, he was fired on. By an expert gunman, at that, he could guess. A common marksman would have made the horse the first target, and the man the second, no doubt. But this fellow had shot for the head, both times, and was probably back there in the green gloom of the trees cursing his bad luck.

Both misses had been extremely narrow. Aye, the man was an expert. And there was Rippon, without so much as a revolver in his possession.

He galloped the horse swiftly away toward the house, but as the first wall of trees closed behind him and he dipped into the bottom of the next slough, he halted the animal abruptly. To get to the house, he would have to pass across open fields, and the would-be slayer, from any treetop, easily could mark his course both in going and in the return, and ambush him again. A man of that sort would not miss the target if he had a second opportunity anywhere near as good as the first.

How long and how stealthily had the fellow been stalking across the fields and through the trees of the ranch, waiting to get in his shot?

Rippon dismounted, tethered the horse to the limb of a tree, and turned straight up the course of the slough. He had made up his mind, almost insanely, to return as he was, without a gun, and try to track down the gunman.

At least, he had the knife at his belt and the loaded quirt in his hand. Working through the green gloom of the creek bottoms, the encounter was very apt to be hand to hand, and very close. In that case, the quirt as a club would be almost as good as the bullet from a revolver.

This creek bottom ran into that in which he had been fired upon. The moment that he entered the latter and turned up the stream, he began to walk like a cat. He pulled off his boots. His feet were still sore, inside their double pair of socks. But he was very glad of the soreness. It made him go more gingerly over the small stones and pebbles.

Besides, there was such a cold and constant fury in his heart that he would have walked on knife edges in order to get at the assassin who was hidden somewhere in the brush.

At every corner of the bank, at every gradual turn, Rippon lingered for a moment and listened, with his ear close to the ground, and then erect, making his eyes blind for the instant so that he could hear the better. So doing, all the small sounds of the place seemed to grow greater. The whisper of the water became a distinctly musical and lonely bubbling noise. The scraping of the boughs together in the faint breeze made almost human hushing and groaning sounds. And, now and then, the far-off lowing of cattle came solemnly across the fields and drifted through the woods to his ear.

He had now come, he estimated, almost to the point at which the bullets had been fired at him. He increased his stealthy caution. He went without breathing, almost. Often he stopped, and flashed behind him the bright, guilty look of a stalking beast of prey. And then he went on.

The pebbles were no longer underfoot, and for that he gave praise, not because they hurt his wet feet, but because the sand was a footing far more silent. So, creeping about a sharply angled corner, it seemed to him that a rifleman started out of the still face of the water at his feet.

He could neither shrink back nor step forward. The shock

and the amazement of the thing held him frozen fast to the spot. And then he saw the truth. It was simply that the creek water, at this point, was spread out in a small pool, the surface of which was utterly quiet, and, therefore, it took perfectly the reflection that fell into it.

The green of the overhanging leaves was here repeated almost more brightly than they offered themselves to the actual eye. And in the design of the interwoven branches and the leaves there was a central figure placed as by a skillful artist of a canvas. It was a man on one knee, with a cap on his head, and rifle propping him on one side, a man with his head canted a little sway in the attitude of one listening. And this was he.

Silently—more silently than a shadow sliding over the ground—Rippon drew to one side, so that the reflection of the rifleman almost disappeared. Then he crouched down and began to move forward, inch by inch.

Chapter Twenty-Six

What was in the mind of Rippon was what is in the mind of the cat when it sees the songbird bending on the spray, just above its head, singing, unconscious of danger beneath. But it was no singing bird that he approached. It was a bearded, grizzled, dour-looking man whose cap topped him off with an unseasonable touch of youth.

Coming closer to the corner of the bank where it turned sharply back, Rippon lost the reflection of the stranger in the pool, for the reason that he had shifted his position many angles forward. Besides, he would hardly have looked at it even if he could, so intent was he in soundlessly creeping forward, with the knife haft gripped, hard, in his hand.

He was so enraged by this new attempt upon his life that he intended neither warning nor hesitation. He meant to strike straight to the heart and have done with the incipient murderer at a single blow.

The intensity of his anger, cold and steady as it was, had blinded him the slightest shade. But the small difference was that degree that lies sometimes between success and failure, life and death. He was at the very verge of the corner, where the tall bank of gravel lifted high above his head and sloped outward above him when a rifle barrel was thrust against his head, and, looking straight down it, he saw the contorted and savage face of the stranger of the cap.

Neither of them moved nor spoke for a moment. Then the

contortion of the rifleman's face extended, rather than altered, into a leering smile.

"So here you are," he said. He whispered the words, as though a louder use of his voice might somehow unsteady the surety of his aim and position.

The quick, desperate impulse in the heart of Rippon was to attempt the impossible in order to attack the man—a swift upward movement of the arm to throw the rifle barrel aside, and then a keen stroke of the knife. So eager and keen was the battle impulse in him that perhaps he would have done the thing even at the cost of his own life. He had ceased being a human. He was only a savage intent on destroying. But the ready wit of Rippon as an old frontiersman and hunter told him that he would only be a fool. This other was not a fellow lightly to be taken off his guard.

"So here you are," the man of the cap said again with his horrible smile.

And Rippon, mastering his great heart with a mighty effort, answered: "So here I am, old-timer."

The address caused a fresh convulsion of the face of the stranger. His very teeth showed through his gray-black beard. Hate drew his eyes to little points of light. "Come right on, then, Tom," he said sternly.

He actually drew his rifle muzzle a few inches from the head of Rippon, and backed up slowly, inviting Rippon forward. And the latter obeyed. He felt that the slightest thwarting of the will of the stranger would end his own existence in a trice. He rounded the corner.

"Set down and make yourself easy," the man of the cap said.

Big Rippon sat down, with the gravel bank at his back. Now that he was around the corner, he saw that the place seemed to have been used as a gravel pit. There was no sign of wagon tracks coming down to the edge of the water, to be sure, but there was plenty of evidence of digging that had taken place, the sand having been turned up or carted away for a matter of fifty feet or so. The gravel under it had been gouged out, also.

Just before him, the man of the cap sat on a stone.

"Well, you recollect the place," he said. "It ain't a bad idea that we should meet again here, is it, Tom?"

"Maybe not," Rippon said, wondering who the fellow could be, or what might have been his relations to Tom Palding. It was very patent that the stranger felt he was known to his victim. Then Rippon pointed a little down the stream. The lifting of his hand brought the instant tightening of the other's watchful finger around the trigger of the rifle. "You missed me already," said Rippon. "I'm more surprised that you could have missed me twice, so close, than that I should meet you here."

"I reckon you're surprised," said the other. "There was a time when the boys had to take off their hats to Jude O'Malley, wasn't there?"

"Of course there was," said Rippon. He was very glad to have got at the name. It gave him a somewhat less tenuous hold upon the attention of the stranger, but all the while he knew by the grin and the twitching lips of O'Malley that the latter was playing with him, and allowing him a moment of life, as a cat allows it to a mouse.

"I still am a shot, pretty fair enough," said Jude O'Malley. "But not like in those days. And what made me miss you, so close, was that, when I seen you, I said to myself . . . 'It ain't him.' And then I says . . . 'It is.' And then I says . . . 'No, he's got a cleaner look than Tom ever had.' But then I knew it was you from the way that they had all described you. I thought you was in jail, about to have your neck stretched by the mob. But there I seen you riding into the sights of my rifle and making them bulge, you might say. And somehow the good feeling was too much for me, and I missed you . . . I still can't hardly say why. Well, here I see you close enough to know that you're Tom Palding, right enough. The finger markings of evil are right there in the corners of your eyes."

"You might have sung out and given me some chance," said Rippon. "You shot at me like a beast. I'd give even a deer some sort of a chance."

"You ain't a deer. You're a swine," Jude O'Malley said solemnly. "Only, I wanna know why you ain't having your neck stretched back there in Tyndal, and why you're riding Bill Workman's horse?"

And with this, he peered earnestly, hatefully into the face of Rippon, as one might look into a dark cave, filled with many squirming, twisting rattlesnakes.

"They would have lynched me," Rippon said, "but the sheriff fought for me, and the sheriff's cook, George, and finally big Jeremy Barrett came in, and he turned the balance. We fought through the crowd, got to their horses, and came away from Tyndal pretty fast. That's the story, Jude." He smiled a little at the other.

"Go on and smile," O'Malley said, actually turning pale with hatred as he stared at Rippon. "Go on and smile. It reminds me of the last time that we was here at the corner of the bank of the stream, picking blackberries, and how we came down here to the cool of the stream and ate the berries. We didn't know, while we sat on our heels, that we were resting right over a gold mine, did we?"

"No," said Rippon. "A gold mine of what?"

"Why, you innocent, what would a gold mine be of except gold, can you tell me?"

Rippon blinked, and looked at the shallow work of excavation that had been going on.

"You didn't know, did you?" O'Malley asked. "You didn't even guess. You thought that Charlie Barrett wanted to buy the place from you for fun, or because he liked you so dashed much, didn't you?"

Still, Rippon stared at the gleaming sands of the creek bottom. It seemed to him that he could see the gold appear suddenly, but it was only the reflected sheen from the foliage above his head. "So that's it?" he said.

"Oh, that's it," O'Malley said. "You can scoop up a handful of sand and wash it out in the water, right there beside you. Go ahead and do it, son. Go right ahead and do it, old-timer. And then you'll see how it might have been if you'd lived, Tom. You'll see how it might've been with you if you had got back into owning the ranch, and had found this place, like you were sure to find it, once Charlie Barrett had begun to work it, this way. He'd opened the book. He'd put the bookmark in, you might say. I've always told him that he was foolish to do any work at all here, no matter how secret. But he couldn't help it, and you'll see why. He was like a hungry boy, and he had to taste the pie. He couldn't let it cool, safe and sound. You wash out a handful of that sand, and you'll see the reason."

Rippon, as he was instructed, scooped up a handful of the sand, and, placing it in the hollow of his palm, just under the softly running surface of the stream, he allowed the water to wash the sand away. It diminished. Swiftly diluted, the sand floated away down the stream, and then, as the cloud cleared and the skin of his hand appeared, he saw that something remained in the small wrinkles of his bended palm. And the substance that remained looked back at him, as it were, with little glittering eyes of yellow. He raised it up through the water. He held it close to his eyes. So incredibly rich was this deposit that there was an appreciable pinch of gold in every handful of the sand and gravel.

He looked at Jude O'Malley. The latter had a leering gaze, his lips parted a little. He looked like a man half dead with thirst, and about to drink.

"That's what you might have had, Tom. You might've been rich. You might've bought up the whole damned valley, Tyndal and all. You might've become famous, for all of that. But you see how it is, Tom. You come back here, and you have your bit of luck, and you get away from the jail . . . I would've liked to see that fight, I must say . . . and then you come out here, and just where you meet your fortune, you meet a bullet between the eyes." He grinned, and then he began chuckling. It was like the mirth of a madman, there was such a fiendish malevolence in the sound.

"Aye," said Rippon. "You've got me safe, I know."

"Yes," said the other. "I've got you safe. I missed you on the horse, but I ain't going to miss you now. Between the eyes is the place where I'm going to put the slug. I wouldn't've missed you, if it hadn't been that I wanted to get you through the head, where your damned ideas are bred like worms. These years, I've always had the picture of you, and between the eyes is where I'm going to plant you."

Rippon listened partly to him, and partly he stared at the gold and dreamed a strange dream. For the time would come, of course, when the real Tom Palding would ride down there into the valley and find his way cleared for him by the foolish emissary who he had sent before him.

For $500 that emissary would have fought for the name of Tom Palding. For $500 he would have died. And the hands of the Barretts would be clogged and burdened by the massacre.

So the real Tom Palding would come, after all, and at the end of his worthless, evil life, he would inherit this wealth that lay hidden there in the bed of the creek.

There was so much of the irony of fate in this, that the head of big Rippon tipped back suddenly, and he began to laugh.

CHAPTER TWENTY-SEVEN

He laughed with such a real heartiness that the tears trickled down his cheeks. Perhaps there was some trace of hysteria in his mirth.

Then, as he wiped his eyes, throwing away the grains of the gold dust, he found that the other was watching him curiously, incredulously.

"You've got a good nerve with you, Tom," commented O'Malley. "Your nerve has improved a whole lot, since those old days."

"Has it?" asked Rippon almost carelessly. And he looked at the man, and he looked at the rifle, and he knew that all the danger from the men at the jail had been little or nothing compared with the danger in the face of which he sat now. For the others, all of them, had wanted to take his life when they were filled with a trembling fire of hatred. But this man's hate made him cold and still as frozen water. This man would be sure in the work of his hands so long as he was in this humor.

"Aye, it has," the other said. "The time was, Tom, when you were pretty much of a cur and a bully. You've growed up into a man that could fight his way through a crowd. And that's what pleases me. There wouldn't't've been so much pleasure for me in ramming a bullet right straight between your eyes, if you were now what you used to be. Now the finishing off of you is almost enough to make up for what you've done to me."

"Why, what have I done to you?" Rippon asked, so utterly

past hope that he could be almost impersonal.

"What have you done to me?" said the other with that same ghastly look of a famished man about to drink.

"Yes, what have I done to you?"

"Oh, you'd forget, I suppose," O'Malley said. "A little thing like that, it hardly would still stick in your brain. You've done the same thing such a lot, since them days."

"Go on and tell me what it was."

"Why, you'd still hardly remember, how we sat here and I told you about little Mary Worth, while we were sitting and eating the blackberries in the cool of the shade. Eating the blackberries and drinking the good, cold water. You'd forget what I talked to you about, I suppose, because it didn't really matter."

"Mary Worth?" Rippon echoed blankly.

"Aye, Mary Worth. Ever know anybody by that name?"

"No, never in my life." He forgot, for the instant, that he was supposed to be Tom Palding. There was, naturally, a ring of reality in the remark.

It had an odd effect upon the other. For O'Malley gritted his teeth until the sound was very audible to Rippon. "By gum," he said, "I think you mean it."

"Of course I mean it."

"Even the letters that you wrote to her afterward, about how your heart was breaking because you couldn't get back into the valley to her, on account of the Barretts. You've forgot them, too, I suppose?"

Rippon was silent.

Apparently there had been something between that arrant rascal, Tom Palding, and a girl named Mary Worth. How could he be expected to know the details? But it was useless to pretend ignorance unless he could convince this man, on murder bent, that he was not really Tom Palding.

As for the latter course, he knew that the thing was impossible now. He had done too much under the name of Tom Palding and been too widely accepted as the real man. No man in Tyndal Valley would be prepared to accept any story to the contrary, unless there were actual proofs and the testimony of witnesses to hand to that effect. Even then, it would be considered, no doubt, a typical Tom Palding scheme of evasion and given no consideration.

So he compressed his lips for a moment, looked straight into the face of Jude O'Malley, and said not a word.

"You see that I ain't such a fool as you thought," said the latter. "But I've wanted, all these years, to know why you done it? What was Mary Worth to you, except the girl that I loved?"

Swiftly Rippon estimated the age of the stranger. In spite of his worn face and his grizzled hair, he could not be much more than thirty-five, or -eight.

"Why, man," he said, "you were only a boy. How was I to think that you really were so mighty and lastingly fond of her?"

"Because I'm not the kind to change," said the other. "You knew that, too. You knew that when old Badger, my dog, died, I wouldn't have another. I never would have another one. No, sir, you knew all of those things, and a lot more. No man in the world ever knew me as well as you did, Tom, and you were only a kid, at that. But you knew me. And you knew that Mary meant a lot to me and always would. I tell you, that I never really looked at any other girl from that time to this. When she left the valley, I tagged after her. But she wouldn't have anything to do with me. She married that Denver man, finally. Then I came back here. But there's never been any woman for me except her. What made you go and talk to her the way that you did, and tell her the lies about me that turned her ag'in' me?" He spoke almost plaintively, but there was a building fire of wrath in his eyes.

"Well," Rippon said, "you know how a boy is. He wants to make mischief. That was all that it was. Only mischief."

"You lie," said the other.

"No, I don't lie."

"You lie. So out and tell me the truth, now, will you?"

A sudden scheme came into the mind of Rippon. The longer they talked, the more coldly fixed in his purpose was Jude O'Malley. There must be some way to upset him, the least trifle, if Rippon were to live.

"Come and out with it," O'Malley said harshly. "There ain't much time left. It's already getting sort of twilight here and hard for good shooting. Though there's a kind of a special light that I can see you by, Tom. But you'll live while you talk to me and tell me the shameful truth about yourself."

"Well, I'll tell you," said Rippon. "It's a pretty plain thing that I've come to the finish of the trail."

"Aye," said the other. "You've come to the finish, and all that matters to you is to tell the truth, because heaven itself is apt to be harkening to you now."

There seemed a spice of madness not only in the face and eyes but in the words of O'Malley, and it was plain that in the days of his life he had suffered more than should be the portion of one man.

"I'm going to tell you the truth," Rippon said. "Matter of fact, I'll sort of enjoy telling you. You didn't think it was Mary's pretty face that made me interested in her?"

"She never was a beauty," said the other. "No, she was a right nice and quiet girl. I guess that some folks thought that she was on the plain side. There was freckles across her nose, I recollect."

There was desire in the heart of Rippon to laugh, but he forced a sneering chuckle to his lips. "I'll tell you the fact, Jude," he said. "I didn't give a rap about her. I simply wanted to cut you out with her. I wanted to see what a fool you'd be."

O'Malley stared. He said nothing, but there was a quick alteration of his color. Stains of purple appeared upon his forehead, and his mouth twitched.

"And you were enough of a fool about it to tickle me," continued Rippon.

"It ain't likely . . . it ain't possible that you got the nerve to say it to me now," O'Malley said half to himself.

"What difference does it make?" answered Rippon. "I know that I'm a goner in another few minutes. Why shouldn't I tell you the truth? It won't make you feel any better."

"Aye," said the other, through his teeth. "Why shouldn't you talk out?"

"I mean to," Rippon said.

"You and me being friends," said O'Malley, "that didn't hold you back any?"

"How good of friends were we, anyway?" Rippon asked coldly. And, all the while, he watched the face of the other like a fox, intently.

"Friends enough," O'Malley answered, "for me to loan you my horse to ride, my guns to shoot, even my dog to hunt with. What more friends could I be to you than that, when I was only a kid?"

Rippon chuckled again. "You don't see that you've answered yourself," he said. "That's the sort of friends that we were. You were pretty useful to have around. That's why I had you. Otherwise, would I have bothered with such a lunkhead?"

O'Malley was silent for another moment. He was beginning to tremble, and the twitching of his upper lip allowed his teeth to be seen, glinting. "Ah, damn your heart," he said softly, his teeth hard-gripped together. His whole body shuddered as he added: "A bullet's too quick and easy for you. I'll like to roast you, inch by inch. I'd like to burn you black as a crust, you snake. You ain't a man, Tom. You never was. Now say whatever kind of a prayer you gotta say before your finish." He leveled the rifle more carefully as he spoke. But, in spite of his care, his quick breathing and the extremity of the rage he was in made the muzzle of the weapon waver from side to side. It was not a large degree of uncertainty, but enough to give Rippon a fierce, keen touch of hope.

Straight for his head the rifle was pointed, and the head is not a large target, after all. He made his plan on the instant.

"All right, Jude," he said. "I'll say my prayer. Just back off a little to give me a chance to kneel, will you?"

"Kneel?" O'Malley said. "Aye, and I will. It'll be something to remember . . . you kneeling, and me in front of you, and the rifle ready to give you an answer. It'll be something to remember, all right." As he spoke, he started to rise to his feet, erect, and, as he moved, Rippon acted.

He jerked his head to the side and at the same time kicked upward for the rifle. The gun exploded. The flash and the roar of it half dazed him, but he knew that the bullet had sped past and left him untouched.

Another shot would follow instantly. He had kicked the barrel well up, out of line, but the muzzle would drop and cover him in the next fraction of a second. He had not the time to rise to his feet and attack, but he threw himself, half risen, sidelong at the knees of Jude O'Malley.

The rifle clanged again, and then both men tumbled over and over on the bed of the creek.

CHAPTER TWENTY-EIGHT

The rifle impeded Jude O'Malley. He tried to bring its muzzle in line with his enemy. When he found that it was too long for that purpose, he attempted to wield it as a club. Then a bruising short-arm blow landed on the end of his chin and knocked sparks from his brain. He relaxed his hold on the rifle and pulled out the good hunting knife from his belt. With it he jabbed upward at the body of the enemy, but his knife hand was caught at the wrist by a grip that burned into the tough sinews and the very bone of his arm.

The knife dropped. He caught up a rock with the free hand and strove to batter the head of the other with it. But now with a sting like a hornet, the point of his own knife was in the hollow of his throat. Above him appeared the lean, fierce face of Rippon. He saw the bony hand, brown-black from exposure to the sun. He was aware of the gleam of the knife blade. He dared not stir; he hardly dared to breathe before that blade would be driven through his neck. So he lay still, and glared up into the face of Rippon.

"I dunno . . . ," O'Malley said, "I dunno how it could've happened. I missed. I missed twice." He gaped with horror, not of the death that was at his throat, but of the mystery that had caused him to fail four times. Limp and helpless with astonishment, he allowed himself to be tied securely, the wrists being lashed together behind his back.

"I should've thought of that," O'Malley murmured in an

almost drowsy voice. "I should've tied you up while I had the drop on you. But you talked me out of it. You always talked me out of everything from the beginning. What made that damned gun miss? A curse on it!"

"You were mad," the other said calmly. "You were shaking, you were so crazy. That's why you missed. It's simple enough. Your hands were shaking, old son. You've seen a dog shake that way, because it wanted to get its teeth into the throat of the other dog. But a shaking hand is a mighty poor tool . . . when you're aiming a gun for the head. Sit up, Jude, and we'll have a chat."

He removed the menace of the knife; he even leaned and helped O'Malley to sit up in the constantly dimming light of the ravine. Above them, the sun had entered into its last phase of brightness, changing its dazzling white face for a golden one, so that gold seemed to be flowing across the blue of the heavens, ready to pour through the interstices among the leaves. And the green gloom under all this outer brilliance grew deeper and cooler all the while, so that they seemed almost to be sitting there in pallid, translucent water.

O'Malley, looking slowly above and about him, felt the trickle of a single drop of blood from the place where the knife point had pricked his throat. It would, he felt, be like the first drop of a thundershower that would drain the life from his heart.

The victor squatted on his heels and made a cigarette.

"You're thinking it out," said O'Malley. "You'll get a mighty better idea than just shooting a man through the brain."

"Yes, I'm thinking it out," Rippon admitted. "It's not so dog-gone' easy."

"I've got a kind of a child-like trust that you'll beat the dickens itself when you want to get a fine way for a murder."

"Tell me," said Rippon, almost more curious than angered. "Tell me if you really would call it murder now, Jude? After you've laid for me here, and tried four shots at me, without any return . . . tell me if you'd call it murder if I killed you?"

"Not death by a bullet, I wouldn't. But what you'll think up, that'll be murder."

"I suppose you were down there at the house, the other night, with the rest of the boys?"

"Why, you're crazy," the other said, almost in wonder. "D'you think that I would be able to get away from here? D'you think that I would get free from the creek?"

"You live here day and night?"

"Of course I do. Suppose that somebody else was to come along down here and find what we've found . . . Barrett and me?"

"He and you both found it, eh? Out hunting together?"

"No, but I found it, and I knew that I wouldn't have enough money to get hold of the place. So I let Barrett in."

"On half shares?"

"Why, we never talked much about the details."

"Didn't you?" Rippon said. "Then I've an idea that you would've done the discovering and the most part of the early work, and Barrett would pay for the ranch . . . and keep it. But let that go."

"Aye, it's all gone," said the other. He seemed rather weary than afraid. And, each moment, the light softly darkened, and the green gloom became more complete.

"It's hard . . . it's hard." said Rippon. "Dog-gone me if it isn't mighty hard."

"What? To skin me alive or feed me feet first into a fire? Yeah, it's hard to think of better ways than that."

"What would happen if I let you go, man?"

The other laughed harshly. "Aye, there's a grand chance of that," he said.

"There's a grand chance of that," Rippon said slowly. "But I don't know what you'd do. Stick on my trail, maybe? Come at me again from behind? Lie in wait for me with a gun?" He did not expect the answer that he received.

"Aye," said the prisoner, "for as long as I live and breathe, Tom, I'm going to hunt you and hound you. I stayed on here at the creek to guard the place, rather than go after you. But now that I know what's in your brain, and what's always been there about me, I'm gonna hunt you and hound you down, if ever you let me live. There's honest, so finish me off now." He added with a sudden burst of despair: "What's the real good of life to me, anyway? I'm smashed. If this here sand was all gold, and all the gold was mine, what good would it be to me?"

Rippon stood up. He made and lit another cigarette and began to pace back and forth with short steps, pausing now and again as fresh thoughts came to him. At last, he paused before the captive.

"I'll tell you one thing," he said. "What I said about the girl was made out of whole cloth. There wasn't a word of truth in what I said."

"You lie, you know you do," declared the prisoner.

"What good is it to me to lie to you, man?" Rippon asked curiously.

"That I dunno. You were always too deep for me, though. I would easier follow a snake down its hole than your ways of thinking and working."

"You didn't see my scheme in talking to you. I wanted to get you white-hot. I wanted you to burn. I wanted you to burn so fast that the fire would shake you. And it did. It shook your body and it shook your hand. When I saw that, I took my chance with you, and the chance just came off."

"Hold on," said the captive. "Say that again."

"If I hadn't talked the way I did, you would have stayed pretty cool, Jude. And as long as you were cool, I was no better than a dead man."

Jude O'Malley drew a short, quick breath. "Deep. I always knew that you were deep," he said. "I see the scheme that you worked on me now."

"Matter of fact, Jude, I liked you. It was pretty hard to pull out from the valley, twenty years ago. It was hard to pull away from you, too. I counted you as a friend, even after Mary. I wanted you as a friend." He paused.

Said the other, after the pause: "I guess I see. You work up my hopes. You make me think that I'm free. Then you turn around and laugh in my face and put me in the fire. Man, the devil must be a first cousin of yours, all right enough." He actually laughed as he ended.

Then Rippon leaned, and, with a touch of the knife, he made the hands of O'Malley free. He stood back, and stared down at the man, and through the shadow he saw the white face and the staring eyes of O'Malley, gaping at him as at a frightful vision.

"There's your gun," Rippon said, placing it on the edge of the bank. "I'll put it away a bit, so you won't follow a first idea that might be wrong. You're full of wrong ideas about me, Jude. Whatever Tom Palding was in the old days, I'm a different man. I've done bad things. I've done things that I hate to think back to. But I'm not the sort of fellow that you think, Jude. I don't blame you for hating the Tom Palding of twenty years ago. But twenty years is a pretty long step. You're wrong to hate me now. Think it over. Think a couple or three times about it. That's all, Jude."

He stepped straight past Jude O'Malley, who had not stirred or altered his expression in the least. Down the bed of the ravine, stepping carefully to avoid the water, went Rippon, with a strange feeling of heaviness for the man he left behind him, and yet a slight touch of happiness because he had left the fellow unharmed.

The sand was silent under his striding. And, after he had gone a little distance, he thought that he heard behind him a moaning sound, as of a distant wind. He stopped and listened.

It was not a sound of wind, because there was a regular pulsation in it. It had, moreover, a vibrancy that could only come from the throat of a human being in agony of body, or of spirit.

When that thought came to him, Rippon went on again hastily with a cold perspiration starting out on his forehead. He came to his boots and he put them on. He reached the bay horse, and untethered and mounted it.

He rode up out of the draw and went rapidly across the sunset fields toward the ranch house, which he could see in the distance with its clustering darkness of trees.

In spite of the gallop of the horse, the wind in his face, and all the picture that rolled upon the eye, he could not rid himself of another picture that filled his mind—the thought of poor Jude O'Malley lying face downward in the cold, damp sand of the creek bottom, and sobbing out the miseries of his heart.

CHAPTER TWENTY-NINE

When Rippon came to the corral and passed into it through the bars that led into the pasture field, he was startled by the sight of half a dozen men, horses, and a buckboard outside the gate to the ranch house. He reined in his horse suddenly, and bitterly wished that he had brought with him O'Malley's rifle. It seemed that every moment of his day was to be filled with unspeakable danger.

Then a voice called out in ringing tones: "Palding, Palding! We're friends, Palding!"

It might be a trap, of course. But so much danger had made him somewhat callous. He went forward to take the chance, and, as he came nearer, the horse in front of the buckboard whinnied softly.

It was Baldy! He knew that whinny as well as he knew any human voice. So he whistled a low note, and Baldy whinnied again, loud and long, stretching out his neck, throwing up his tail.

The men who were standing about, at the heads of their horses, laughed a little. And that laughter took the alarm and the suspicion out of the mind of Rippon. Laughter does not go with treason, stratagems, and spoils.

As he came up, a tall fellow gave the lead rope of his horse to another, and stepped out to meet him.

The light was quite dim now. Still, dimly, he could make out the figures and the faces of typical men of the mountains.

"You're Palding?"

"Well?"

"Aye. I see you are. My name is Bascom."

Rippon dismounted.

Bascom went on: "I'm one of the rats who tried to lynch you today, Palding. And I've come out here, with some of my friends from Tyndal, to let you know that we realize that we were a pack of fools. I'd like to start in by shaking hands and asking if we could be friends."

The hand of Rippon went out instantly. He knew how to value a man who spoke in this manner. "Why, Bascom," he said, "every man in the world is likely to drift downwind and get into trouble. Everybody has done it, one time or another. I'm mighty willing to forget today, if the rest of you people can."

"We can't," said Bascom, taking the proffered hand of Rippon with a mighty pressure. "We can't forget. We don't even want to forget how we tried to do a murder, and how a white man inside the jail held us off. You could have slaughtered a dozen of those men. You didn't. You singed our faces for us, though!" And he laughed.

They all laughed together. A world of relief and of good feeling was in the air.

The others crowded up and took Rippon's hand in turn. His brain was rather in a whirl, and he did not catch all their names. Bascom, at any rate, seemed the appointed leader and speechmaker.

"Bud Caswell," said Bascom, "told the doctor some things that were mighty worth hearing. And the doctor told them back to us. Palding, we've all been wrong about you. Twenty years back, you left us kind of in a hurry. Since then we've heard some stories . . . but they were crooked lies and gossip. We know that now. No man does what you've done the last twenty-four hours unless he's right . . . unless he's always been right. We've come out here to ask you to forgive us for being fools, and to thank you and heaven many times for keeping us from being criminal fools!"

"Why," Rippon said, really touched, "I've explained before. I've forgotten today. Besides, I have to go back to the jail tonight. I promised the sheriff that I would, when things settled down."

Six voices told him hastily: "There's no jail in Tyndal big enough to hold you, Palding."

Bascom explained: "The sheriff doesn't want you, except as a friend. That's the way that we all feel. That is, everybody that is in Tyndal feels that way, and everybody in the country around Tyndal, except maybe the Barretts." There was a faint growl from the others. "Well," went on Bascom, "I ain't going to say how much ground the Barretts have lost by this day's work. Charlie Barrett could have had anything he wanted out of almost any ma, yesterday. Tonight, he's not so high. Nowhere damn' near so high."

A man with a heavy bass growl of a voice said: "Look here, Tom Palding. You were alone the first day. You're not alone now. We know that you're in trouble. We've come here for you to pick out any three of us. And we'll stay and see you through for a few days, until the Barretts have a chance to understand that they can't do what they please."

Rippon listened with the weight of worlds falling from his shoulders. The danger seemed to be ending. The beginning of a new and easy time was in sight. To be sure, the second day had not quite ended, and three days remained before him. But with public opinion turning so strongly against the Barretts and their ways, he felt that from then on he would be comparatively secure.

So thought Rippon, not knowing what the future held immediately in store for him. He thanked the bearers of the message. They represented practically the entire vote of the people in Tyndal and the surrounding district. Some of those who had directly suffered in the attack upon the jail might still be sullen, to be sure. And then there was the danger from the Barretts, always. But the assured support of the townsmen, the law, the sheriff, was expressed by this delegation.

"Now, then," went on Bascom, "when we took a look at your mustang, it seemed like he could have worn a better harness, so we went and got him fitted with one. The old buckboard didn't seem to want to roll altogether in the same direction, and so we stepped across to the Peabody brothers' store and there we got hold of a pretty good buckboard that might be handy to you. But when we got the horse and the buckboard, it seemed kind of a foolish thing to take an empty rig out to a rancher that had come all the way to town at a walk to bring in a wounded man and that hadn't had a chance to do his shopping. So we just put in a few trifles there in the buckboard that may be useful in your kitchen, old-timer. And none of these things comes from anybody in particular. It's the way of Tyndal town to say that it's sorry for what it's done. It asks pardon and would've sent flowers, but it didn't think you might like flowers as well as bacon and eggs. Boys, trundle that stuff in and leave it at the house. Hack, you help me get this horse out of the harness."

There on the spot, with the greatest goodwill, they unloaded the buckboard and carted the contents—a great heap of them—to the kitchen of the house. The new harness was taken off Baldy by Bascom and Hack, and Rippon was quite prevented from expressing thanks to anyone. They merely slapped him on the shoulder and pushed him out of the way.

And at last he sat down on the back porch of the little ranch house and watched the last of the comings and goings. Bascom joined him there, after a moment, and Rippon asked after

George, the Negro, and the little sheriff.

"The Negro, from now on," said Bascom, "is as good as any white man in Tyndal. Not a man in the town but would be proud to call him a friend. He was the most scared chap that I ever saw, when he charged out of the jail, but he fought himself into pretty good shape. He was a regular black wildcat before the end. There's no question about the sheriff. There never should have been. He wouldn't let us have you. And he was right. He kept us from shaming ourselves and murdering a good man. And he hasn't jailed a single man in the mob. No, Palding, whatever folks may have felt about you when you left us, twenty years ago, when you came back this time, you've more than made up."

Rippon, profoundly touched, would have had them all come in to supper with him, but Bascom refused for them all. They were needed back in Tyndal. They were needed to report that the peace-offering had been accepted, and that all was well between the cowpunchers of that range and the newcomer into Tyndal Valley.

So, one by one, they shook hands with Rippon again and went out to their horses.

Leaning his arms upon the sharp pickets of the corral gate, he saw them gallop off into the twilight. One of the horses began to buck. The other riders, with a great, cheerful whooping, scattered before and behind. And presently, being properly subdued, the rebel mustang galloped away at full speed and the whole troop with it. Rippon saw them disappear. He heard the last of the hoof beats floating back to him out of the distance, and his heart sank a little.

He could hardly tell why he was so troubled. It was not, mainly, that he missed the protection they had offered to him— their protection against an unnamed danger, that clearly was from the Barretts. He had refused that proffer. It was not numbers that could save him, so much as keen wits and a ready eye and ear. They had helped him before and probably he would have to rely upon them again. Numbers give to each member of a group a false sense of security that dulls the eye and makes numb the wit. No, it would be far better to remain by himself. Numbers could not defend him from a shot fired from ambush; numbers were simply more likely to lead him blindly into the peril.

No, it was not for this reason that he regretted the departure of the men from Tyndal. It was, rather, the feeling that he had made for himself a place and a name in the hearts of a whole community, and that place was his own, but the name was not. He had risked his life, not once but many times. And at the end of three more days, if he were still alive, he would have to slink out of the picture like a ghost, a bodiless phantom, while the real Tom Palding rode into the picture to remain there forever. The real Tom Palding would get the use of that treasure that was scattered through the sands of the creek. Neither Charles Barrett nor poor Jude O'Malley would get a penny from the hoard.

But above all, Rippon would become no more than a ghost, a strange interlude in the story of Tyndal Valley, and after his going, men would shake their heads at one another and comment upon him to the effect that, after all, he had been simply a hireling and a crook.

It stung the very soul of Rippon. All his days he had been a rather unconsidered wanderer. He had been a respectable obscurity. Now, for the first time, he had put himself on a pedestal of public esteem. They looked up to him as the bravest of the brave. And the position was to Rippon like the breath of life in his nostrils.

Jeremy Barrett—the sheriff—the doctor—strange Jude O'Malley—and finally Maisry herself, all these must fade away like pictures of smoke and never be seen again. He had for them three remaining days of existence, and then a long sleep forever.

CHAPTER THIRTY

So, dark in his mind and melancholy, Rippon went to the fence of the pasture and whistled for Baldy. The mustang came and, sticking his head across the upper wire of the fence, tried to catch his master's forelock inside the prehensile twitching of his upper lip.

Rippon rubbed the nose of the horse with a faint smile and went back toward the house.

The bang of the gate, as he went through it, made him jump a little, as though it were a distinct signal, cutting him off from what he had been doing and thinking before. It was like an announcement that the danger of which he had stopped thinking was now begun again. He went into the kitchen, lit the lantern, and looked around him at what had been brought. And his eye lit as he saw.

Someone with a practical mind must have picked out this lot—someone who knew the desires of lone trailers, and lone ranchers, too. He found bacon, white flour, self-rising pancake flour, coffee, tea, bar chocolate in thick slabs, a quantity of beans, some jerky of the best sort of venison, and a very handy thing to have at all times, canned tomatoes, the camper's essential and luxury, potatoes, Irish and sweet, sardines, crackers, canned milk, dried apples, some plum jam and other varieties, and, above all, the king of all jams, that which is made from black currants.

The mouth of Rippon watered as he looked into the stoutly

wrapped packages, and examined the titles of the cans. The food supply was by no means all. There was an excellent rope, forty-five feet long, of the very best quality and suppleness. And there was a quantity of ammunition both for a Winchester and a .45 Colt revolver. There was a jackknife, a pair of soft, warm blankets that made him yawn when he looked at them, half a dozen bandannas as big as sheets, made of the finest sort of silk. There was a complete sewing kit, some woolen socks, and slippers that make Sunday life a shuffling luxury.

"They must've figured that I was both naked and starved," Rippon said aloud.

He felt rich as he looked around him at these heaps. Instantly he made a fire and started supper cooking. It was more than a supper. It was a feast. They had not forgotten to bring from the butcher some choice cuts of fresh meat. There was a ten-pound section of sirloin that made him turn up his eyes as if in prayer, and there was a leg of lamb, and three of the fattest capons he ever had seen. Their breasts were as round and as firm as sculptured marble.

Among this wealth he hardly knew how to pick and choose. All was his. He was like a small child. He went about his cookery with a continual faint smile and decided that he would reward himself for that day's work in exactly the fashion in which the good fellows of Tyndal had seemed to hope that he would make festival.

He made a mulligan stew. Well, there are mulligans and mulligans, but the sort of a mulligan that he constructed was an edifice, a work of art, a musical theme, and a gourmand's delight. Its component parts were not lightly and casually thought up by Rippon. They were things for which he had hungered and thirsted at various times and in various places. When he had kept a frozen camp in the mountain, walled in by the white iron of the snow and the necessity of nursing a sick companion, he had thought constantly of nothing so much as the morsels of tender chicken that should drift in a proper chicken mulligan. So, as the pot steamed over the roaring fire, he cut up one of the capons small. As he did so, he reflected that there would be three meals in this mulligan, by the time the proportions were all perfectly added. Well, that did not dismay him. No, not if there were thirty meals, for the pot could be freshened each time with a touch of something new and a rewarming would give it life. The eternal beauty of mulligan stew is that if it differs little in itself, the appetite that one brings to it varies, and the varying component parts are sufficient to satisfy the most critical, are they not?

Be it noted that Rippon was no headlong, hodge-podge blunderer. Once, carrying a pack, leaning under the weight of it, stunned and bruised by the beating of the sun against the back of his head, his feet tormented in cowpuncher's boots, he had slogged his way down a railroad, stretching his stride to cross two ties or shortening it maddeningly to make only one at a time, and in that day of hunger, thirst, famine, exhaustion, and then starvation pangs again, he had thought of onions, fried brown, simmering in the pan, throwing out their spirit through an entire camp. Because of that day of longing, onions now were rapidly simmering in a frying pan over the fire in the Palding house.

Once, on the verge of timberline, burned and dazzled as he toiled into the barren snows, he told himself that water, beer, and wine never could quench the thirst. Tomatoes were the only thing for that. At the root of his tongue, and deeper, from that day there had lingered a love for tomatoes. Was it any wonder, then, that he opened a quart can of them?

He peeled potatoes with dexterous hands of speed, and diced them in little translucent cubes. Potatoes were necessary, but they should not be allowed to boil into a sticky mass of thin starch. Instead, they were put off in a small pot by themselves.

He cut off some lean bacon and fried it by itself. Only the crisp lean of that bacon should go to the flavoring of the mulligan. Some canned beans could warm there in their can, at the back of the stove, waiting for the critical moment.

Then, remembering that he had seen some parsley in the yard, he caught down the lantern from the nail and ran out to find it. He got that parsley, his mouth watering as he picked it. There were two or three other herbs whose fragrance and sharpness were familiar in the annals of his diet. He found two of these, along the path, standing up and shimmering in the light of the lantern, inviting his eyes. He took some of each and went back still further enriched.

Presently the top of the stove was covered with little pans and cans, each containing a portion for the great ensemble. In the meantime, sweet potatoes were roasting in the oven, and the herbs, tied to the clothesline, were drying above the stove. No one but a fool puts wet green things into a masterful stew.

The coffee pot was on, too, as a matter of course.

And finally, as he leaned hot and anxious above the stove, moving this pan to the rear, away from the fire, bringing that one forward to greater heat, peering through the steam at the cooking chicken, Rippon decided that the great moment for the combination had come.

All swiftly and yet softly now. No dashing together of ingredients, like a brutal barbarian, but each thing added to the big stew pot in turn gently. He composed like a musician, adding theme to theme to make the harmony grow.

And now all was in. Some of the herbs had been added, some remained for garnishing of the plate. But there still remained certain dexterous touches to make perfection more perfect.

Heaven bless the wise and forethoughtful man who, in the grocery store, had reminded him of tabasco sauce, which puts in a dish the little necessary thread of red fire and piquancy. Let him be likewise blessed who took care to add some cloves of garlic, which has the tang of pepper and the smoothness of olive oil.

Then all was ended.

He laid out on the table the sweet potatoes, a loaf of the fresh, brown-crusted baker's bread that those generous men had brought out to him. He put out the deep, big, tin plate, cast for the appetite of a real he-man; he furnished that plate with knife, fork, and huge iron spoon.

In the meantime, over a very low fire, the ingredients of the pot were blending with one another, each giving to its neighbor and receiving in turn. The fragrance of the cookery went up to the ceiling in a steam and spread through the kitchen. He breathed of it, and controlled his appetite, and waited for the crucial moment.

At last it came. He guarded his hand from the hot handle of the pot with a wrapping of rag. He had barely seized that handle when he heard a faint squeak on the boards of the back porch. Instantly the stew was abandoned. A gun was in his hand. And a cold, unfrightened wariness was in his brain. He slid to the kitchen door, and waited there a moment. Yes, across the porch, softly, carefully someone was making his way, some one man.

Then Rippon took thought that from where the strong lantern hung on the wall, it would cast a diagonal shaft of light across the porch, once the door was opened. No sooner had the idea occurred to him than he threw the door wide, and standing at the edge of the doorjamb, the wall covering his body except the projecting head and shoulder, he leveled the revolver on this night stalker.

There in the midst of the darkness he saw the man—a huge, towering bulk with great shoulders, and a long, pale face, sodden with the luxury of an easy life, and pale—unhealthily pale.

He had thrown up one hand, as though to shield himself from the sudden shaft of the lantern light. He had crouched a little, ready to leap away into the sheltering darkness, but the trap had been sprung too suddenly and had taken him too unawares. He saw the flare of the light, and in it he saw the steady gleam of the revolver, covering him, watching him like an evil eye.

"You!" said Rippon. The thrill of the thing left him suddenly. He stepped out onto the porch and lowered the mouth of the gun. "It's you, Palding, is it?" he said.

Tom Palding lowered his warding hand, straightened, took a deep breath, and shrugged back his shoulders. He seemed to be trying to fit himself into a more manly attitude for a more courageous rôle.

"It's me, all right," he said. "Glad to see you, Rippon. A mighty lot gladder than you seem able to see me."

For the voice of Rippon had been rich with disgust.

He stepped aside, and gestured to Palding to come in. The man was so big that he filled the doorway and shut out the light as he entered. And darkness fell like the swift rushing of a shadow across the heart of Rippon. He had looked forward to three more days of danger, of glory, of joy—three days of Tyndal, and the men of Tyndal—three days of Jeremy Barrett, the giant, and of Maisry. Now all the three days were gone, snuffed out like three paltry candles. The end seemed to have come at this moment.

He entered behind Palding and closed the door, slowly, and keeping his face toward it for a long moment as he pressed the handle and let the latch click.

CHAPTER THIRTY-ONE

At the stove, Palding stood stretching out his hands over it, to warm them. There was a perceptible shiver running up and down his back. He rubbed his hands together and kept nodding his head, as though to reassure himself.

"Well, you've gone and spent a big slice of that five hundred on chuck," he suggested, casting his eyes toward the open doors of the cupboard and the loaded, bending shelves inside.

Rippon made no answer. He could not have spoken in reply to any query at that moment.

Palding went on with increasing smoothness. "That's the trouble with a lot of you fellows," he said. "You work like the dickens, starve, burn in the sun, stew in the shade, freeze in the snow, and, when you're through with burning, stewing, freezing, you take the few little dollars that you've got your hands on and you blow it all . . . to please your stomach. Booze, mostly, and then a big feed . . . a stew." He laughed softly, uncertainly, and then with a hearty roar, as though he were finding himself at home more and more every instant.

"It's funny, I guess," Rippon was able to say. He had forgotten how distasteful the man was to him. A deep and infinite loathing came up from his very heart and enveloped him as he stared at the broad, hulking back, sagging with weakness. There was nothing to the man. He was merely able to support his own weight.

"Yeah. It's funny," the other said. "It's mighty funny." He

turned around, to give his back the benefit of the heat of the stove, and, as he turned, he was seen to be frowning. "I had the dickens of a march down here . . . without so much as a mule. I've hoofed it till I was footsore." He looked down at the big, clumsy shoes that were on his feet.

"Where did you get those?" asked Rippon.

"Heaven provides for its own," said the vagabond. "I stopped in at a cabin where the owner was out, and I borrowed a pair of his extra shoes."

"Stole 'em, eh?" Rippon suggested.

Palding looked straight at him. "You think that I'd be a fool to steal a pair of shoes? Why, you can go to prison as quick for a pair of shoes as for a pair of diamonds. No, I left five dollars in place of the shoes, and then I went on. He'll feel rich when he finds that five dollars."

Rippon made no answer. He put on the table another tin plate, knife, fork, and spoon. He laid out another tin cup for coffee. He cut the loaf of bread squarely in two. Then he took the pot of stew and began to ladle out huge portions for each of them.

"That looks good," Palding said. He leaned and sniffed it.

"It is good," said Rippon coldly.

"You're a cook," Palding said critically. "You've got some garlic in that. What dago taught you to put garlic into a mulligan?"

"I dunno," Rippon answered. "Sit down."

"You bet I'll sit down," said Palding. "I could eat that whole pot myself. I ain't had a proper meal for three days . . . four days. Not a real one. Camp food is a joke. This is more like the real thing." He began to attack the stew.

His life in the East had not taught him better manners. He ate more greedily, more disgustingly than the rudest cowhand. He took the chicken bones with his fingers. He sliced off the meat that was easily come at, carried it to his mouth on the end of his knife, and then finished off the shreds of chicken with his teeth at work. He ate noisily. When he was thirsty, he poured a third of a tin of canned milk into the coffee cup and filled it with coffee. He drank noisily, also.

"We oughta have beer for a meal like this," said Palding. "That's what we oughta have. If you really were in the know, son, you'd have beer for a meal like this, I'm telling you. Well, it's good coffee, though. It has a fist in it that a man can feel, and that's the right sort of coffee to make."

He attacked the meatless portion of his plateful with the wad of his half loaf in one hand and the spoon in the other. His fingers were still greasy from eating the chicken. The grease spread onto the handle of the spoon, and from that to the palm of his hand. He took great spoonfuls that left bright traces of the grease, again, as far as the center of his cheek. And these attacks on the food he varied by biting vast mouthfuls from the loaf that he kept poised. He took a second helping. He fished in the pot and got himself most of the bits of chicken that remained.

Rippon, watching, felt the incredible fury of a small boy, outraged and imposed upon. But he would not make trouble about such a thing as the table manners of a natural hog.

As the second plateful began to disappear, big Palding started to talk. He talked between, and through, and around mouthfuls. He rested both his elbows on the edge of the table and lowered his face toward his portion, and still he talked, grunting and growling over what he ate like a dog.

"You seen Charlie Barrett?"

"Yes."

"What did he want?"

"To buy this ranch," Rippon responded coldly.

"Was he serious?" grunted Palding through a mouthful.

"Yes."

"How much does he offer?" the big fellow asked, more interested in mulligan than in money apparently.

"Ten thousand dollars."

"Hey! You got him up to that?" Palding raised his greasy face now and looked at his table companion with amazement.

"Yes. I got him up there."

"Ten thousand for this old rock pile?"

"Yeah."

"Why, he's crazy."

"He said that he wanted to round out his land and, I suppose, that he wanted to wipe the name of Palding out of the valley."

"Something in that. Yeah, there's something in that. He hates the name all right. He has a reason to, damn him." He put back his head and shouted with a sort of triumphant laughter. "Ten thousand dollars!" he repeated, when his laughter had subsided a little.

Rippon looked down at his plate. He detested the man so much that out of human decency he wished to keep from letting Palding see the loathing in his eyes. But the taste had departed from the food. It was not a feast; it was a torment. He could not help thinking how Jeremy Barrett and he could have had a glorious time there at that table, a quiet, genial, hard-eating time, with a sympathy like brotherhood between them. And Maisry sitting, perhaps, at an end of the table, presiding.

He wondered how many years it would take some man, some good man, to smooth the look of fear and worry from the forehead of Maisry. But if she married a brute who took advantage of her gentleness, her submission, Rippon would return from the ends of the world and strangle the man with his hands.

"Tell me," said the voice of Palding. Rippon looked suddenly up. "What were you thinking about?" Palding asked, half sneering in anticipation. "Daydreaming, eh? Dreaming about what you're gonna do with that five hundred dollars that you've got so cheap."

"No, I'm not thinking of that."

"You were, though."

"Palding, don't tell me what I'm thinking about."

Palding stiffened. Then he shrugged his shoulders and remarked: "Gonna use the high hand, are you? Well, you can keep the high road, if you want to. You've got five hundred dollars of pretty soft money."

Rippon said quietly: "You've got two hundred and twenty pounds of pretty soft life, Palding."

The other winced. He peered at Rippon as though to make out whether or not there was some innate threat conveyed by this remark. "You mean that you could have cut my throat and that you didn't. Well, that time's past. You told Barrett that you wouldn't take the coin?"

"Yes."

"And then what did he do?"

"He wanted to murder me. But they called in Jeremy, and Jeremy asked the cook, Maisry, and between them they decided that I was not to be murdered."

"Jeremy . . . the bull . . . the lion. He's with you, eh? How did you get him on your side?"

"By trying to be decent, perhaps," Rippon said, looking straight at Palding.

But the brazen front of Palding was not troubled. "So you got away, and then they tackled you in the night and you gave them the run. I've heard the whole story. The valley's full of it. A poor chap that I met on the road, he told me the story this evening. He says that there never was a thing done in Tyndal Valley like that jail break. I guess that there never was. You've pretty near earned that money of yours, that five hundred." He waited, grinning.

"Yes. I've earned it," replied Rippon.

"You thought that I was sending you down here to a lot of soft, woolly lambs, didn't you?" Palding grinned. "You didn't believe that they were wolves. But tell me, when you seen the length of Barrett's teeth, why didn't you skin out of the valley and take the five hundred dollars along with you? That's what I can't understand. Why did you stay on here at the house, like a rat in a trap?"

"You wouldn't understand," Rippon said.

"Well, try me. It's gotta be something deep."

"I've given you my promise. I stuck to it."

"Promise? I wouldn't understand?" said Palding.

The bully rose hot in his face and made his eyes bulge. He shoved himself halfway up out of his chair. But when he saw that this demonstration of fury had not the slightest effect upon his host, and, as he saw the calm, judicial eye of Rippon watching him, he gave up his bluff and, with a grunt, slumped back into his chair.

"You trying to make trouble or a joke?" he demanded heavily.

"Not either one of 'em," Rippon said, and made himself a cigarette. Still he watched the other curiously. It was like sitting at the table with a beast, not a man.

CHAPTER THIRTY-TWO

Among the last pieces of wood that had been put into the stove was a pine stick with a resinous knot in it, and the fire at this point had heated the knot and its gums and moistures until it exploded with such force that the lids lifted a little and fell clattering back into place, and all the pans jangled, and the stove itself tottered a little on its ruined feet.

At the sound, big Tom Palding leaped out of his chair and bounded back into the darkest corner of the room. His pale face grew whiter still. His knees shook and bent under the weight of his gross body and of his fear. And yet he was not harmless even at this moment. The lift of his lip showed his teeth. His eyes were pointed with light. He was like a cornered rat, and a dangerous one. One hand was thrust inside his coat, obviously gripping the handle of a gun.

Rippon continued to watch him for a second before he said: "Something blew up in the stove. That was all."

Palding looked carefully around him. Then he mopped his forehead and came back to the table almost unwillingly. He sat down and poured himself another big drink of coffee. "I thought they were at me," he said. "I thought, for a minute, that they were coming for me. Damn them!" He shook his fist malignantly at the world in general. It was extraordinary that he cared not in the least to show his terror before another man. But he was plainly unique. Never had Rippon sat opposite such a fellow.

"They're not likely to come tonight," Rippon said. "They're

more apt to be at home, thinking things over and making new plans."

"They'll have no more plans," Palding said, full of confidence. "They see that public opinion is against them. They see that they've played their cards. And they've failed. They've brains. I'll say that for the Barretts. They'll know when they're beaten. It would have been just as good for me, though, if they'd murdered you. That would've cleared the path for me, just as well. They would kill one. They couldn't kill two. They could murder the false king, but, after that, they wouldn't dare to lay hands on me."

He leaned back in his chair. With his own words, he had warmed his heart, and now he rubbed his hands heartily together and chuckled, a rumbling bass laughter of content.

"It's going to be all right," Palding said. "And I don't need you any more. It's going to be quite all right now. You've pulled the fangs out of the snakes' heads. Now they're harmless, I guess. You can make your pack and start now, if you want. And tomorrow I'll ride in and see the sheriff, and prove who I am, and show that I need protection, and make him give it to me . . . why, it's perfectly simple. The game is all in my hands from now on."

"You want me to start now?" repeated Rippon.

"Yes. I don't want you around any longer. You've been the hero. Well, I'm not a hero. I don't want to have you about. I don't want you around when I appear. They'll make comparisons. They'll begin to talk down about me."

"You're a fool if you let me go before the five days are up," Rippon said.

"A fool, am I?" the other said, ugly at once.

"Yes, a fool. You'd better ask me to stay thirty days more rather than to stay three."

"You can start right in explaining," said Palding. "I don't

understand."

"I won't argue. I'll show you," Rippon said.

"What'll you show me?"

"The reason why Charlie Barrett will never stop until he's killed you."

"You can show me that reason?"

"Yes."

"Then show it now."

"You'll have to walk a bit to see it."

He got up and took the lantern from the wall. At the door, Palding held back for a moment. The night wind was rather sharp in its touch, and Palding groaned.

"I'm tired and cold," he said. "Wait till the morning."

"You'd better look at this in the dark than in the daylight," Rippon said.

So the other followed after him, still groaning faintly, and cursing the soreness of his feet, for they had been badly hurt by the wearing of unfitted shoes during the last day's march.

The wind that had greeted them at the door of the kitchen fell. The face of the night was open and still, all freckled with brightness above and marked across the fields with the soft piles of shadow where the trees grew up along the watercourses.

"It's my own ground," Palding said with an air of triumph. "I'm walking on my own, at last. I'll see them get an inch of it away from me! I'll stick to it. It's better than wife and children to me. It's my life. That's what it is."

He began to expand as the exercise warmed his blood once more. And the bright stillness of the sky restored his confidence.

"The grass is wet as the dickens," he complained a moment later. "I'm going to get cold. I don't see why we have to go out like this through the middle of the night. What's your game, Rippon? What are you driving at? By gosh, I don't trust you. What's in your head?"

Rippon looked away from his companion. It seemed to him that he could not endure the sense of physical nearness with the man, to say nothing of meeting his eyes. So he glanced off across the fields. The grass was wet with a fall of dew so heavy that, here and there in places where the grass grew close together, the starlight touched upon the beads of water and made streaks of dimmest mother-of-pearl.

"I'm giving you a chance to open your eyes," said Rippon. "If I had a game, it would be an easy thing. If I wanted this place, I could have shot you through the head back there at the house."

"Hold on," Palding barked. "What are you saying? No, you're not the kind that does murder. You've got the fear of the noose always dangling in the back of your mind. You haven't got the grit for murder. I saw that before. I saw it up there in the mountains." And his sneering laughter rang loudly through the night. There was so much ugliness in the man that he could not help letting it boil over, now and again.

"There'd be no rope for me to fear," said Rippon. "In this valley, I'm Tom Palding now. You're nothing. You haven't got a name. I could shoot you through the head and call in the sheriff the next day and show the body to him. Tell him that you'd attacked me. There have been plenty of attacks, recently. People would lay it to the schemes of the Barretts. I could kill you out of hand, Palding, and then take your land for my own. Nobody would question me."

Tom Palding could not answer at once. He swayed a little from side to side. Rippon could see the movement against the stars of the horizon.

"I guess you're right," Palding admitted.

"I know I'm right," answered Rippon. "Now, come on with me and I'll show you why the Barretts will never let up on you."

He conducted his companion straight across the fields to a bend in the creek before them. Through the brush he made his way, and, going down the bank with the other behind him, he heard big Tom Palding muttering and whispering under his breath.

"What's up?" he gasped when they stood together in the creek bottom.

"You'll see pretty soon," answered Rippon. He pushed up the chimney of the lantern, scratched a match, and touched it to the oil-soaked wick. As the flame rose, he pressed down the chimney, the guards of it squeaking loudly. At once a clear, steady light shone, and the green, damp leaves gleamed about them, and the water at their feet flashed like glass, or mercury.

Palding's pale face turned quickly from side to side. He turned and looked behind him. "A damned fine place for a murder," he said, half to himself. Then he added: "What's all the mummery for? Tell me that, will you?"

"I won't have to tell you. I can show you," Rippon said, and he kneeled by the stream and picked from the shallow bottom a handful of the sand.

As he had done before, earlier in that day, he allowed the gently running water to wash the lighter particles away. Like a dust cloud in a street, so in the shining water the stain rose and cleared and passed. Then Rippon stood up and showed the palm of his hand to his companion. It was veined across, in the wrinkles, with the glittering yellow marks.

Palding stared mutely at it. He blinked. He could not understand. "Well, what's it about?" he asked.

"It's the reason for murdering you," Rippon explained. "Take a good look at it. It's the reason for most murdering, I reckon. Look at it, man!"

Palding touched some of the particles. He held those that adhered to his fingertip to the eye of the lantern and stared at them more closely. Then his hand fell suddenly to his side. He jerked about and faced Rippon. "By Godfrey!" he cried. "Gold!"

"Yes, gold."

"The old creek. . . . Who would ever have dreamed it? Gold
. . . gold! Who knows about this, man? Who knows that this
stuff is here?"

"I'll tell you one who knows. Charlie Barrett knows that it's
here."

There had been a wildfire springing up into the face of Palding, but that fire diminished at once. "If Barrett knows it, then I
know why he was willing to pay ten thousand for the land."

"Of course you know. And now you know why he'll try ten
times harder to kill Tom Palding."

"I'll sneak into town and get the news of it filed. I'll. . . ."

"They're probably watching this place with twenty men,"
Rippon said. "Perhaps they've already closed us off from the
house."

"You're right," Palding muttered. "Let's get back."

"And what if we do? That's the place where they expect to
find us. That's the trap that they expect will take us and hold
us."

"What will we do?" Palding moaned.

"We? We won't do the same thing. You'll slip away somewhere
and wait till the shooting's over. And I'll go back to the house
and sit through the party that's bound to come."

CHAPTER THIRTY-THREE

When they had come back so far that they could see the loom of the house, Tom Palding said: "What's your first name, Rippon? I mean, really?"

"Name of Ed," said Rippon. "Sometimes Ned. And there's been a few girls that have made it Edward now and then, but never for very long."

The other did not laugh. "Ned," he said, "you're the stuff. That's what you are. You've got nerve . . . and I'm dishwater. That's what I am. Just dishwater. I'm going to stay out here, but maybe I'll ring in before the game's over. . . ."

"Sure you will," said Rippon. "You're a lot better than you think. That's all that's wrong with you . . . thinking." He stepped on through the darkness toward the house, wondering at the pity he felt for the man who he was leaving behind him, like a coward, to stand there outside, while the danger would be closing on the house itself. But there was an honest pity in him for Palding. The man had been almost right, it seemed. He perhaps had reached for decency, and missed it when the tips of his fingers were already upon it. As he went forward, it seemed to him that he was not only leaving Tom Palding behind him, but that the man was sinking into a darkness, into a great oblivion, as into black, bottomless water.

When Rippon was near the back of the house, he climbed through the barbed-wire fence and made a short cut. It was very black under the trees, and through this shadow he saw the pulsing of a cigarette like the gleam of a red star. He halted.

"Who's there?" he called.

"Harry Barrett," said the voice of a man.

Rippon peered to either side, and even glanced over his shoulder. It did not seem likely that a lone Barrett would come to him. "Who's with you?" asked Rippon.

"I came alone," Harry Barrett said rather sullenly.

"And what for?"

"They want you at the house."

"Who wants me? Charles Barrett?"

"Yeah. That's it."

"So he sends for me. Is that it?"

"Yeah. That's it."

"Well, you take him back an answer from me. Take him an evasive answer. Tell him to go to the deuce."

The other replied: "I knew it wouldn't be any good. I said it was a fool thing to send for you, but I had to come. He sent me. That's why I came. It wasn't my idea."

"And what was his idea?" Rippon asked. "Does he think that I'm a half-wit, or worse? Does he think that I'll go over there and let the Barretts have another chance at me, all of them?"

Harry Barrett paused for an instant. Then he said: "That's right. I knew that you'd say that. I told him so. I knew it would turn out that way, but he sent me just the same. He said that there was a chance."

"A chance for what, even if I went?"

"Well," said the messenger, "he wants to make it up. He wants to call everything off and you and him be friends."

"Oh, he'll call everything off, will he?" Rippon said bitterly. "That's an easy break for me, I guess."

"Yeah. I know," said Harry. "Of course you're sore. No wonder. You got a reason. I said so, that it wouldn't do any good for me to come. But I was sent. His idea is that you've had a rough road, just about, from all of us. That's recently. In the old days, you gave us the rough road. Well, I mean that you killed poor Sam. So that's the idea. We've tried to get back at you, and you've slammed us some more, but now he wants to call it quits, because he says that public opinion is with you. I'm telling you exactly what he told me. I'm not trying to persuade you. I told them all that you would never come."

Rippon hesitated. If he had been the real Tom Palding, he might well have refused to heal the breach. But he was not Tom Palding, except for three more days. And, of course, if he could spike the guns of Charles Barrett in the meantime, why should he not? It was only that he could not believe that the other had actually changed his mind. To conceive of Charles Barrett divorced from his hatred of Palding was like trying to conceive the moon without light, or the sky without stars. There might be a trick behind this. There probably was a trick.

"Does Charles Barrett take me for a fool?" he snapped harshly.

"Aw, you don't have to take it out on me," said Harry. "You're quits with me beforehand. I've got a sore jaw where you slammed me today, beating through the crowd. You're quits with me. You don't have to yap at me about the Barretts. And I tell you that, when I rode over here, I didn't really expect that I could take you back with me. So long, Tom." He turned and took a stride or two along the narrow board walk toward the corral gate.

"Wait a minute!" Rippon called.

"Yeah?" The other paused.

"I'm going to ask you, man to man, Harry . . . do you think that Charlie means this? Do you think that he's aiming to be square and aboveboard with me?"

"Why," Harry Barrett said with an amazing frankness, "I never know just what is going on in his head. He don't bother to tell me. But this time I would guess that he meant well."

"What makes you think so? Will you tell me that?"

"Why, the way he argued it out with me. I didn't want to come over here and wave no white flag. I wanted to fight it out. My jaw is still pretty sore. It's swelled up nearly the whole side of my face. I didn't want to have no peace declared. But he told me how we had tried our best and our worst to get you, and that both luck and Jeremy was against us, and, with Jeremy on the wrong side of the fence, how could we ever hope to clean you out? Well, he persuaded me so well, I agreed with him. And here I am. But I don't expect you to believe me."

"Hold on," Rippon said. "Every time that I've come near to you, your family, I mean, I've been in danger of breaking my neck. But I sort of half believe that he means to play straight this time."

"I sort of believe that he does, too," said the boy.

Suddenly Rippon laughed. "I'll throw a saddle on that horse of mine and go back with you," he said.

"You can't go back with me," said the boy. "I've got to ride on to Uncle Lew Barrett's place. That's why I think that you'll be safe, all right. You go and patch up things with Father, and you'll be all right, I guess. Because he told me no matter what you answered, I was to go straight on to Uncle Lew's and tell him that everything was off, and you were not to be touched."

"Did he say that?"

"Yes, he said that."

"So long, then, Harry. Thanks for coming over. I'll go and make up with Charlie Barrett, because I think it'll be a lot better for all of us."

"Yeah," said Harry. "It will. It's spoiled a jail door already, and pretty near busted my jaw. I don't want the fighting to go on no longer. So long!" He laughed as he spoke, and turned away, calling the last words over his shoulder.

Rippon went on to the porch and sat down for a moment on the edge of it with his head in his hands, trying to puzzle out the problem. Then it seemed to him that he saw a ray of light that invited him to a solution of the mystery.

There was poor Jude O'Malley, of course. What would he have done since he was spared by Rippon? Why, naturally he would have gone to his partner in the business and declared to him that Tom Palding now knew the value of his place and that there was no use in attempting, any longer, to make a secret of the treasure that lay in the ground.

The natural reaction of Barrett would be rage and spite, at first, but afterward, thinking the matter over calmly, he must surely agree that there was little more that he could do to make trouble for the Tom Palding of his hatred. So, like a sensible man, Charles Barrett was attempting to make peace and inviting the enemy to come and shake hands.

This was the logical explanation of the invitation that Rippon had just received. It was this that he wished, also, to believe in. But he could not. With his outward mind, so to speak, he felt that Barrett was aboveboard. With an instinct rooted close to his soul he was sure that the old fox was devising new evil and harm for him, greater than ever before.

Twice he started to his feet; twice he sat down again.

But then he remembered that he actually had told Harry Barrett, the messenger, that he was going to ride over to the Charles Barrett house. The memory that he had committed himself now stirred him forward. He got up, made a cigarette in the dark of the night, lit it, and went out to the pasture, where he caught Baldy and brought him in for saddling.

Insuppressible Baldy! Even now, there was mischief in him. There was a wild mischief that made him pitch clear across the corral as soon as he was mounted. But Rippon kept his grip, and laughed grimly. Then he gave Baldy a good lashing with the quirt, opened the gate, and rode out into the lane.

It was still early in the night. It was so early that, when he looked back upon all that had happened since sunset time, or thereabouts, he could hardly give credence to the thing. For had he not had his encounter with Jude O'Malley, and confronted Palding with the truth, and now taken the message of Harry Barrett at its full worth?

He would not think forward. But there was an instinct that told him something important lay ahead of him, whether good or evil. Before the morning he would meet it face to face.

Well, at least he was in no hurry to find the crisis, for a crisis he felt it would be, the like of which he never had encountered before—the danger he had faced in the jail would be as nothing compared with that toward which he now jogged the mustang. Or else—there was a sudden and blessed release from all troubles forever. So he felt, womanishly keen of instinct at the moment, and then despised himself for admitting such tremors of the mind, such hopes and such fears.

He swore into the empty dark of the night and galloped the mustang on, with a resolute brow.

CHAPTER THIRTY-FOUR

When Rippon saw the dark outlines of the Charles Barrett house, he did not allow the horse to pause or even fall to a walk. He knew, somehow, that if he let the horse slow up, the courage would run out of his heart like water out of a sieve, and he would need all the spirit he possessed perhaps, before he was through with cunning Mr. Charlie Barrett.

So he cantered Baldy up to the hitching rack, tethered him, and then permitted himself to pause and consider the house. There was no light burning in the whole of it, except in the kitchen. And what would Charles Barrett be doing in the kitchen, on a night as warm as this? And if not in the kitchen, why should he be sitting in the dark, awaiting the coming of the man who he had invited?

A little flicker of fear, like a thrust of blue flame, jumped in his mind. He brushed that away and went to the kitchen door.

Maisry opened it for him. She dragged the door open, with her head drooping, and her eyes on his boots. But from them, she ran up her glance swiftly to his face, and her eyes opened. She stepped back quickly, with a sort of guilt about her manner.

"Why, hello," said Rippon.

"Hello," said the girl.

"You act sort of scared of me, Maisry."

"No. I'm not scared," she said. She clung to the doorknob. She still gaped at him in a manner so startled and so stupid—he could think of no other word—that his temper went up like a flame.

"Shall I come in or stay out?" he asked her briskly.

Perhaps Charles Barrett bludgeoned her with far curter speeches than this one, but she seemed to feel it. She blinked at him, and her forehead darkened with a little frown, puckering in pain. How well he remembered that look.

"You wouldn't wish to come inside of the house, would you?" she asked him.

"Well, I've got an invitation from Charlie Barrett to come inside."

She looked over her shoulder. "Oh," she said. "He invited you again, did he?"

Again? Well, for that matter he had been invited to enter that house once before, and he found himself on the verge of his death day when he went inside. Perhaps he would discover himself in a peril just as grim as that tonight. And yet? Well, the message from Harry Barrett had rung true. If there were treachery in the mind of Charles Barrett, there was none, he was sure, in the mind of Harry. All the air was not black against him, he could really hope.

He went into the kitchen with a long stride. He took the edge of the door and flung it shut with a crash behind him. Then he took a breath. "I feel better, now that I've taken the plunge," he told her. "You tell Barrett that I've come, will you?"

"He's not here," said the girl.

"Hold on! Not here?"

"No. He's not here."

"Well, he's out at the barn, maybe?"

"No, he's gone away."

"Away?"

"Yes."

He stared fixedly down into her face. He saw her eyes widen, in their usual way, as she attempted to meet his glance. But her look shifted to the side and down.

"Did he leave any sort of a message for me, Maisry?" he asked her.

She sighed. She drew her glance up from the floor. "You'd better go away," she advised.

"By thunder," broke out Rippon, "he did leave a message for me. What was it?"

She sighed again, and then she faltered out: "He said that if you were to come while he was away at Chester Powers's house, you were to stay a few minutes, please, and he would be right back."

When she had finished the message, her head fell back a trifle. She looked so white that Rippon was half afraid that she might faint.

"Hey, Maisry," he said. "What's the matter that you look so bad about?"

"Oh, I dunno. Oh, nothing, I guess," she said. "It's all right. It'll be all right."

"You look sort of sick. You better take a drink of water," he said.

"No, I wouldn't better take a drink of water, I guess," she said. "I'm all right, thanks." She said it wearily, the words trailing slowly from her tongue. And she turned back toward the other door, saying: "I'll put on a light in the dining room. That's got about the most comfortable chairs in it. I think there's a newspaper that came in the mail, today, besides."

She dried her hands with a clean dish towel, but the pores of the skin of her fingers were so filled with moisture from the dishwater she had been using that her hand left a wet print upon the chimney of the lamp, after she had lit it.

He studied her carefully. She was something like a good book—a good book with battered covers, but with known contents. What a kitchen wench she was, to be sure. The smudge of soot was not on her nose. It would have to be somewhere, though. Yes, there across her left elbow—just where the elbow dimpled when she straightened her arm. Her hair was more straggling than usual, also. Stray, thin locks of it floated on the air. And the knot at the back of her head was twisted so tightly and hard that the compacted coils shone. Suppose that it were combed and brushed to lightness, how much there would be of it. He looked down toward her feet. They were shod in the cast-off shoes of a man. No, not a man. They were the shoes of a boy. He had kicked the toes away until the copper tips were visible, shining with a red glint. He had run down the heels on the outside edges. He must have been a shiftless, wild, harum-scarum child. Now Maisry wore his cast-off shoes, as she scuffed her way through the house and about the kitchen. She wore cheap cotton stockings that wrinkled a good deal just above the shoes. She had on the same dress that he had seen her wearing before, and in front of her she was guarded by an apron of most faded calico. It was so faded that there was not a distinguishable design left in it. It simply looked like a soiled white. Where she had been leaning against the edge of the sink, there was a heavy, sharply defined line of wet.

She had just finished fitting the lamp's chimney back into it when he said: "Look here, Maisry."

She turned her head with a slight jerk, like one who is accustomed to hear voices of command and obey them swiftly. "Yes," she said.

"Your hand is shaking a good deal. I guess I'd better carry the lamp."

"No, I'll carry it, all right."

"I'd better carry it," he insisted.

He took the lamp from her. She tried to resist, as though she insisted upon doing her duty, but her hand was still a little moist with the dishwater and the glass standard of the lamp slipped from her.

He held it, now, but he did not carry it at once into the dining room. For, as he poised it, the light shone down into her eyes. He looked into a well, as it were. An odd dizziness and breathlessness troubled Rippon. As long as he cared to stand there, it did not seem to occur to her to say anything. A long moment drew out; they still were gazing at one another.

"Look here, Maisry," he said again.

"Yes?" she said.

"Look here. What frightened you? Or were you only tired?"

"I guess I was only tired," she said.

He nodded at her. "I frightened you. I scared you, Maisry. No, you tell me the truth."

"Yes. I guess you kind of did," Maisry responded, and stepped back from him a little. She seemed to want a protective distance.

"But look here," he said, "why should you be scared about me? Why should you be afraid of me?"

He saw her swallow; she blinked a little. "No, I'm not afraid of you," she said.

"You are, though."

She would not persist in her denial. She seemed to be standing there waiting, like a child about to be punished. The heart of Rippon swelled. "I wish . . . ," he began. Then he stopped, for he thought that he could not be altogether sure of the steadiness of his voice.

"Yes?" she said faintly, after a moment.

"I wish that you wouldn't act this way," he said.

"I'm not trying to act any way," she said. "What am I doing?"

He set his teeth so hard that his jaw ached. "Tell me something!" he commanded brusquely.

"Yes?" she said.

"I want to ask you something," he repeated. "Charles Barrett . . . you tell me the truth, now . . . did Charles Barrett ever hit you? Did he ever strike you?"

She looked at Rippon. She looked down at her own hand, slender as the palm of a child. "Oh, no," said Maisry. "He never struck me with his hand. He wouldn't do that." She shook her head. "I'd better be getting ahead with the dishes," she said.

But Rippon remained there, standing with the lamp in his hand, feeling like a tyrant because she seemed unable to turn away as long as he was before her. He took a sad, sad pleasure in the power he exerted over her.

"You're tired out," he said.

"Oh, yes, I'm mighty tired," she said.

"And you're feeling sad, too."

"No, I am not sad," she told him.

"You're feeling pretty blue and sad," he insisted.

And she explained: "Well, it's kind of the end of the day, you know."

"Maisry," he said, "what's the matter?"

She did not answer. Her mouth twitched at the corners, and then puckered a trifle. Tears ran down her face and she bent her head a little to hide them.

CHAPTER THIRTY-FIVE

When Rippon saw her weeping so quietly, a strange pang went through him like a hard-driven knife. He put down the lamp on the table and stepped closer to her. "Maisry," he said, "don't be crying, will you?"

"I'll not cry," Maisry said, her head bending a little lower than before.

He slipped a hand beneath her chin and pressed her face slowly and gently upward until it was tilted toward him, blindly, for the lids covered the eyes and the tears still streamed. "I'm making you cry," he said. "I'm no comfort to you, Maisry, not a bit."

"You are," said Maisry. "You're a lot. . . ." Sobbing got into her voice and stopped her, but she bit a corner of her lip and forced the weeping away.

Rippon put his arms about her and drew her to him by degrees, for she seemed as fragile and breakable as a child, and, instead of resisting, suddenly she clung to him and looked up in a wild and wondering way.

"I love you, Maisry," he said.

"No," she said.

"The way that I love you," said Rippon, "the rest of the world is nothing compared to it."

"You're only comforting me. You don't mean it, and you can't mean it," said Maisry.

But she drew herself still closer to him, and on her blinded face a smile trembled. Rippon leaned and kissed her. Then, gradually, her eyes could open. To see her smile and the brightening of her eyes so changed her that he almost felt she had been touched by enchantment in the moment when he was close to her.

"You're laughing at me, really," she said.

"I'm laughing, almost, for the joy of you, Maisry," he said.

"But how first could you have looked at me?" asked Maisry.

"The first look was a long one," he told her. "And that was enough for me, but, afterward, when I knew what you'd done this very day for me. . . ."

"I?"

"You saved me," said Rippon. "You saved me, because you sent in Jeremy Barrett. And if it hadn't been for him, I'd now be either hanged or a murderer in fact. But Jeremy. . . ."

At the first mention of that name, she had winced. Now she thrust herself back from him with a spasmodic strength and stood against the wall with her head a bit on one side and her eyes both wild and blank, like someone risen out of a sickbed, delirious.

"Jeremy!" she cried. "And I forgot all about him. Jeremy . . . Jeremy. . . ."

"What in the name of heaven is the matter?" Rippon asked.

She beat her hands together in a helpless agony. "I forgot him! I didn't remember. All at once I was so happy that I was blind with it, and I couldn't think. Will you believe me?"

"About what?" He had stepped into a sort of sad, sweet heaven of expectation, and now heaven seemed to be withdrawing from around about him.

He followed her a little half step, but she stretched out her arms and shook her head and her hands to keep him away. She was in a frenzy of grief and of fear.

"I didn't remember. I forgot about Jeremy," she lamented.

"Jeremy?" Rippon repeated, stunned at last by the word and the thought that went with it. "I know that Jeremy wants you. But you don't want him, do you? I know you don't. You never did. He knows that you never did. Look here at me, Maisry. You're tearing my heart in me. Tell me what it's all about? You never loved Jeremy. Say that, before you say anything else."

"I never loved Jeremy," she repeated almost mechanically.

"You only like him, sort of?"

"I only liked him . . . sort of."

"And you pitied him, sort of, too. Because he's kind of slow, and stupid, and honest, eh?"

"How could I pity anyone?" said the girl. "I did pity him, though. Because he was so strong that he could kill people with his fingertips, I suppose, but he was gentle with me. He followed me around with his eyes. I knew he loved me, and that made me pity him, too. I never tried to make him. I really never did."

"I know you didn't," said Rippon. "You wouldn't have to be explaining to me, Maisry. Not a word of it. You kind of pitied him and liked him, and partly because he loved you. Because you're such a kind of a girl, Maisry, that, if a man loved you, you couldn't be anything but gentle and kind to him. That's the way of it."

"Charles Barrett," she said, "swore that I was making eyes at him. He said that, if I did, he'd do something terrible to me. But I never did, even Charles Barrett believes that, finally."

"Hold on," said Rippon, all the blood rushing out of his brain and leaving him dizzy. "You're not going to say that you ever told Jeremy . . . I mean, you never pitied him so much that you told him you cared about him a lot? You never. . . ."

"I never told him that I cared a lot. I only told him that I liked him. I terribly did like him, too."

"And me," Rippon said, heaving a great sigh of relief. "I like him, too. I like him a mortal lot. You never said that you loved him, then?"

"No, I never said that."

"Thank heaven," he said. "Then, Maisry, why are you keeping me away from you? Is it that you don't really love me, either?"

"No, no," she said.

"And there's nothing to tie you away from me, is there?"

"There is!" she cried out. Now she put those slender hands of hers together, one clasped above the other, on that place where the pulse was throbbing and aching in her throat. She did not need her hands to defend herself from him or keep him at a distance now. With a word she had done that, and built a wall, and dug a trench to separate her from him, forever, perhaps.

He got hold of the edge of the table and steadied himself. It had seemed, a while ago, that there was something wonderfully appealing about her, but something almost ridiculously beneath notice, too. In her sloppy clothes, with her ill-done hair, she was the sort that other girls would shrug their shoulders at. There had seemed nothing clever about her. One would hardly expect her even to dance well. There had only been something that had fitted into his heart with exactness and something that passed into his blood with a sad sweetness. But now there was a distance between them, and she was transformed. He had kissed her; he had felt her hands clinging to him, and now they were pressed together at the base of her throat, and he was far away.

He had been blind, but fear now cleansed his eyes and he saw that she was not only good, but that she would be forever gentle and forever true. What did an ancient and patched dress, and a faded apron matter, or disarray of the hair, when her beauty was shining all the while, quietly, and he had been in the darkness and had not seen it? She was all that he wanted. She was everything desirable in the world.

So he steadied himself, one hand behind him, gripping the edge of the table.

"There's something that ties you away from me," he repeated. "Well, you tell me what that is . . . what it can be, when you care for me, Maisry."

"Ah," the girl said, "it's because I was born to be unhappy."

"Don't cry," he said, "or I'll be coming to you again."

"I won't cry," Maisry insisted. "I won't . . . a bit." She fought back the sobs. All sign of weeping, and even strain, passed out of her voice, so gallantly did she master herself.

"Now tell me," he said. "Jeremy has something to do with it. I gather that's what you mean. Jeremy's somewhere in it."

"Yes. It's all Jeremy. I promised him."

"Wait a minute," said Rippon.

"Don't look so white," Maisry said. "It kills me to see you look like that because of me. I wish that I never had lived. Oh, why ever was I born for such sorrow all my life? My heart is dying when I see you look like that."

"Wait a minute," Rippon said hoarsely, feeling his way through a frightful fog of the mind. "You say that you promised him?"

"I did."

"You promised Jeremy that you'd marry him, didn't you?"

"Yes. I did promise."

"Don't cry, Maisry, for a minute, but talk to me."

"I'm working hard," she said.

"Now you tell me . . . it was this same afternoon that you gave him the promise, wasn't it?"

"Yes. I don't know how you could guess that. Jeremy hasn't told you, surely."

He stood up, leaving the table behind him, a sort of rage making him tense. "It was right after he came home from the town that you promised that you'd marry him. Isn't that the truth?"

"Yes, it was then."

"It was because you'd sent him in to help me at the jail. He came back to you like a hired man and he asked for his pay, and you paid him off. You told him that you'd marry him. Tell me if I'm not right?"

She said nothing at all, for a moment, but then she whispered: "Why are you hating me so much? I couldn't do anything else. I could see the bruises on his face. His clothes, they were all so ripped to pieces, and I knew that he'd been fighting to save your life, and that I'd sent him. . . ."

"I know," Rippon said. "It's a true thing, too. He saved my life. He went in and saved me. It's twice that he's saved me, and both times because of you. He saved me here in this house. And now I'm standing here trying to take his happiness away from him. I'm not a man. I'm worse than a dog. Maisry, do you hear me? He's better than I'll ever be. Heaven be good to both of you. He's the finest man and you're the loveliest girl that I ever knew in my life."

She only said, as she stared at him with great, wide eyes: "Are you going to go away now?"

"It'll be no easier five minutes later. Kiss me good bye, Maisry."

She lifted her face to him, and, holding her strongly, he turned a little with her in his arms and kissed her, and she him, as though all their love and their grief might be expressed and forgotten in that instant.

It was because he had turned that Rippon saw past her how the door to the dining room softly swayed open, as though a draft were blowing against it, and then, into the dark square of the opening, came the broad shoulders and the white, convulsed face of Jeremy Barrett.

CHAPTER THIRTY-SIX

He thrust the girl away and behind him and she, turning, saw big Jeremy like a crouching lion in the doorway. Her scream went like a lightning stroke through his brain.

"Jeremy! Jeremy! We were saying good bye forever. . . ."

She might as well have shouted at the ear of the lion he resembled. With both hands he gripped the edges of the door and flung himself forward at Rippon.

The latter had snatched out a gun and leveled it at that contorted face, but he could not fire. His finger was frozen upon the trigger. Instead, he raised the gun and flung it full into the face of the other.

He saw Jeremy stagger to the side. A streak of crimson slashed his face, but instantly he was in again.

Rippon used the length of his legs to side-step. As he stepped, he struck with all his might, and found the bone of the jaw with his knuckles, and jarred all the weight of his body after it. He did not stop the rush of Jeremy with that blow. By him went Barrett, and Rippon turned quickly, expecting to see his man topple headlong, for it seemed surely that no human brain and nerves could receive two such shocks as Jeremy Barrett had endured.

He was wrong. For Jeremy did not fall, but, swerving as he reached the wall and pushing himself away with the thrust of both arms, he hurled himself back at Rippon. The blow of the ponderous revolver had cut his face, but had neither stopped nor apparently stunned him. The punch that carried all of Rippon's power behind it was to him no more than a tap from a child. All elastic and supple with padded masses of muscle, the body of Jeremy and his massive jaw disdained such strokes as these. Silently he came in, with the screaming of the girl like a thread of fire tangled in the thoughts of Rippon.

He wished that he had pulled the trigger of his revolver now. It was the killing of big Jeremy, or else his own destruction, for nothing less than a death would ever satisfy the silent rage of Barrett.

In the instant that Jeremy needed to cross the floor, Rippon looked brightly and clearly into the mind of Charles Barrett and saw all his motives. He had failed with numbers, against his enemy. Now he determined to use a power greater than any numbers, the hatred of the most formidable man in Tyndal Valley. What all the rest of the clan could not perform, what they had been foiled in performing by the prowess of this single arm of Jeremy's, would perhaps now be done by Jeremy himself.

The girl was the lever through which Barrett would topple all the ponderous and crushing weight of Jeremy's resentment upon the head of Rippon. How Charles Barrett had guessed that there was an interest between him and the girl, Rippon could not tell. Or how he had persuaded Jeremy to lurk hidden in the dark of the silent house, and then to play the wretched part of an eavesdropper—these were mysteries to Rippon. But the fact remained that Charles Barrett had accomplished these things.

With his consummate hypocrisy, he had sent the special message of invitation to Rippon, and other messages had been forwarded by his means to the remainder of the clan, telling them that the war against the supposed Tom Palding must be ended instantly. It was a consummate stroke. The hands of Charles Barrett would be clean, no matter how the meeting ended. If Jeremy died, it repaid him for the opposition that he had given to the former plans of his kinsmen. Nothing was lost, on the other hand, if Rippon were the victor in the battle.

In one split part of a second, as the monster rushed at him across the floor of the kitchen, Rippon saw these truths, blindingly bright. At the same time, he caught up a chair by the top rung and would have used it as a club—but, somehow, he could not take an advantage over Jeremy—not even then. Instead, he braced himself and struck for the head with all his force. He reached Jeremy with a whipping left. The blow was a little high. It struck the cheek bone and laid open the flesh to the bone, and the impact did for one of Rippon's knuckles. He felt it go in like a thing made of putty. Instantly after, he jerked over the right, a good blow, a cleaner one, and one that landed again on the desired point of the chin, and a little to the side.

The shock of it should have struck the brain of Jeremy like a club stroke landing at the base of the skull. It merely stopped and straightened him for half an instant. Then he fell forward and firmly grasped Rippon in his arms.

It was not the force of the hug that crushed the breath from his lungs that amazed and paralyzed the very heart of Rippon, however. It was the tearing power in the hands of the man. They were not like hands. They were as armed claws of a beast, reaching into his vitals and tearing him to the life. He struggled. His arms were pinioned to his side. He was utterly helpless and numbed by the grasp that held him. He was as a child in the clutches of a monster. It seemed to him that this was not a man against whom he fought, but a ravening beast.

Then he saw a greater marvel still, as he was whirled lightly from his feet. He saw little Maisry grasp up a copper pot and swing it above her head with all the strength of both her hands. And she ran forward, her face white and desperate, her eyes with such a light in them as he never before had seen in the eyes of a human being.

She struck, but her blow failed, for Jeremy had swung about, heaving up Rippon as he did so, and the force of the blow she had attempted toppled the girl off balance and brought her to the floor.

The same sway brought Rippon's back crashing heavily against the nearby stove. It was a big stove, but one on a most uneasy footing, and it could not stand for an instant under the blow that it now received. It simply broke in two and toppled from its four little pedestals. Into the hot wreckage rolled Jeremy and his victim. And out of the well-crammed firebox rolled burning embers, and a mass of showering, red-hot coals.

Not even the vengeance of Jeremy could make him immune to such a happening as this. He bounded to his feet with a shout, and Rippon, twisting away, was at the door in a single stride.

He reached it; he was through it; he felt the flying shadow of the monster behind him and slammed the door shut in his very face. There was a crash. Looking over his shoulder, Rippon saw the door split into fragments, and the body of Jeremy thrusting through, halfway clear of the wreckage, but stuck and delayed there an instant.

That instant got Ned Rippon onto the back of Baldy. Then next moment the mustang was speeding away.

A great, unhuman shout rose up, roaring behind him like a storm wind. It was the voice of Jeremy, he knew. Then a gun began barking, and bullets flew through the air about him, but he was away. If there had been daylight for that shooting, as he very well knew, it would have been the end of him. Battle and battle fury did not make the hand of Jeremy shake. That much was plain.

But now Rippon was out on the road. He sped Baldy down it at a furious speed. Before long, Jeremy would be on the back of one of those strong, hard-galloping horses that he kept as his own string. He would be rushing across the night, red as a comet in his wrath. And heaven help Rippon if the man found him during the course of that hunt.

When he reached the crossroads, he paused. If he turned to the left, he would be heading for the tangled tree and rock wilderness of the mountains. If he turned to the right, he would be launched in the direction of the old Palding home.

Two things he debated. First, where would Jeremy hunt for him? Second, how much did his promise to Tom Palding bind him? He had vowed to Palding that he would remain for five days in the valley. Did he dare attempt to remain there another three, with such a terror as the awakened Jeremy on his trail?

He ground his teeth together with a groan. Yes, it might well be that Jeremy would ride straight down the road toward the Palding house, but, on the other hand, he might not search at once in such an obvious direction. He would know that he had thoroughly imprinted the dread of his hands upon the body and the mind of Rippon. Perhaps he could envision his new enemy fleeing toward the heights.

As Rippon turned these ideas in a sort of agony through his mind, he looked back, and, where the house of Charles Barrett squatted black in the night, he saw an eye of red appear. It broadened. It grew deeper. It cast out a ray of red, straight at Rippon, like a pointing finger, and then, with a rush, it ran up the side of the house.

Suddenly flames were spouting from the side of the building. The mass of coals and burning wood, fallen upon the wooden floor of the kitchen, would of course ignite it almost instantly. And then to run to the wall of the house would take very few seconds, where it could feed upon the time-dried and rotted timbers.

Up to the roof the hand of the fire had now reached, and instantly it sped along the roof to either side. Would that red flag call back the giant to undo what he had started?

Rippon guessed that it would not. It would be a red banner the sight of which would bring all the other Barretts from a great distance, gathering to the help of the leader of their clan. But it would not call back Jeremy from the wild pursuit of his vengeance.

How the heart of the man must be bursting at the thought of the treason of Rippon—the treachery of the man whose life he twice had saved, and once at the risk of his own.

To answer the last of Rippon's thoughts, he heard the beating of hoofs coming down the road toward him. If he rode on, now, the direction of his flight would be known. But if he did not ride on, the other might sweep by. So he pulled in the horse to the side of the road, crowding its flank against the brush.

Straight up to the crossroads pushed the other rider at a swinging gallop, but when he came to the corner, without hesitation he took the left-hand turn and rushed away toward the mountains.

It was Jeremy, beyond a doubt. He had taken the wrong chance. How long would it be before a doubt came to him and brought him raging back into the valley again?

CHAPTER THIRTY-SEVEN

The Charles Barrett house went up like a torch. The flames ate down into the cellar; they rushed to the roof. The whole thing became crimson and yellow, and the arms of the fire thrust out through the doorways, through the windows. A wild, changing light was shaken in great waves across the countryside.

Rippon sat his horse and watched. Sometimes he looked up to where the heads of the fire masses broke away, shot loftily against the sky in the form of branches and leaping horses, then disappeared against the cold faces of the stars. Sometimes he scanned the roads. And presently, from every direction, he saw the riders coming. Men spurred past him, racing down the lane on which he was sheltered by the shadows. They shouted to one another in excitement and dismay. Like rats running to a granary, so they ran toward the house of Charles Barrett.

In a way, it was a strange and foolish affair. The house was such a shack that it was hardly worth the name of a dwelling. It was a mere huddle of loose boards. Nevertheless, it was the residence of a man. In that house might be documents, records of life and death, papers of an untold value in sentiment and partly in hard cash.

There in the dimly red-lighted shadows, Rippon smiled a little to himself. For once more the schemes of Charles Barrett had reverted upon his own head. He had arranged the meeting because of which his own house went up in flames. What a black bitterness, what a rage must be in the soul of Charles

Barrett at this moment.

The thought of it made Rippon actually laugh aloud. And then he suddenly turned his horse for the house itself. He knew that it was rash. He knew that nothing could be in a higher degree more dangerous than for him to go near this nest and swarming place of his enemies. There would be fifty men there, perhaps, and every one of them ready to send a bullet through his brains and be respected, honored by the rest for the performance.

Yet he could not keep away. The sting was in the heart of Charles Barrett, now, and there was a malicious pleasure in the chance of seeing Barrett suffer.

A better and a nobler desire drew Rippon back more strongly still. Little Maisry was there at the house, or among those rough fellows. He must see her again, if she really cared to look at him, now that he had shown the white feather and run from the violent hands of big Jeremy. Would she not be shamed by that exhibition of cowardice?

It was not until he remembered Maisry that it so much as occurred to him that there might be cowardice shown in the thing. He had run from Jeremy as any man without weapons would run from a wild beast. Yet now, thinking of Maisry, a little knife of remorse and of shame was plunged under his fifth rib. He grew hot in the face. He writhed in the shadow. All the more reason for trying to get back and to see her again. All the more reason for that, to be sure.

Straight back he rode. He attempted no subterfuge to come close to that news of trouble. But he went straight up to the side of the barn, where the mass of the horses was gathered, tied to the posts and the upper rail of the corral fence. Among all the rest he left his own mount. As for himself, he would have to trust to the utter darkness to cover him, and, when the light came in wild, high-breaking waves, he would have to trust to the strangeness of it. Not every man of them could be really familiar with his face. A few had seen him man to man; most of them would know him merely by a glimpse of a rushing fighter in a throng as they had seen him earlier that day in Tyndal.

Earlier that day. It seemed that half a life had been concentrated in the interval between midnight before and this moment.

He left Baldy not at the farthest end of the horse group but near at hand. He tied him with a slipknot that a single jerk would dissolve. That done, he went around the corner of the barn. He stopped at the doorway.

"You're too late, partner," said the voice of a man he did not recognize. "The old place is going to be a cinder, pretty shortly."

"I reckon it is," said Rippon.

There was no question about the ultimate destruction of the house. But a water line had been formed, running from the pump at the watering trough to a corner of the building, and a long succession of water buckets was being relayed from hand to hand. One man stood at the head of the line, and that was Harry Barrett. Into the flames he threw a steady succession of great, silver splashes, and it seemed for a time that he might make some progress. Near him worked a group of half a dozen with axes, under the supervision of a smaller man, who wielded an axe himself.

The smaller man was Charles Barrett. The venomous sense of him seemed to strike into the face of Rippon even from the distance. He did not exactly hate Charles Barrett. There was so much more malice in him than in any other human being of Rippon's knowledge of men and their ways that he could only loathe and detest the man as one would a viper.

The axe work sent up vast showers of sparks, and fresh clouds of smoke arose in stifling masses from the newly thrown water. The smoke and the steam throttled the head of the water line and the axe men repeatedly. They gave back, only to have Harry Barrett and Charles dart into the confusion and the dimness again.

With the water they tried to clear a way into a certain room of the house. With the axes they tried to chop a passage. But presently, as Rippon reached the door of the big barn, he heard the stranger nearby saying: "The old place is going to be a cinder shortly, I reckon." And, at the same time, the line of the water bearers and the group of the axe wielders gave suddenly away and retreated from the glare of the fire.

Old Charles Barrett, in a sort of frenzy, was seen to drag himself away from the men who tried to restrain him. He brandished an axe over his head. He turned and shook it in the faces of his recent allies. Then he charged at the flames.

But he could do nothing alone. The instant that the steady pouring of the water ended, the flames took rapid hold upon the remnant of the place. They cast up a red and yellow wall in the very face of the householder. Even the indomitable will of Charles Barrett could not deal with such an answer as this, and, little by little, he took backward steps, his face ever to the flames.

"He mighty well hates to give up," said the stranger in the darkness of the barn.

"He mighty well does hate it," Rippon agreed. "He acts like he'd about as soon be burned himself as to have his house burned."

The other chuckled. "Have a smoke?" he said.

"No," Rippon replied hastily. He did not want the flare of a lit match to reveal his face. But the other scratched a match and put the flame of it to the end of a cigar.

That light showed to Rippon a man well past middle age, with an old-fashioned and semi-patriarchal beard that flowed down his breast to a square edge at the bottom, a dense, a glorious beard, such as one rarely sees in these degenerate days. He had a bush of heavy eyebrows as glistening white as his beard was black. The beard curled thickly, and the brows were a silver tangle of great size. Withal, something wrinkled and pointed about his nose gave him, in the first glimpse of his features, an expression of comic insight.

"I reckon," said the stranger, pulling upon his cigar and smacking his lips loudly as he did so, "that Charlie would pretty nigh as soon go up in smoke himself, body and boots, as to see all of that house burn."

"I've heard he was kind of fond of it," Rippon commented.

"The dickens you have," the stranger said with an amazing frankness. "He ain't fond of nothing, except his hard cash, and his revenges, and his hates. It ain't the house that he's fond of. It's the things that are in it. He never had no use for banks. He never would trust them. He always would rather've trusted himself. Well, he's trusted himself. You see how."

"He must've had some money in the place," said Rippon.

"Oh, mighty little of that. He wasn't fool enough to keep much cash around. He wouldn't do that, but he's got a stack of mortgages in there with the fire playing with 'em, by this time. I reckon that by now the insides of that old safe of his is getting pretty hot. By this time, the edges of some of them mortgage papers is beginning to curl up and to turn brown."

"He's got a lot of mortgages, has he?" Rippon said.

"Aw, he's had half the hearts and the souls of Tyndal Valley inside of that safe of his," said the stranger. "He's got my heart and soul in there now."

Rippon did not know how to comment. "Maybe he'll lose a lot of money out of this," he said.

"Maybe he will," said the stranger with a mysterious frankness. "Maybe he'll lose five thousand that I owe him . . . damn his poison heart for him." He said it without bitterness of accent. Then he chuckled softly.

"Hold on," said Rippon. "You don't want to be confessing like that. Somebody might hear you that would stand a witness for Barrett that you owed him the money even though the mortgage was burned."

"Somebody might," agreed the stranger. "But I pick and choose the gents that I talk to."

"Do you?" Rippon said, amazed. "Do you know me, partner?"

"I don't aim to know you exactly," said the other. "But I know a mite about you. There ain't much to this idea of knowing a man. All that anyone ever can know is the title page and the footnotes. That's about all, I guess."

"Well," said Rippon, "I'm not a talking kind." He even felt encouraged to add: "I'm no particular friend of Charlie Barrett."

"I reckon you ain't," said the other. "But he's the one that planted the Barretts here. He's the one that herded them out here like a flock of sheep, and loaned them the money to get land, and to farm it. He's been the dad to the whole valley. I don't reckon that many of them love him for it, though." He broke off, chuckling again. "Some of 'em," he continued, "find it kind of hard to love a man that they owe money to. I'm one of that kind. I reckon that some folks here in Tyndal Valley that wear the Barrett name don't like Charlie much better than you do."

"Better than me?" exclaimed Rippon.

"Or maybe I'm wrong," said the man of the beard. "Ain't you Tom Palding?"

CHAPTER THIRTY-EIGHT

The last sentence clanged like a hammer stroke through the brain and through all the consciousness of Rippon. He started. He wished, at that moment, with a fervent desire, that he had a gun close to his hand. He probed the darkness about him. It seemed to him that many phantom fingers were reaching for him out of the shadows.

"No," said this odd fellow beside him. "I got nobody with me. The rest . . . they've all gone up there to show Charlie how much they love him, and how glad they are to labor for him. And all the while they're kind of wishing that he was in the fire himself." He paused, and laughed again. "We're a kind lot, we Barretts," he said. "I'm old Will Barrett, if my face has sort of slipped out of your mind."

"What gave you a sight of me?" asked Rippon. "The firelight from the house?"

"Just a glint at you. But I got good eyes. I used to foller the sea. I could see the loom of land before most. I trained my eyes at sea, son. Well," he went on, "it's a funny world. Here we've been trying to cut your throat, and you've come right in and burned down Charlie's house for him, and his papers along with it, and a better turn was never done for all the Barretts of Tyndal Valley, I reckon."

"I burned the house?" Rippon exclaimed, amazed at this turn.

"Well, didn't you, now? Wasn't you here when the fire started?"

Rippon paused. Murder they had accused him of, and his hands had been washed clean of the charge, certainly. Arson was a crime even more detestable, and how could he prove that he had not kindled the fire? Ah, there was little Maisry, of course. He had come to save her. Would she end by saving him?

"I didn't start the fire," Rippon said shortly.

"Why, likely you didn't," said Will Barrett. "But a good thing that it got to going, anyway. And how glad old Charlie must be that he wrote and asked you to come down here into Tyndal Valley. He must be kind of glad and proud about that. Coupla days back, he was a pretty big man. He stood kind of on a mountain. But he's off the mountain now. The sheriff's no use for him. He's made the Barretts bump their heads against a stone wall, and they ain't likely to forget that jail day soon. He's got them accused of trying murder in the dark of the night, and other things. And I guess he wouldn't poll a vote in this valley . . . not if those mortgages will only burn inside of the safe. Go on, fire. Burn. Whoop it up! Ride, ride! Ten degrees more, and the papers begin to cook. Ah, that's a good thing, too. That'll pack in some fuel around that old safe."

The entire roof had given way and crashed. The uprush of the sparks put out the stars, and spilled a wave of blinding light far and wide. The trees of the distant creek, for instance, were in that second clearly to be seen by Rippon.

As the wave of brilliance passed, in a twinkling, he turned toward his companion, with a feeling that eyes had been upon him.

"I guess pretty good," Will Barrett said. "I'm glad that I ain't lost my eyes. You're Tom Palding, all right."

So the old fox had not known for sure, after all. Rippon bit his lip.

He watched the men about the house. They had stopped their hurrying back and forth and their maneuverings around the fire. They were simply standing to gaze, and as the fire settled, with the falling of the roof, and tended to cast the heat farther out to the sides instead of straight up into the air, the crowd of watchers gave back slowly, until they were ranged along the edge of the corral. Some youngsters who had ridden over to view the blaze, remained perilously close to the verge of it. Some women had come, also, and stood about, pulling shawls closer about their shoulders, as though they felt the calamity like a cold wind.

One would have said that that crowd was watching the last struggles of a living thing rather than the fall of a building and its destruction. The flames were not abating. They raged more furiously through a smaller compass. Now and again there were sharp explosions that sometimes made the sparks leap on the surface of the sea of flames. There had been ammunition left in various rooms throughout the house.

Someone came riding up the lane, dismounted, and approached the group.

"That's the sheriff, I reckon," said Will Barrett. "He had the loom of the sheriff. Kind of small, and thin enough to cut the wind dead easy. There's a lot of men with a sharp entrance that can carry a cargo pretty fast, and a big cargo, too, when it comes to that." He added: "Charlie'll be saying something to him about you pretty soon, I guess."

"I'll go hear it," Rippon said.

"If you ain't a fool, you'll stay out here on the edge of the dark," said Will Barrett. "House burning ain't a safe way of using up your time in Tyndal Valley, maybe."

But Rippon went. He trusted the irregularity of the light. This old fox had made him out partly through a practiced keenness of vision and partly by guesswork; there were not apt to be other eyes like his among that crowd. Besides, he would be standing at the rear of the entire mass. So he crossed the corral and took up his place behind a number of tall men who stood together, leaning against the fence, silently watching the work of the flames.

Charles Barrett, making his way through the tangle of people, was already close to the sheriff. He pointed, called out: "Hey, Joe! Joe Clark! I wanna talk to you!"

Joe Clark came a few steps to meet him.

Everyone else grew silent. There was only the dull roaring and the occasional crackling of the fire. It was no longer a towering conflagration. It was like a fire kindled on a hearth for the household gratification of gigantic and unseen spirits.

"I seen the light as I was jogging back to town this evening," said Clark. "So I came along out. Sorry it happened, Barrett. Know how the thing started?"

"I know every mite of how it started," said the other. "It never would've begun, if you hadn't turned loose the worst crook that ever rode and murdered and done arson in Tyndal Valley."

"Hold on," the sheriff said. "I don't know who you mean."

"You don't know Tom Palding, I guess?" said Barrett bitterly.

"I know Tom Palding," the sheriff said. His manner became more coldly aloof than before. He even added: "Are you getting ready for another lynching scene, Charlie? Is that your game? I've got a thinner neck than Palding's, but I guess that a rope could be fitted to it, all right."

"Don't try to make a fool out of me," said Charles Barrett. "You know that I don't mean anything like that." He waved his hand toward his clansmen. "They made a mistake today. We all made a mistake. It's forgotten. You said it would be forgotten. Well, then, here's a new thing. You don't let your pets ride around the place and burn down houses, I guess? Not even your pets, Clark."

"I've got no pets," said the sheriff. "What's your proof against that man?"

"I'll tell you my proofs," said Charles Barrett. "After today in Tyndal, I says to myself that we've been wrong, and that we've got to go right, from now on. I say it so strong that I make up my mind to call an end to the trouble with Tom Palding. I admired, sort of, the way that the snake came out and wriggled through the crowd of us. Harry, stand out here."

Harry Barrett stood out, a grimy, blackened figure. He had been very close to the worst of the fire.

"Did you take a message to Tom Palding this evening?" Charles Barrett asked him.

"I did that."

"What did you tell him?"

"I told him that there was an end to the fighting, and that you wanted to have a peaceful talk with him, here. That's what I told him. He said that he'd come. I went on to spread the word to everybody that hands were to be kept off Palding."

"He did come," said Barrett. "He did come, and, when he came, he found out that I was away. I was off like Harry, telling everybody near me that they were to keep their hands off Tom Palding. I was trying to make a peace. He came and found nobody home. I hadn't expected him so soon."

"If nobody was home," the sheriff said, coldly still, "who saw him here?"

"Nobody except the little goose of a kitchen maid, Maisry. That's the only one that was there. But she saw him come."

"Maisry's not a goose," the sheriff declared. "Go on, Charlie."

"Well, you know what went through his head when he came into the house. He saw that there was nobody there but the girl. What was she? Nothing! Nothing to him. And he remembered that I had money in my safe. If he'd had the time, he would've tried to crack that safe, I guess. He was always half a yegg. But instead, he figgered that he would do worse by me. There was more than cash in that safe. There was a hundred thousand dollars of mortgages and notes in there. So he takes and says to himself, that, if he can't help himself, at least, he'll ruin me. And he sets fire to the house."

"The girl saw him, eh?" the sheriff asked sharply.

"Of course she saw him. D'you think that I'm talking through my hat? D'you think that I'm making it up, man? I tell you, it's arson. He's burned down my house, and I'm a wrecked man!"

"You've said a lot against him," said the sheriff.

"Are you going to stand there, only?" said the rancher. "You're not going to raise the country and hunt him down, the dog?"

"I'll see Maisry and hear the stuff from her," said the sheriff. "That's my duty."

"With him getting more miles away, you're going to talk to a chit of a half-wit servant girl?"

"She's not stupid. She could talk well enough to make you think that Palding burned down your house. I'll hear from her, too."

"She's out of her head," the rancher insisted. "She couldn't talk sense now. She's over at Dick Barrett's house, with a fever, and raving. You couldn't get anything out of her. I've heard the yarn from her already. You act like you don't trust my word for anything, Clark."

"I don't," Clark said calmly. "I don't trust your word for a thing. I'll have a talk with Maisry."

Charles Barrett, stunned by this retort, stood glaring.

"I'm here," said a small, trembling voice from the edge of the crowd.

Rippon started, almost with a groan. For it was Maisry's voice that he heard.

CHAPTER THIRTY-NINE

There was a mild sensation through the group of onlookers. But Charles Barrett gave back a little from the sheriff, and, turning toward the direction of Maisry's voice, there was enough firelight for Rippon to see the corrugations of his scowl. He could see Maisry, too, in the dimmer distance, mounted on a little wretch of a shambling, knock-kneed mule.

"Who let you go?" called out Barrett. "You oughta be in bed. Here, Harry, you and some of the rest get hold of her and see her back to Dick's place. They'll take care of her. She needs nursing. Don't let her be raving around here."

It was the calmness of Maisry that stunned Rippon.

She said, after the roar of the rancher's voice, very calmly to Clark: "Sheriff Clark, I'm not raving. They took me away by force, and they locked me up, but I managed to slip away. I had an idea, sort of, that they'd try something like this."

Harry Barrett was already at the head of her mule, but the sheriff warned him back sharply.

"There'll be no force," said the sheriff. "Barrett, I don't want to think what I'm starting to think now. Maisry, come over here closer to me. You've got something to say, and I want to hear it."

"She's out of her head!" shouted Charles Barrett. "Is this your justice? It's a damned travesty. If there's law in the land. . . ."

"Aye, there's law in the land," Clark assured him. "There is so much law in the land that you're liable to learn the taste of it all for yourself pretty soon. Maisry, tell me what happened?"

She had come much closer to the sheriff and to the firelight, and Rippon saw a pale, weary, calm face. "I was alone in the house, I thought," she began. "But I was wrong. Jeremy was there, too, hidden. And Charles Barrett knew he was there, of course, and had sent for Tom Palding."

"Now, if that ain't raving," Barrett cried, "what is it? I told you that she was out of her head!"

"Kind of interesting to me," the sheriff said. "What makes you think that Charlie Barrett knew that Jeremy was left in the house?"

"Because he wanted Jeremy to see me when I was with Tom Palding alone . . . when I thought that I was alone with him. That was all. He hoped that Jeremy would grow angry. That was what he wanted. He wanted to leave Tom to Jerry's handling."

Her simplicity and her clear statement made an instant impression even on the prejudiced crowd.

"Will you go on, Maisry?" the sheriff coaxed kindly.

"I'll tell you everything," she said. "I'd told Jeremy this afternoon that I'd marry him. It was after he got Tom out of the jail, with you helping. And when I saw Tom this evening, I told him about it. He said that I was right to stay with Jeremy. He said good bye to me. And just then Jeremy opened the door and saw Tom . . . kiss me."

Only at that point did the confession seem to trouble her. Her head bowed a little, but only for a moment, and in that moment a low, stern murmur went through the crowd.

She raised her head, at that, and looked fearlessly about her. "They fought together," Maisry continued. "Jeremy was like a madman. They fought terribly. They crashed against the stove and knocked it to pieces, and the burning wood and the red-hot

241

coals poured out onto the floor. Then Tom ran for the door, got out, and rode off on his horse, and Jeremy fired shots after him, and then I heard his horse galloping after.

"I tried to put out the fire, but the floor was burning in front of the sink and I couldn't get at the water there. I ran out to the watering trough and carried in a bucketful, and I screamed for help. But when I got back, the fire was running up the side of the wall. I threw on the water, but it didn't seem to do much good. I went back and got more. When I came, that time, the whole kitchen was like an oven, and where I threw in the water, it only made a dark spot, and then the flames closed right over that spot again.

"I knew that I couldn't put out the fire then. So I went in to try to save what I could. I thought I might carry out clothes and things. But when I got into Charles Barrett's room, I must have fainted. I woke up on the floor. This lump on my forehead, that's where I must have knocked my head when I fell. I heard a lot of voices. I ran outside, and the house was half in flame, and a lot of people were there. And Charles Barrett had me taken away to Dick Barrett's house, and they locked me into a room and said that I was to keep still. But I managed to pry the window open and climb down from the second story. That's the whole story, I think."

"A crazy woman's story!" Charles Barrett shouted. "Would anyone in the world take any stock in it?"

"I'm one who would," Clark stated. "And I'm one who says that there's crimes that no law is quite right to get at. Men stay out of jail, even, that ought to hang. You hear me, Barrett? Men stay out of jail that ought to hang. Maisry, you come to Tyndal with me."

There was another deep-throated murmur from the crowd. The sins of Charles Barrett were only too apparent, but, after all, he was of their clan, he was the confessed head of it. They hated the sheriff at that moment, not because he was wrong, but because he was right. More Barrett shame would now be published to the world. They hated Maisry, too. Even poor Maisry. At least the women glowered at her, and whispered ug-linesses to one another.

"I'm not going to Tyndal," Maisry said in the same quiet, dead voice out of which the softness and the caress had gone together with the tremor of fear.

"Where'll you head for, then?" asked the sheriff. "You can't go far on that mule."

"I know it," she said. "But I'm going. I won't have to go far. And it will be away from Tyndal."

"Well," Clark said, "you know your own business a lot better than I do. Do you own that mule?"

"I bought it from Mister Barrett," she told him. "I gave him four months of my wages for it, and two more months for the saddle. He was going to shoot the mule and feed it to his dogs, but it's plenty good enough to carry me."

The sheriff glared at the girl, at the saddle, and then at the cartoon of a worked-out, broken-down animal she was mounted upon. After that inspection, he turned to the crowd.

And they forgot Maisry and her revelation, of which the last seemed, perhaps, more damaging than all the rest put together, such a wretched state of parsimonious meanness did it show in the mind of Charles Barrett.

Even Rippon forgot the girl, in his intense interest as he stared at Barrett. He knew that this was no weak man. But he watched the direction of Barrett's glance, as the other looked around, and felt that he was able to read the man's soul. For Barrett looked to his clansmen, and their faces were hard as iron, and their eyes looked back on him with a cold and penetrating contempt and disgust. How many of these debtors would acknowledge the money they owed to this man, since the security by which he held them had been destroyed by the fire? How many of them would acknowledge his old leadership, since he had shamed his kinsmen in the eyes of the world?

His little empire was gone. The money that had sweetened his life and rewarded his labor had disappeared. Yonder was Jude O'Malley, leaning with a sour face upon the haft of an axe. No doubt he had told his confederate that their schemes to get the gold of the Palding place had gone awry, and that everything was known. Nothing remained to Charles Barrett except the consciousness of his villainy. His following deserted him. He was alone in the world. Yet he maintained a grim face, and gave back look for look with those around him. Only death could weaken him.

The sheriff was speaking, and what he said enthralled those listeners. It was something worth recording in their innermost minds.

"You people," Clark said, "or all of you that hold with Charles Barrett, and his people, I've got to tell you something. You've stood high, here in Tyndal Valley. You don't stand high now. The rest of the valley ain't with you. I'm not with you. The law's against you. If I'd known then what I know now about the lot of you, you wouldn't've come off so easy after what you tried at the jail today. You look to me like a bad lot. I'll keep my eye on you for being that. The first wrong move that any one of you makes, I'm after him. The first hand that's raised against Tom Palding, for one thing, I'll have the lot of you in jail. You've tried murder by night. You've tried murder in a mob and the open day. And nothing's happened to you for it.

"I'm ashamed that I can sit in the saddle, here, and say so. I've let you ride right over me. But the next time, some of you will trip . . . and break your necks. That's all."

He turned his horse away, and a snarling sound rose from those big men as they looked after him.

He jerked his horse around. "You can bark and you can even howl," he said, "but mind what I've told you. I don't fear you. Not you and all your sneaking ways. An Indian on the trail for scalps was a gentleman compared with you murdering sneaks. Now howl again, if you want."

But they did not howl—they did not even whisper as he turned his mustang's head and rode slowly away, for each of them was saying to himself that the hand of the world was against the Barretts, and, when the hand of the world is raised, no man may prosper under the shadow of it. They felt the weight of this truth, pressing down upon their very souls, and then they turned and stared at Charles Barrett, who had led them into these troubles.

He, however, was not abashed. In the bitterness of his own woes, he had small care for theirs. And what put the taste of dust and ashes in his mouth was the knowledge that he had brought all his undoing about with his own mind, his own actions. Each of his crooked schemes had failed. Destiny and Rippon had been too much for him.

It was the slight pause that comes before a company breaks up, but, before this one dissolved into the broad night, another thing happened that drew them back close to one another for a little while.

Rippon himself was turning to slip back among the horses and collect Baldy. Though, for that matter, after the speech of the sheriff he felt that he would be reasonably safe even among the Barretts, letting them see his face openly. But it was not a time to take such chances. There was Maisry to think of, Maisry to follow.

But before he could start, came the other thing that startled even the thought of Maisry out of his mind, for a moment. Out of the dark of the night, across the fields, came a gigantic rider on a gigantic horse. And Jeremy Barrett loomed near with a strange thing carried before him over the pommel of the saddle.

CHAPTER FORTY

When he was well inside the circle of the firelight, and close to the rest of the Barretts, big Jeremy heaved the thing from across his horse's back and flung it down.

Staggering, reeling, nevertheless that limp and seemingly inanimate bulk kept its feet and took on the form of big, clumsy, fat-faced Tom Palding. Here was the real Tom Palding, at last, face to face with his enemies. Whatever fight might have been in him, whatever courage of the cornered-rat type seemed to have been extracted. He stood like a dead man before them—a dead man, a corpse artificially supported. His very mouth sagged open, but not for speech. His eyes were like the eyes of a dead fish.

Well Rippon himself had felt the mighty grasp of Jeremy; he still ached to the core of his bones from that dreadful grip, and he could well imagine what had happened to Tom Palding, that ignominious hulk of a man.

"Who's that?" demanded Jeremy of the rest. "Take a look at him, all of you. Tell me who that is?"

How they stared. Twenty years had passed over the head of Palding, to be sure. They had been willing to take another man for him. But now that they confronted the true Tom Palding, there was a sudden cry from a man at the rear of the pack: "If that ain't a Palding, I'm not a Barrett!"

And then another shouted: "It's Tom Palding! It's Tom Palding!"

That cry silenced the others. There was enough significance in it, to be sure, to crush them all. And from the side, his hands in his coat pockets, sauntering in the most leisurely fashion, came the man of the great curling black beard and the bushy brows, Will Barrett. He was smiling beneath his beard.

"If that's Tom Palding, Charlie," he said, "then who's the man that you've tried to murder by night, that you tried to smash down the jail to get at? Who's the man that made you wreck the good Barrett name and burn down your own house? It ain't likely that you've been just a plain fool all this time, is it?"

With a sudden rush they closed around Palding. He was so tall that Rippon could see him, his head looming above the rest.

What was his duty now to the wretched fellow? Should he show himself and stand by the man in this final pinch? Perhaps it was not his duty. His part of the contract had merely been to represent the name of Palding there in the valley. For the discovery, Palding alone was guilty and at fault. But Rippon was no man to go by the sheer letter of the law. He cinched up his belt a notch. He laid his hand on the top rail of the fence. But before he could vault over came the tragedy.

"Palding! Tom Palding! D'you remember me? Remember Jude O'Malley?"

The voice had a screech in it, almost like the cry of a woman, and there was a sudden commotion, with Palding yelling frantically: "Keep him off! He'll murder me! Murder . . . !"

The last word was a frightful scream that stopped suddenly in the middle. And Rippon, in the act of vaulting, was frozen in his place. He knew what had happened, though the mass of swirling people had shut him off from the sight of it.

That crowd now gave back. They washed apart like a wave from a high place on a shore and left the picture in full view. As if on purpose to illuminate it the better, the dying fire put up a crimson hand loftily into the air. It showed to Rippon the forms of Jude O'Malley and big Tom Palding lying in a tangled heap, and neither of them ever would move again. Near the outflung hand of Palding lay a crimson knife. He must have struck out to defend himself, but both strokes had gone home at the same instant, it appeared.

The Barretts stared helplessly down at the spectacle.

And then Charles Barrett exclaimed: "If it had been the real Tom Palding that had come back at the first, I never would have missed a trick! But a man came in his place. A man that beat us all. It's kind of as though fate was against me."

Big Jeremy on his great horse pushed straight up to Charles Barrett. It seemed as though the fall of the two men meant nothing to him.

"Now, where's Maisry?" Jeremy said. "Where's Maisry, Charles?"

"Maisry?" Charles Barrett said slowly. "Why. . . ." He started back a step or two. Then he answered. "Maisry's gone, and a good thing for all of us, and a better thing for you, Jeremy. She kind of had you hypnotized, but. . . ."

Jeremy lurched suddenly forward, and, as his horse made one step, he gripped the older man by the shoulder.

"Damn you," said Charles Barrett. "You're breaking the bones!"

"Where's Maisry?" Jeremy repeated. "D'you hear me? You said that you'd keep her safe for me. Where's Maisry?"

"Gone to the demons or the angels, and I don't care which!" Charles Barrett shouted. "Gone to thunder, for all that I care, you wooden lout, you blunderer!"

Rippon, tense and on his toes with expectancy, merely saw Jeremy Barrett straighten in his saddle, and turn the head of his horse toward the outer darkness.

To look for Maisry, of course, but where was Maisry now?

And who would find her, Jeremy or himself? Or would either of them be able to overtake her?

Rippon ran back across the corral to the place where he had tied his mustang. He jerked the reins loose from the slipknot that held them lightly. He flung himself into the saddle and headed for the side gate that gave upon the fields. He jerked it open and was presently passing over the soundless grass of the pasture land.

It seemed that nearly everyone else was scattering away from that plague spot where the two men had killed one another. Horses and riders streamed off in all directions, taking short cuts across the fields or thronging down the lane.

Jeremy would be far away, now, following some mental clue to the spot where he might find the girl.

Rippon dared to ride quite close to the edge of the firelight, close enough to see Charles Barrett standing with folded arms beside the body of Tom Palding. The body had been laid face up, the arms and legs straightened, and now there was light enough for Rippon to see the long hair sweeping back from the forehead of Palding; there was light enough for him to see, or imagine he saw, the sneering smile on the face of the dead man.

Poor Jude O'Malley, as though he did not matter one way or another, lay crumpled against the dark earth, left face down in the dew of the grass, his sadness ended and his heart still forever.

But there was Charles Barrett, left alone with the body of the man he had tried to trap, rob, destroy. And in the end, Tom Palding had fallen, but not through all the malice of Barrett, and not through all the cunning of his wiles. Accident had struck down the real Tom Palding, and it was Charles Barrett himself who was trapped, robbed, and destroyed. Here, at the end of his trail, as the accumulated triumph to crown the work of his life, he was permitted to see the face of the dead enemy, by the light of his own burning house. They had gone down together, in a truer sense.

For Tom Palding was utter destruction, in death. For Charles Barrett, there was a more real agony, death in life.

The history of the man lay unfolded before the eye of Rippon as clearly as though, from a great height, he looked down upon a vast landscape of time, and saw the traveler passing along the road of the years. He had filled his days with work. His mind and his hand had been busy. He had constructed a building of power over men, of power in the form of wealth. Nearly all had been snatched from him in two short days, and by the hand of a stranger.

Now it seemed to Rippon, as he stared in passing at that lonely figure against the dying red of the fire, that an invincible destiny had seized him far away across the mountains, across the desert, and plucked him by the hair of the head, as it were, and dragged him straight over the sands, over the mountain rocks, over the ice, down into this green valley for the sheer purpose of wrecking the pride and the strength of Barrett.

No man would respect him from this day forward. No man ever would trust his word or his bond. The very heart and depth of his meanness and his villainy had been laid open. The wealth had been snatched away from him. He was left like a young son, with barren land, and nothing else.

It was no particular gratification to Rippon to see the downfall of the man. He who had hired him lay dead on the ground. He against whom he had been hired stood by, worse than dead. His pride kept him erect. Perhaps misery already was bowing the shoulders a little. And Rippon pitied him with all his heart.

He rode on slowly into the darkness.

He looked back. There was the fire, drawn smaller by distance, heaped together in a single blur of red, and against it still loomed the motionless form of the watcher.

CHAPTER FORTY-ONE

When Rippon looked back again, the fire was no longer in sight. He tried to cast all thought of it behind him, and faced forward only to the problem of poor little Maisry, lost and alone in this dark of the night. *Where would she go?*

A hill loomed on his left. He sent Baldy up it, the little mustang dexterously picking his way among the boulders and the sharp-edged smaller rocks. At the top of the hill he paused, shaking his head at the dimness of the starlight. But, at least, the height enabled him to see the dim, tarnished silver of the Tyndal River, gleaming faintly at the elbow bend beyond the trees, and farther to the west he could see the walls of the valley widening, sloping outward with smooth shoulders that presently disappeared.

Had she gone down there, wandering out toward the big plain where she would find many houses, many kindly people to take her in and help her on her way?

Aye, but what was her way, after all? That thing troubled Rippon and made him shake his head. Jeremy must have some clues. He had known her a long time. He would be conversant with her past, understand from what region and from what people she came, and to whom she would be likely to return. But Rippon knew nothing at all. There was not a single thread, no matter how slight, that he could follow.

He sighed as he turned in the saddle and scanned the mists that were rising in the lowlands. Then he looked up to the east, along the course of the upper valley, and sighed more bitterly still.

Certainly she never would take that way of leaving Tyndal Valley. Tyndal Valley, he echoed to himself, as he stared through the night at the starlit outlines of the mountains. Tyndal Valley that had a curse on it.

What would come of them all? What would come of the Barretts? What would be the future fortune of the sheriff, the old, wise doctor, Bud Caswell, Harry Barrett, and all the rest? And what would come of Jeremy, honest in all things, but unluckily cursed by his love for poor little Maisry?

He thought, also, of the provisions heaped in the old house of the Paldings, which had been brought out to him by the grateful and repentant townsmen from Tyndal village. He thought of the gold that was there on the Palding ranch, its secret now known only to him and to that wise but baffled fox, Barrett.

As he turned the picture in his mind, and as it seemed to him that a broad curse rested upon the entire valley, and made night doubly dark, he happened to look to the east again, up the narrowing reaches of the upper valley, where it faded away into the heights of the Tyndal range, and there he saw the glistening top of Mount Tyndal itself, the king of the region, and between the shoulder of Tyndal and the shoulder of Granger Peak, he saw a bright silver eye wink down at him.

He stared at it in bewilderment for an instant. Then it widened with a dazzling brightness, a slender arc appeared, a broader rim followed, a half disk, and then the whole brilliant shield of the moon was clear. It shone fully in his face. It set the snows of Granger and Tyndal glimmering with magic, and it flooded with light the way into the mountains.

That's the way that she's traveled, he thought suddenly and with conviction. For it appeared, all at once, as clear as day to him that Maisry must have taken her course to the east.

Why? It was a mad thing for her to attempt, of course. She had had in her saddle pack neither blanket nor food or weapon, so far as he had seen. Then what would become of her up there in the winds that went through the body like volleyed spears? What would she do when the mule was slipping on the iced faces of the rocks? What would she do for food and shelter? She was not likely to possess the talents of a dweller in the wilderness. Her only courage was patience; her strength was a mild and persistent will.

And yet Rippon was confident that she had gone up into the mountains. She must have felt, as he did himself somewhat, that black curse that filled the valley from lip to lip. She must have looked, as he did, to the upper range as to a better and a promised land. She would go that way, also, because others would not be likely to suspect her of attempting to ride the pass by night. All those reasons must be working in her mind. She was fleeing as if from sin.

Rippon, nodding as he turned over these ideas in his mind, prepared to follow her. He had a grim satisfaction in feeling that huge Jeremy Barrett would never have the cleverness to plunge so deeply into the motives and the ways of a girl's mind. He would as soon suspect her of plunging into an icy ocean as of riding up there into the dangers of the Tyndal Pass.

He did not drive straight up the pass, nevertheless. In the first place, there was no very considerable reason for hurry. Mounted as she was, he was sure to overtake her. And it was all the better to let her get a short distance the start of him. If her mule grew very tired, and she herself were somewhat numbed by cold and fatigue, she would be more apt to go carelessly on, not seeking covert, and regardless of pursuit. Besides, in a little while, the moon would be rising higher and giving to Rippon a better light for his search.

So he failed to start straight up the valley. The Palding house was somewhat to the side of the direct trail. But he went to it, first of all.

For two days it had been home to him. And as he came in through corral gate and walked down the boardwalk to the rear porch, a certain feeling of melancholy came over him. A home could be made here. Cattle could be grazing on that shallow, inhospitable soil. Even without the gold, something could be made of the ranch. But now the last Palding was dead.

He went around the house to the windmill, and, pulling down on the lever, he dragged the fan with a screech out of the wind and sent it clanging home close against the wheel. Then he hooked the lever under its bent iron holder. That windmill would work no longer, for how many days? For years, perhaps.

He went from this into the house itself, lit a lantern, and looked about the kitchen. He thought of how he had cooked that mulligan stew earlier in the evening. It was scant midnight, now, and the man who had helped him to eat that meal was dead. The soiled pans were piled in the sink, half filled with water. The odor of coffee hung faintly in the air, and the smell of the potato sack, rank and raw, and of the onions.

His melancholy grew. It was impossible for him to avoid wondering what might have happened if Tom Palding never had appeared in the valley.

Suppose, let us say, that Tom had slipped in climbing over the rocks of the pass, and tumbled into a depth beneath? Or suppose that the cottager had returned and found Tom as a thief stealing the shoes from the house, and settled him with a .45-caliber bullet through the heart—if any of these things were true, then Rippon would have been left alone and victorious in the valley to bear the name of Palding. He had won the respect of the townsmen. He had gained the name of a fine and straightforward fellow. The ranch could have been his, to make rich with his husbandry. There was the gold mine that he could have exploited. As for the Barretts, they would have lived in terror at the mere thought of his power and his knowledge of their baseness.

He saw this dream shine for an instant, and then it vanished. He never could have lived for any period under any other than his own honest name. No, and there was evil in Tyndal Valley, and it breathed up out of the ground in his face.

He set about making a pack. He did not build a heavy or a cumbersome one. He merely took some coffee, bacon, flour, sugar. He took a rifle and ammunition for it. He took a blanket that might be needed sorely by poor Maisry. These things he bundled together. Then he stepped out onto the back porch and closed the door behind him softly. He went on tiptoe over the porch and down the steps. The boards of the walk were creaking faintly under him before he remembered that there was no one in that house to hear his going. Perhaps there never again would be. The weather and the weight of the wind would beat down the roof. The decay and the ruin would follow, spreading rapidly. Mold and dry rot would alternately consume the wood. The walls would bulge. In time, it would sink into a shapeless heap where not even a wolf could find adequate harborage.

He remembered, then, what Palding had said of the men of Tyndal Valley—they were wolves. And Rippon had seen their teeth.

When he got out to the corral, he lashed the pack behind the saddle on Baldy. That little Trojan had done a good bit of work already on this day, but now he flattened his ears and humped his back, in protest against the unexpected burden. For when, before this, had his master ridden with such a pack as this in addition to his own sufficient weight?

But, when Rippon mounted, Baldy merely shook his head, and, with a philosophical resignation, he jogged to the outer gate of the corral, allowed the bar to be slid back and the gate pushed open, swaying and creaking. Then Rippon rode out into the open lane.

There was no need of closing the gate behind him. The ranch was a hollow shell. Nothing remained in it worthy of plundering, except the remains of the provisions that the generous repentance of the townsmen of Tyndal had provided for him. Let the next vagrant take them and use them, washing out the many stale pans that were piled high in the sink before he started his cookery.

Rippon faced the moon in the east and headed up the valley. Still he did not press the mustang. There was time before him. There was almost a lifetime, perhaps. For if he missed Maisry among the wilderness of rocks in the upper pass, he never would stop his searching, surely, until he had located her on a later day.

He set his jaw, as he had set it many a time before when he had faced a long and bitter test. He set his jaw, and, settling himself comfortably into the saddle, he allowed the mustang to break into the little dog-trot that was its habitual gait. It was hardly faster than a walk, but Baldy would stick to it all night long, he knew, except on the steep slopes.

So they wound up the valley, with the moonlight brightening every moment before them. They began to climb. The trees grew smaller. And then an icy wind came out from the pass and struck at their faces.

CHAPTER FORTY-TWO

They were fairly committed to the heights now. And from the moment that the wind began to blow, the weather grew worse and worse. Even Baldy, tough as he was, trembled as the cold, knife-like blast thrust through him to the core of the bones.

Then the trees vanished altogether. They mounted into the icy region above timberline, and the worst of the march began. It was bad enough to have to cling to the trail. It was far worse to have to search continually on all sides for sign of the girl. There was not a single trail in many places. There were half a dozen ways of winding among the rocks, any one of which she might have taken. And he had ridden such a distance that, taking the difference between Baldy and her broken-down mule, he might be passing her at any given moment.

The wind brought tears to his eyes. He winked them out and shook his head at fatigue and cold. His body might be daunted, but never his spirit so long as he followed along this quest. Again and again, he left the back of the mustang, and, clambering to the top of some pinnacle, he stared into the recesses among the smaller rocks. It seemed impossible that, dressed as she was, her fragile body could have endured the cold as far as this. And he found no trace of her.

The moonlight was not constantly with him now. For the usual cloud masses were piled high around the tops of the Tyndal range. They were like new and monstrous mountains in the air. Some of them were as dark as the heart of a black night.

Some of them were gray as slate, impenetrable, and crowns of fluffy, translucent snow appeared above them. It was as though the top of the pass were merely the foot and beginning of a loftier climb, represented towering there, far above the head of Rippon.

As he failed to find any trace of the girl, waves of sick despair rushed over the soul of Rippon again and again. He blinded himself to such thoughts. But there was so little sweetness in her life, happiness was so untasted, that was she not likely simply to give up the battle and lie down beside the trail to wait for the end?

It would not do to delay now. The bitter frost and the urge of the wind would find her life in half an hour, he was sure. And though he strove to keep the thing from his mind, again and again he could see the pitiful picture of the huddled body, cramped forever by the mountain cold, and, downwind, a hunting wolf at work upon the trail.

By degrees, this vision so occupied his thoughts that he became convinced that he would fail. He knew and had tasted failure all his life long, but there never had been a bitterness so great as this one. He would fail. He had always failed. Never had he succeeded in any great adventure, except that one in which he had participated in the Tyndal Valley. But even that had ended in ruin. If it had not been for him, poor Maisry would not have fled.

At last, at the very top of the pass, he halted the mustang. She had not come farther than this. Of that he was convinced. Either he had passed her along the trail, or else she had ridden down the valley, in spite of the emotions that he was sure she must have felt. She had taken the easier and the more sensible way, and he had ridden all this distance for nothing. He immediately determined to retrace his steps.

But, at that moment, a deep ocean of clouds poured across

the face of the moon. As fast as a horse gallops, those clouds were rushing westward, not fifty feet above his head. They were neither gray nor white. They were so thick that they blotted out the moon and were themselves totally black. Only, on the front margin of the advance where the light of the moon still struck through the mass, there was a fringe of luminous white, like the crooked line of white that forms and re-forms along an ocean beach.

He decided to wait for a moment, hoping that these clouds would clear, and the moon again give him its light. He needed that light bitterly by this time. Trickles of water that thawed in the daytime were now frozen again during the night, and everywhere Baldy was stepping on ice as treacherous as wet glass. Baldy was sure as a mountain goat, but even a mountain goat would not choose to be abroad in such a time and such a place as this.

So he waited, looking anxiously upward. As he waited, as though to repay his vigilance with a sneer, a great glistening arm of hail reached down from the cloud and struck him. It cut the skin of his face. At the same time, the wind freshened, and the roar of the great hailstones sounded like a dry thunder on the rocks about him. Real thunder followed. A storm was coming up. It was already upon him, and it was thickening every instant. He could not go on. It was impossible to ride the pass through such weather as this.

So he cast about him for a place where he could find shelter. He got out of the saddle and led the mustang forward, feeling his way step by step. For all was as dark as the inside of a room at night—a room with shutters drawn against even the starlight.

He was making cautious steps over an icy stretch when, looking to the right, he saw, or thought he saw, the blink of an eye of red. It stopped him. He turned and stared fixedly, but saw nothing. He moved to the right and the left, stood on tiptoes, squatted a little, but it did not appear again.

A hallucination, he told himself. The cold must have soaked through his body to the core. Before long, he would begin to have other and wilder visions, and after these would come the fatal desire for sleep.

He was about to step on again, when the same eye of red looked at him, and again from the right. This time he spotted it instantly, and halted. It was a mere trembling ray of light, but he turned toward it with a sudden wild hope in his heart.

It was not the girl, of course. It was some wanderer through the pass, benighted as he was. It might even be Jeremy Barrett. An odd freak of chance if Jeremy were up there in the rock wilderness searching as he was for the girl.

When he thought of Jeremy, he got his rifle out of its long holster. It was loaded, he knew. His hands were very numb, so he beat them together, and then, as he walked slowly on, he held his right hand under the pit of his left arm that it might be warmed. At last he felt that the trigger finger could respond to his will. So he took the gun under his arm, but still he kept his right hand in a coat pocket. That trigger finger must remain supple, or he was apt to die if he met Jeremy Barrett.

And yet he knew that he felt no anger against Jeremy. He had felt the insane strength of Jeremy's hands in fight. But, on the other hand, he had seen Jeremy Barrett cleave a way through the mob, fighting for him as a friend, and he never could forget.

It was strange that in that place of crime, hatred, suspicion, foul attempts, he had found the man who he preferred above all he had known as a friend. But they loved one woman, and that was the ruin of their friendship.

Step by step, cautiously alert as a stalking cat, he approached the red eye of the fire. It hardly gained in size. It was not until he had come very close that he could see why. It was built inside of a nest of rocks, perhaps to shelter the flame from the wind. It was only the light that escaped through a single chink that had taken his attention. A very odd thing, this. To be sure, the rocks might keep the wind out, but they also kept the heat in. Of what good was such a fire as this to a half-frozen wanderer?

In the next moment he saw a form bent above the stones of the fireplace. He came still closer, his rifle ready. Then he breathed a sigh of relief. No, it could not be Jeremy. Even through the night he could have made out the bulkier outlines of big Jeremy Barrett.

A stone was removed from the face of the fireplace and a bit of wood was thrust in. It had begun to rain, a cold shower, coming aslant upon the wind. And, looking through the sparkles of that rain, most dimly and like a ghost, he made out the features of the stranger who kneeled by the fire, and saw that it was Maisry.

The very knees of Rippon weakened. He was no man for prayer, but he could have given thanks, then, with an uprush of spirit and from the bottom of his heart.

"Maisry," he tried to call. The voice died in his throat to a whisper.

"Maisry!" he called, and the sound of the cry startled his own ears, there was such joy and agony in it.

She started up, leaving the face of the fireplace open, and so he could see her more clearly as he came lunging on through the rain. He came to her and found her with both arms stretched stiffly before her, her lips parted, her eyes frightened. Perhaps those arms were meant to keep him away?

He stood holding her.

"I thought it would be Jeremy," she kept saying. "I thought it would surely be Jeremy. Even when I heard your voice, something said Jeremy inside me. I thought that Jeremy would be sure to find me."

"He'll never find you now," Rippon said. "And if he does, I'll take care of that. You're as wet as a muskrat. Do you know that? You're soaked to the skin."

"I'm a little damp only," she said.

"Oh, Maisry," he said, "God bless you. God bless your pretty face and your sweet soul." He picked her up from the ground and kissed her again and again.

"You're dripping," she said. "You'll catch your death. You're dripping wet."

"Me? That doesn't matter. I'm a water rat. I'm used to water. My skin is tanned leather, Maisry. Now wait here a minute."

Baldy had come straight up to the fire and, standing alongside Maisry's old mule, he was pricking his wet ears at the flame and letting the light of it shine in his eyes. From his back, the master hastened to undo the pack. He took out the blanket. Then he hesitated.

"You're sopping," he said to the girl. "Stay here for half a minute. There's a better rock there. You see the height of it and the slant of its face. It'll keep you as dry as a tent. Wait a minute now."

He took a few live brands from the fire, holding them by the ends that were unburned. These he carried under the brow of the rock that he had pointed out. It sloped far out in the direction of the blowing rain and made an almost ideal shelter and windbreak. There he placed the burning sticks. There was a quantity of low-growing brush nearby. He tore it up. He could have torn up trees in the same manner, he felt, there was such a fury of strength in his hands. And these bushes, shallowly rooted in crevices of the rock, came away easily. He knocked the water from some of them and fed them gently to the fire. It caught, it took hold, it began to rush up through the branches with a loud crackling, and he felt as though he had found and rekindled the spark of life.

CHAPTER FORTY-THREE

When that fire was roaring, he got Maisry beside it and brought the animals. In her drenched clothes, she looked as small as a child, so that he wondered at her and loved her more than ever, it seemed.

"You're sopping . . . you're just sopping," he said. "Now, I'm going out there to get some more brush together. You've got ten minutes to peel your clothes off and wring them as dry as your hands can twist. Don't be afraid. The fire'll keep you warm enough till you get them on once more. When you're inside them, take this blanket and give it a tight wrap around you. Look at me, Maisry. You look mighty kind of blue in the gills. Do you feel the cold inside of you, or only outside? D'you feel it like cold water in your stomach, maybe?"

He took her by the shoulders, yearning over her.

She was blue-white, and shaking violently. A dreadful fear came over him in a wave far colder than snow water.

"No. I'm going to be all right. I'm not cold inside. Not very cold. I'm going to be all right."

He turned away from her. He shouted cheerfully over his shoulder: "Peel, and wring those clothes! Be pretty smart about it. I'll be soon back." He went stamping off through the storm. It struck him like a club across the shoulders, but he merely shook his head and went on.

"She's gotta be all right," Rippon mumbled to himself. "She says so herself. She says that she'll be all right. She oughta know. She's going to be all right." But this talk to himself was not convincing. There was still a vast dread in his heart, chilling and numbing it.

On the verge of the firelight, with his back still turned to the fire, he found more brush and tore it up. The roots came away in thick mattings of lichens and fern-like growths, and he nodded over them, for they would make a hot and low fire. He worked feverishly.

It seemed to him that he had far overstayed his time, when he straightened and, cupping a hand over his mouth, thundered, without turning his head: "All right, Maisry?"

Like the tinkle of a distant bell he clearly heard the answer: "One more minute!"

And he stood there with the force of the wind rocking his body and laughed with joy, for it seemed to him he could see a sun-bathed house, and that sweet voice somewhere in it calling: "One more minute!"

Melancholy followed. She was too beautiful. She was too good. Heaven would not leave her in the wretched cold and darkness of this earth among mere humans.

He tore up more shrubbery, and then heard, more faintly still, her hail to him. With a great load of fire material, a staggering burden of it, he leaned against the wind and came back to her. She was wrapped in the blanket like a mummy. It seemed to him that already some of the blue had left her face. Surely there was not the same stone-like whiteness about her mouth. And her eyes shone at him. How brightly they shone at him.

He fell to work in a sort of joyous frenzy, as hope leaped high again.

He knocked the water out of some of the brush. More of it, already, had been drying beside the fire while he was away. He made a bed, the wetter brush beneath, the dryer on top. It was a good bed, springy and soft. The constant wind current of the heights had blown out and flattened the bushes to the ground, so that they acted like boughs of good evergreen. All in a moment, it seemed, that bed was ready, and he made Maisry lie down on it.

He built up another fire on the other side of her. Soon it was comfortably warm. The work and the fire heat made him perspire a little. There was no danger of freezing then. He went on the other side of one of the fires, and beyond the place where Baldy stood patiently alongside the mule. He took off his own clothes, wrung them out, dragged them on again. Then he returned to the girl.

He started cooking. Most of the time he kept his back to her. For he dared not, somehow, look at her too much. He liked to have her at his back, like a delightful dream, a thing too beautiful to be true, too true to be a vision. Only, now and again, he went and kneeled by her on one knee and bowed close above her face. And, every time, he could see the color more and more strong in it. The stone-like pallor diminished. And into the cheeks came a fresh tint of rose. He thought her eyes were like stars. Stars reflected in deep, still water. Stars with dew on them. And he would go back to his cookery.

She hardly stirred. She hardly spoke. He could see, when he glanced at her, that she was looking deeply into the future, and that the beauty of it enthralled her.

Then the food was ready. He placed it before her, and they ate their first meal together. She was propped against the wall of the rock on a dry bundle of brush at the small of her back, and he, cross-legged, sat just beside her. And before them the rain slanted down in a steady wall, white as smoke, almost, under the firelight, and solid as a dense smoke, too.

Suppose someone should find them here? Well, he had the rifle. And, besides, he felt that happiness had made him a giant capable of coping even with Jeremy Barrett.

At last, that meal was ended. They had not spoken a single word during all of it. He lit a cigarette and began to smoke. She was flat again, wrapped in the blanket closely, smiling like a child at the white, down-rushing wall of rain.

"Maisry," he said, "I don't want to know all that you're thinking. I only want to know a little bit of it, if you feel like talking."

She waited a long moment. He thought that she was not going to answer at all, but finally she said: "Well, suppose that you could turn one place and one moment into forever. . . ."

And he knew that she meant that moment.

"Say, Maisry," he said, "you're kind of happy? You're a little happy?"

"I never was once happy before," she said.

"By heaven," he said through his teeth, "you're going to be happy all the rest of the days of your life."

She shook her head. She did not look at him, but steadily at the pouring of the rain. "I couldn't stand it," said Maisry. "Not like this. To be happy like this, for very long, that would kill me, I think. I couldn't stand it, I think."

"You know," Rippon said, leaping a bit toward her, "you know that I'm really Ned Rippon. I mean, I don't own anything."

She nodded slowly. "I know," she said, and smiled a little, as though at his folly in thinking that he needed to tell her that, or that it mattered.

"Where were you going?" he asked her after a time.

"Away. I don't know. I just wanted to get out of the arms of Tyndal Valley."

"You might have died, Maisry, if I hadn't found you."

"I'd as soon have died," Maisry said, "if you hadn't found me. That was the way it was."

Tears stung the eyes of Rippon. Bitterly, fiercely almost, he made swift and silent vows. He made them in his heart where a good man and a strong man registers thoughts stronger than prayers.

"Maisry," he said after a time, "are you still warm?"

She did not answer. He looked at her and saw that she was fast asleep. But, as though the sound of his voice had gradually penetrated to her consciousness, without opening her eyes, she turned her head toward him and smiled, and a hand came out from beneath the blanket and made a faint, slow, small gesture toward him.

Rippon made another cigarette. He lit and smoked it. He had to keep his jaws locked hard, not against pain, but against raging joy that kept welling up into the hollow of his throat, and making the corners of his mouth twitch.

It was while he sat there like that, staring blankly, straight before him, that he saw something move through the wall of rain. The rain dissolved. The form turned into the black outline of a man, and Rippon, without stirring, caught up the rifle and covered the other.

The blackness of the approaching body took on detail, took on color. And then, stepping up to the rim of the rainfall, but keeping just inside it, he saw Jeremy Barrett. He could make out, really, not much more than the great bulk of the man and the shining of his eyes. But through the last few inches of rapidly descending rainfall, his face was like a face seen under a film of fast-flowing water.

Rippon gripped the rifle hard. But, in spite of himself, he felt as though a mountain were leaning toward him. Then he saw that the glance of Jeremy was not for him—not for a single instant. It was fixed steadily upon the sleeping girl, with her head turned to her lover, and her hand put out a little toward him.

He stood there only for a moment, then the veil of rainfall grew thicker, whiter, before him. His silhouette turned black. It disappeared to a shadow. It was gone altogether, and left Rippon forever alone with his happiness.

ABOUT THE AUTHOR

Max Brand is the best-known pen name of Frederick Faust, creator of Dr. Kildare, Destry, and many other fictional characters popular with readers and viewers worldwide. Faust wrote for a variety of audiences in many genres. His enormous output, totaling approximately thirty million words or the equivalent of five hundred thirty ordinary books, covered nearly every field: crime, fantasy, historical romance, espionage, Westerns, science fiction, adventure, animal stories, love, war, and fashionable society, big business and big medicine. Eighty motion pictures have been based on his work along with many radio and television programs. For good measure he also published four volumes of poetry. Perhaps no other author has reached more people in more different ways. Born in Seattle in 1892, orphaned early, Faust grew up in the rural San Joaquin Valley of California. At Berkeley he became a student rebel and one-man literary movement, contributing prodigiously to all campus publications. Denied a degree because of unconventional conduct, he embarked on a series of adventures culminating in New York City where, after a period of near starvation, he received simultaneous recognition as a serious poet and successful author of fiction. Later, he traveled widely, making his home in New York, then in Florence, and finally in Los Angeles. Once the United States entered the Second World War, Faust abandoned his lucrative writing career and his work as a screenwriter to serve as a war correspondent with the infantry in Italy, despite his fifty-one years and a bad heart. He was killed during a night attack on a hilltop village held by the German army. New books based on magazine serials or unpublished manuscripts or restored versions continue to appear so that, alive or dead, he has averaged a new book every four months for seventy-five years. Beyond this, some work by him is newly reprinted every week of every year in one or another format somewhere in the world. A great deal more about this author and his work can be found in *The Max Brand Companion* (Greenwood Press, 1997) edited by Jon Tuska and Vicki Piekarski. His next Five Star Western will be *Stagecoach*. His Website is www.MaxBrandOnline.com.